The Kinship Series

# THE EXPERIMENT

**Also by Robin Lamont**

If Thy Right Hand
Wright for America

*The Kinship Series*

The Chain
The Trap

The Kinship Series

# THE EXPERIMENT

## ROBIN LAMONT

Award winning author of *The Chain* and *If Thy Right Hand*

Cover: 99Designs
Interior Design: Jera Publishing

Cover Imagery: Shutterstock/Dreamstime

Grayling Press

ISBN: 978-0-9858485-8-3 (print)

LCCN: 2018913953

# ACKNOWLEDGEMENTS

As I dove into the connecting spheres of pharmaceuticals and animal testing, there were many people who helped me along the way. Many thanks to Michael Budkie, who for decades has worked hard to protect animals in laboratories. Much appreciation to Dr. Aysha Akhtar, Alka Chandna, and Kari Hamerschlag for their referrals and counsel. Special thanks to Michael Hansen, Senior Scientist at the Consumers Union for his expertise. Any errors made with the science are entirely on me. Finally, much gratitude to Matt Swensen for his thoughtful reading of the manuscript and helpful insights.

*The Experiment* is for Ken.

# CHAPTER 1

Jude Brannock strode through the noisy mob. They'd heard her coming. As she advanced the length of the kennel, stepping purposefully along the cracked, concrete floor, the dogs that knew her leapt up on the chain link fencing and barked riotous, happy greetings. The new arrivals barked because everyone else was barking. Jude barely glanced at them.

The one she was looking for was housed at the end. The shelter director made sure that there was an empty pen between him and the others. For good reason. He had backed himself into a corner and pulled his lips back showing a lot of teeth. A black mutt, Jude figured he was a hound mix of some sort. Very thin. Very fearful. And in this state, very dangerous. She stopped in front of his pen. "What up, dude?" she asked.

He answered with a menacing growl at which point she re-thought her strategy. She was armed with a fistful of dog biscuits but now thought they weren't going to do the job alone. If she had any chance of getting through to this fellow, she would also need to compose herself, clear her head of the raging storm of emotions that had been building for days.

She was buffeted by alternating bouts of frustration and anxiety. The undercover investigator that she'd trained and been running for the past two months was going off the rails. She knew what Tim's problem was, but there wasn't much she could do about it. Not from here. And there was no one she could consult with. This was between the two of them.

The rumble of the dog's feral warning sounded again. He had started to drool. Jude pushed aside thoughts of Tim to return to the challenge at hand. Avoiding eye contact, she said, "Okay, bud, I'm all yours," and she lowered herself to the concrete floor outside his pen, keeping her back to him and focusing on her breathing. Before long, the other dogs settled down, but not her new friend.

Finally, she spoke to him, turning her head only slightly in his direction. "I thought we were past this. After all we've been through, you don't remember me? I mean, don't you want to find a nice home? You're not a bad looking guy. You can do better than this place."

He barked harshly.

"I think it's time we give you a name," she said softly. "How about Rocky? You're a fighter with the heart of a marshmallow. Let's see if we can get through to that heart – or at least your stomach. What do you say?" Jude hummed the first few bars of the *Rocky* theme and then began to talk about nothing in particular. All the while she maintained non-confrontational body language. After a few minutes of steady, low-key patter, Rocky stopped panting, though she could hear him padding back and forth, unsure. She had no illusions that he ever took his wary golden eyes off her.

Jude broke some of the biscuits into pieces and pushed one under the chain link gate. After a moment, Rocky snatched it up and dashed back to his corner. Jude gave him another piece, and another. With each successive trip he eased his retreat until finally he hung around by the door, waiting for the next morsel. In slow motion, she stood up and unlatched the pen. Rocky withdrew to the back and snarled. But it was half-hearted.

She edged herself inside and crouched by the gate. Refraining from making eye contact, she resumed her exercise of chatting softly and occasionally leaving a piece of biscuit on the ground. He came closer and closer. From the corner of her eye, she saw the running scar around his neck where his fur had been scraped off – a sure sign he'd been chained up, and for a long time. Finally, he took a treat from her hand. She reached out and touched his shoulder. Rocky trembled but didn't draw away.

Jude said, "We can't keep meeting like this, boy. People will start to talk." The thin dog gazed at her wistfully; he wanted to trust her but was still wary. "It's okay," she reassured him. "There are really good folks here, and they'll help you. You don't have to be afraid."

She fought the urge to stroke his neck. It was enough for today. He needed time.

Back in the shelter office, Madelyn, the ruddy-faced director, greeted her. "It's awfully quiet down there. I really appreciate you coming on such short notice. You're the only one who can get close to him."

"Where did he come from?"

"I have no idea. One morning I found him tied to the fire hydrant out front. I barely escaped with my life getting him into the pen."

Jude dropped into a chair, drained. "I think he'll be okay. He just doesn't know what end is up. Take it slow and bring those treats, he likes them." She brushed off the crumbs and then sniffed her hands. "I'm going to smell like peanut butter all day. Oh, and his name is Rocky."

"You're a saint," exclaimed Madelyn.

"Hardly," replied Jude. A slender lock of auburn hair fell against her neck and she reflexively tucked it back into the messy topknot that languished at the top of her head. Jude paid scant attention to her looks, neglecting what many women would view as minimal hair styling and makeup. Not that she needed it, but a little would have gone a long way toward brightening her pale complexion and bringing out the green in her hazel eyes. Similarly, more thought to her everyday wardrobe would have helped draw attention to her long legs and carved shoulders. Jude preferred to direct the spotlight to matters that needed desperate fixing.

"Do me a favor," Jude said. "Don't send him to County without telling me, okay?"

"I'll do what I can."

"No," insisted Jude, getting up to go. "County is a high kill shelter. He won't last two days, and you know it. Give him some time."

"I promise. You want a cup of coffee?"

"Thanks, I'm late for work," she said distractedly, eyeing her cellphone. She checked for new messages, but still nothing from Tim. The precariousness of their situation came crashing through the storm gate again, and her fingers twitched, a hair's breadth from sending him the code that would pull him off the investigation immediately. That's what her boss Gordon would tell her to do, but he didn't know the whole story and Jude wasn't about to tell him.

She slipped the phone back into the pocket of her jeans. Even knowing some of it was of her own making, Jude couldn't shake the feeling that, like Rocky, she was being pressed into a corner by events spinning out of control and was ready to snap if anyone moved too fast.

# CHAPTER 2

From the minute she laid eyes on Tim, she was conflicted. Jude's physical attraction locked in combat with her sense of professionalism. He had just turned twenty-six and had raw good-looks, with fair Celtic skin that reddened easily in the wind and thick, curly hair. There was a glint in his eyes that saw humor in almost any situation, until, that is, he came face to face with the suffering of animals. Then his brow would furrow, and the glint would crystalize into something hard and brittle. With an athlete's physique, he was lean through the torso and hips, broadening to shoulders and arms that worked hard at the gym. From their first touch, Jude desired him.

"It's an honor to work with you," he told her, shaking her hand enthusiastically. "Everyone says you've done like the most astounding undercovers."

"You make them sound like backflips," she laughed.

He grinned. "Oh, you can do those, too?"

*Shit*, she thought, *I'm in trouble*. But she ignored the warning signs and pushed any misgivings about training the "new guy" into the musty back closet of her mind.

Jude was a senior investigator with The Kinship, a small group dedicated to animal protection. They didn't have the visibility or the financial backing of some of the big organizations like the ASPCA or PETA, preferring to work in the shadows. Their specialty was in undercover investigations to gather and document evidence of industrialized or large-scale animal abuse. Working across the spectrum, they'd send in an investigator to secure a job at a factory farm, a race track, or a puppy mill. Then with film, photos, or witness statements in hand, they'd go to the authorities, or if no one would take action there, to the media.

Tim had come to them recently and seemed well suited for one of the targets The Kinship had in their sights – Amaethon Industries, a private laboratory in Vermont that tested on animals. In the past, the company had been cited for violations of the Animal Welfare Act, which imposed rules on the treatment of animals in laboratories. And in June, Amaethon was due to begin pre-clinical testing on an experimental drug, using dogs and rodents.

They needed to get someone inside, and Jude thought that Tim was the right candidate to land a position as a lab technician, whose primary job was to monitor animal behavior and assist the researcher with handling the animals. Tim was good with dogs, exceptionally good. And a crash course interning with a local veterinarian would give him the necessary skills and vocabulary to pass muster. Meanwhile, the organization's resident computer engineer CJ Malone would take care of creating a checkable identity and a sure-to-be-noticed resume. CJ was wheelchair-bound, but could go anywhere with his coding skills, including hacking into other databases where stored information could be "amended" as he put it. His personal motto was, "my other computer is *your* computer."

There was only one wrinkle. Before he had come to The Kinship, Tim had done a covert operation with another animal protection organization, landing a job at a factory farm that raised pigs in Minnesota. The investigation was a failure. Word had it that he'd blown his cover, although no one knew exactly how it had gone down, least of all Tim. Jude believed him. It could happen to a rookie: a stray wire showing on the hidden camera or one too many questions in a rush to extract an admission. She was sure that under her tutelage, he'd be successful at Amaethon.

When Tim was, in fact, hired to work at Amaethon in the canine section, Jude was anxious to get started. "Yes!" she fist-pumped. "We know for a fact that they've ignored the housing and handling rules, pitifully inadequate as they are. All they got was a slap on the wrist from the U.S. Department of Agriculture, and I'm certain that hasn't stopped them. If we can prove new infractions, the government will have to do more than fine them. I want to *get* these guys."

With four weeks until he had to be in Vermont, they began to work. Except for his mornings at the vet, they were together almost constantly, crafting Tim's backstory – where he grew up, what sport he played in high school, his political leanings, his favorite ice cream. From there, Jude went over the hidden cameras that could be placed in the brim of a cap, a buttonhole, or a wristwatch. "You're going to be there for almost three months, so you'll have plenty of opportunities," she told him. "What we need is *documentation* of the violations."

She hammered home the house rules for maintaining contact. He was to call her every day. Just as important, if he or anyone at The Kinship felt he'd been compromised, he was to heed Jude's message that would signal him to get out of there fast.

Tim was an eager, receptive student and fun to be around. But not a day went by that Jude didn't war with herself. Sometimes she'd stay professionally detached, determined that he would not blow his cover *again* – if in fact, that's what had happened. Not on her watch. At other times, she forgot herself and was drawn into his aura of warmth. He'd say something that would make her laugh and then when she was totally disarmed, he'd put a light hand on the small of her back as they walked through a door, causing her knees to nearly buckle.

It wasn't long before she surrendered and took him into her bed.

\* \* \*

Jude drove back streets from the shelter to The Kinship offices in Brentwood. Anything to avoid the clogged highways of Washington, D.C. at rush hour. It gave her enough time to make her decision. She would give Tim one more day. It was a risky move. Their communication had begun to falter in recent days; he'd sounded distracted and rushed on the phone. Worse, his contact became sporadic, sometimes going two or three days between calls – a serious violation of "the rules." In their last phone conversation, he sounded drunk. They'd fought. But dammit, she couldn't pull him off now. Not after the email he'd sent yesterday morning. *I have something big for you. Still working on it. Will call tonight.*

This was what she'd been waiting for. Finally, he had something – *something big*. Of course, it was disappointing that when she opened the accompanying attachment, she didn't find a video or audio recording. Just two photographs: the first was of a ramshackle yellow house, and the second a photo of an empty field with a jagged rim of hills in the distance. No clarification about what they meant or what connection they had to his mission. She waited for his call to explain, but it never came. Cause for concern perhaps, but not yet cause for alarm, given that he was probably still angry with her. And she rationalized that there was nothing in his email or the seemingly random pictures to indicate that his cover was compromised.

Just one more day. If Tim had something big on Amaethon, he had to see it through. Her job was to find a way to hold off Gordon a little longer.

Jude parked in the community lot across the street from the converted hosiery mill where The Kinship maintained an office. It was a solid brick building with tall windows and old wood floors that were worn and smooth. There were places one could see the embedded edges of metal tracks where two hundred years ago, carts ran between the sewing machines. They shared the third floor with a lawyer, an architect, and a couple of accountants, each of whom had their firm names etched on the glass front door. The Kinship had only the suite number on theirs.

She stopped at the Starbucks on the ground level and ordered coffee, adding a splash of soymilk to the scalding hot liquid before taking the stairs. But as she shouldered her way through the stairwell door, she took a sip from her container and burned her tongue.

Gordon's door was closed. Good. She didn't see CJ and assumed he was hidden behind a computer screen somewhere. She waved to the new intern, a bright-eyed, bubbly girl with grand ambitions to save all animals, and made her way through the loft area peppered with cubicles until she got to her own.

The gray fabric panels that separated the work stations were richly decorated with snapshots of friends and family, pets, and framed slogans like "Don't Think Outside the Box, There Is No Box." All but Jude's. While her desk was piled with files and DVD's, her cubicle walls were bare except for one picture torn from a magazine. It was a photo of a man, holding his scoped high-powered rifle aloft and sitting on the back of a male lion he had just shot in a game park. The animal was thickly-maned, huge and magnificent, the color of the sandy ground where his blood had pooled, his eyes closed forever. The killer atop him was so grotesquely obese, it looked like he might have trouble getting up without help. But he smiled broadly, proud of his accomplishment.

The image, for Jude, captured everything that was wrong in the relationship between man, animals, and nature. Each time she looked at it, she was reminded that trying to change that relationship was something worth fighting for.

She deposited her backpack next to her desk and turned on her computer. While she waited for it to boot up, she ran the tip of her tongue across her teeth, feeling the small screech of the burn. Gordon's voice startled her.

"Hey, there."

Jude quickly swiveled to greet him.

"How was New York?" he asked.

Gordon Silverman was the founder of The Kinship and had hired Jude as an investigator at the outset. Ten years her senior, a silver-haired man with an aquiline nose, nearly hawk-like, he had become Jude's lover for a brief time. They were friends and co-workers now, but it was a relationship built on scarred trust.

"Good."

"You and your friend Alicia have a nice time?"

"Alice."

"Alice, right." He seemed inclined not to ask further about the days off she'd requested, and Jude was fine with that.

"So, what's the word from Tim?" he asked, getting down to business.

"Says he's got something for us," she replied, keeping her voice even. A taut, humming metal wire felt like it was tightening around her chest. She'd prepared what she was going to say but was afraid she might stumble.

"Do you know what it is?"

Jude shook her head. "I'm sure he'll tell me tonight."

"The testing is finished soon, isn't it?"

"A week from Thursday."

"What about his mental state?"

"The job's gotten to him a little, which isn't a surprise," she hedged. "He's become attached to the dogs. We expected that."

"Anything else?"

Jude stared at the ceiling as if trying to summon up concerns she didn't necessarily have. "A few weeks ago, he hinted that he'd met a girl. I warned him not to get involved. I think he heard me, but maybe … I don't know."

Gordon frowned.

"We'll be talking tonight," Jude reassured him.

Eyeing her sternly, he said, "Make sure he gets the message, Jude. Getting involved with civilians on the job is bad news all the way around."

"I know, I know. I'll press it home."

"I thought he had a girlfriend here in D.C.," said Gordon.

"I … don't know," replied Jude innocently. "He never said anything to me."

Gordon looked at her before saying, "Okay, let's talk first thing in the morning. I don't have a good feeling about this."

The rest of the day dragged as Jude obsessively checked her cellphone, convincing herself that there would be a message from Tim next time she looked. She prodded him a few times with a breezy text from his "sister" Emily – their signal to phone in right away – but he wasn't responding. She could feel his resentment resonate in the silence. He'd give her the evidence she wanted, but by God, he was going to make her pay for it. Before she left, she almost went into Gordon's office to show him the photos. But then, she'd have to explain Tim's surly lack of communication and where it was coming from, which would mean revealing their affair, and she didn't want to do that. Not now, not ever.

# CHAPTER 3

Tim didn't call.

When she finally dozed off, she fell into a fitful chase dream. Seeing Tim round a corner in the distance, she'd run to catch up with him. At some point, he turned into Rocky and she knew that she had to get to him before Animal Control did. Both were always just out of reach.

It was still dark when she finally gave up the idea of sleep and got out of bed. She padded barefoot into her apartment's small kitchen and brewed a pot of strong coffee. Her cellphone never more than a few inches from her hand, she drank enough to make her teeth feel tight. At one point, she began tapping out the text that would end the assignment once and for all: *Dad's back in the hospital. Need you home. Emily.* But she couldn't get herself to hit the send button. Maybe, just maybe he'd make contact before she had to talk to Gordon. Her dog Finn gazed up at her with liquid brown eyes, knowing she was troubled but unable to help other than to insert his nose under her hand.

Just before dawn, she took him out for a run. It was going to be hot again today, and it was better to get out before the Arlington joggers and bicyclists descended on the park. Jude trotted the two sparsely-treed blocks from her building to Four Mile Trail. Hardly a wilderness footpath, it was just a stretch of pavement that wound alongside a dirty creek. Nevertheless, there were some leafy spots that felt cool, and after the first mile, the strain of Tim's silence began to fall away.

Jude tried to put things into perspective. Okay, Tim screwed up. It wasn't her fault. Probably it was this girl he met – a girl he seemed to delight in telling her about. None of my business, she told herself; there was never any real future for us. And maybe there was some other girl involved when he bungled the undercover in Minnesota. If that was the case, his days with The Kinship were over. For now, though, hopefully he had footage of the big thing he promised, and if they had to yank him, not the end of the world. With Finn on a loose leash trotting beside her, Jude rationalized herself into a mood that bordered on hopeful.

And then it happened … again.

Patches of black appeared at the outer edges of her vision. They crept in toward the center creating a tunnel-like effect, squeezing the lines and shapes still visible into waves. Jude stopped and lowered her head between her knees. It had worked before. The first time, she shook off the episode, convinced it was dehydration. The summer had been brutally hot. But the same thing happened a few weeks later.

She went to an ophthalmologist who promised there was nothing wrong with her eyes. A long overdue checkup followed, at which her general practitioner said her blood tests had come back fine, but just to be sure, recommended that she get a work-up done by a neurologist. Earlier in the week she'd received the good news: her MRI was clear, he could see nothing wrong. The last few minutes in his office, though, had unnerved her. She could still hear him.

"Have you been under particular stress recently?" asked Dr. Amin, seemingly out of the blue.

"Nothing other than thinking I might have a brain tumor."

He glanced at her open file on his desk. "Mmmn. It says here you're an investigator with an animal protection group."

"So? You think the eyesight thing is related to my work?"

He made a noncommittal wag of his head. "How many times did you say it's happened?"

"A couple," she lied. "I don't think I was drinking enough water."

"Your work must involve some pretty dark stuff. I can't imagine what it must be like." When Jude didn't respond, he added, "Probably very stressful."

"Are you saying that my job is making me go blind?"

"The brain can have a very powerful effect on our physiological–"

Jude stopped him right there. "Look, I've been doing this a long time and nothing like this has ever happened. I love what I do. I'm sure I was just dehydrated. I mean, I take my dog out twice a day no matter what, and it's been incredibly hot."

"Miss Brannock, the problem you've been experiencing is not from dehydration." He gazed at her with stern tolerance. "I recommend that you see somebody."

"See somebody?"

"There are a few other neurological tests we could do, but frankly, I don't think they're necessary. Everything I see so far tells me you're a physically healthy young woman. I'd like to give you the name of a psychologist."

As her mouth dropped open, Dr. Amin wrote a name on his prescription pad, then tore off the page and held it out. "Ruth Harris is very good. She's in Arlington. You'd like her."

Jude took it but had no intention of calling. There was nothing wrong with her. She stuffed the slip of paper into her pocket, relegating the psychologist's name to an inaccessible part of her consciousness, tucked away with certain memories of her childhood that, as far as she was concerned, were best forgotten.

"Is everything okay?"

Jude straightened up to find the shimmering pavement of Four Mile Trail coming back into focus. A middle-aged man stood a few feet from her with a small white terrier who was growling at Finn. Her dog, all ninety pounds of him, looked down at the terrier indifferently. The wavy lines and the tunnel vision were gone.

"Thanks, I'm fine. Just a little light-headed, I guess."

"Happened to me the other day. Really easy to get dehydrated these days," he said.

See? She wasn't the only one.

\* \* \*

By the time she got to the office, she knew she couldn't put Gordon off any longer. Jude steeled herself as she grabbed her coffee and laptop and headed to his office. She was surprised to see that fellow investigator Lucas Matz was already there. She hesitated at the open doorway. "Hi," she offered tentatively.

Gordon called her in. "We're talking about Tim," he said.

Her stomach turned over. Lucas flashed her a guileless smile through his scruffy five-o'clock shadow. It was a smile he reserved for her, the one that seemed to say that it was always just the two of them in this fight. With straightforward features, he wasn't particularly handsome but had an intensity that belied his casual, slouchy demeanor. He was dressed in his usual attire: a black t-shirt, perpetually frayed at the neck, and army-issue cargo pants.

She smiled back, but it felt forced. Why was Lucas conferring with Gordon about her case?

"I was just filling him in," said Gordon.

"Oh yeah, of course," Jude said, as if bringing Lucas in had been her idea all along. She set her coffee on the desk and took the seat next to her co-worker, who was comfortably sprawled in his chair, his runaway, dirty blond hair tied back in a ponytail.

"Anything to report?" Gordon asked her.

Jude shook her head. "He didn't call in last night."

"When is the last time you spoke to him?"

"Well, his communication over the last few days has been spotty."

"Why didn't you tell me yesterday?" accused Gordon.

"I was sure I'd hear from him," replied Jude defensively. "On Tuesday morning he sent me an email that said he had something big on Amaethon. And he attached these." She pulled up the photographs that she'd put on her laptop.

Gordon lifted his hands in bewilderment. "What are they? They make any sense to you, Jude?"

"Not really. He used to talk about wanting to fix up a house in the country someday, and a couple of times he sent me photos of a house or barn for sale. But I don't understand why these photos with that message. I thought he would explain everything when we talked, but … no word."

Gordon looked over at Lucas. "How much do you know about Tim Mains?"

*Why is Gordon bringing Lucas into this?* thought Jude. *Because I'm being pushed out, right? He doesn't want to confront me directly, but he wants me out.* A wave of resentment broke over her.

"He's at a place called Amaethon Industries," Lucas was saying. "They've been cited before, I guess."

"Two last year and at least one before that," interjected Jude, needing to take the reins again. "According to Tim, he's only seen two principals. There's the Chief Scientific Officer who's running the protocol and another guy who's there a lot. He thinks he's involved in financing the project, but it isn't clear."

"How'd you get him in?"

"As a vet tech."

"Don't you have to be licensed to do that?"

"CJ … uh, *found* his state license. But Tim got all the basics from the vet, and so far, he's simply been monitoring them for this test."

"How many?"

"Twenty-four. A standard number of canines for a protocol like this."

"They're just testing on dogs?" asked Lucas.

"No, mice and rats, too."

"What name is he using?" Lucas asked.

"Tyler Jeffries."

Lucas rolled his eyes. "Sounds like he's on a prep school rowing team."

"He picked the name, okay?" Jude bristled.

"How big is Amaethon? I never heard of them 'til now."

Gordon answered, "It's a pharmaceutical start-up. Everyone's getting into the game right now, hoping to get bought out by one of the bigs."

"The lab's in Vermont, right?"

"A place called Half Moon. It's a farming town, a few miles outside of Montpelier. Jude, yesterday you said that the job was getting under his skin. How bad?"

"He was upset that a few of the dogs were severely distressed. They're probably the group on the highest dosage."

"Dosage of what exactly?" Lucas demanded, although his clenched jaw said he wasn't sure he wanted to know.

"They don't tell the techs much, but Tim said he thought it was a drug for stroke or heart attack patients. They put it in the food."

"Fuck, man," muttered Lucas. "Who does this to animals?"

Jude let out an exasperated sigh. "Testing on animals is not breaking news, Lucas. Can we move on?"

For a moment, he looked slightly hurt, then marshaled a comeback, delivered with his usual unhurried drawl. "What makes you think he's still there? Maybe he bailed."

"He wouldn't do that," said Jude flatly, pulling her laptop toward her and snapping it closed.

"It's a lot of pressure, and he's inexperienced," offered Gordon.

"He was ready. And why would he tell me he had something on them and then leave?"

"I can think of one reason," Lucas threw in. "He witnessed violations but couldn't get it on video and he knew you'd be disappointed."

Gordon swiveled in his chair. "Maybe we made a mistake with him," he sighed.

"He *was* ready." Jude leaned forward to press her case, and as she did, she knocked over her Starbucks container, spilling coffee which spread in a rapidly growing pool on her boss's desk. "Oh, shit. Sorry, I ... I didn't see it there." She jumped up and ran to get an armful of paper towels.

On her return, she continued to defend Tim and, in some respects, herself while she sopped up the mess. "Really, he wouldn't quit without telling me. Maybe he was a little stressed out, but he was prepared for that."

Lucas, trying to see all angles, pitched in, "It's possible he got made. Look what happened in Minnesota."

The lift of Gordon's eyebrow said that he saw some sense in this, prompting further commentary by Lucas. "I got the feeling Tim had a reckless streak."

"Undercover work doesn't generally attract the safe, timid type," Jude pointed out sharply.

Gordon pinched the bridge of his nose and Jude could tell that he was re-thinking his decision to hire Tim. Finally, he asked, "What about this girlfriend you mentioned?"

"I don't know who she is." Jude busied herself cleaning up the coffee to forestall further questions on that topic.

"Okay, listen up." Gordon had made his decision. "I'm pulling him. Jude, text him now. And Lucas, I want you to go to Half Moon and see if there's a way to get him out without burning his bridges. If they buy the deceased father story and things aren't as bad as I think they may be, he might be able to get back into Amaethon. Can you leave this morning?"

"No," cried Jude. "He's my trainee. I'll go."

"Lucas should go."

"Gordon, please," exclaimed Jude. "I can handle this."

"You look tired to me, Jude."

She suspected that might be code for, *you fell asleep at the wheel.* "Please, Gordon. I'm fine," she pleaded. "Listen, I'm the one who's been handling him. It's probably this girl. They're hooking up and he's afraid to tell me about it. I know Tim. I mean, I've got a good sense about him. I'm the one who should go up there." Drops of coffee dripped through her white fingers clutching the wet paper towels.

The boss mulled it over for a moment and relented. "All right. Get whatever you need and head out. I want to hear something by tonight."

Jude and Lucas left the office together, tension between them palpable. He gave her a long, hard look as she deposited the paper towels in a waste bin. She felt it through her back and glanced up. "What?"

"Are you all right?"

"Of course, I'm all right," she said, unable to keep her annoyance with the whole situation out of her voice.

"It wouldn't be your fault if he pulled up stakes. It happens. Not everyone is cut out for this work."

"He's fine, Lucas." And that was that.

Except that Lucas was waiting for her in the hall. With the office's open floor plan, it was often hard to get a word in private.

"How was New York?" he asked.

"Good."

"What's Alice up to these days?"

"Same old."

"Listen, I'm not tryin' to muscle in on you," he said. "You know me better than that."

"Yeah, I know," she replied.

"So why the cold shoulder?"

"I'm just worried about Tim." She started down the hall toward the stairs and Lucas kept pace with her.

"He's a big boy. He can take care of himself."

"But you always thought he was a lightweight."

"I never said that."

"You thought it."

Lucas laughed. "Okay, I *thought* it. I'm only sayin' that I don't want you to be hard on yourself. Gordon hired him; you just got tagged to train him. And knowing you, the CIA couldn't have done a better job. The people who come to us because they want to help animals, they bring a lot of passion and idealism. And he had balls, I'll give him that–"

"What's your point?"

"Going 'undercover,'" he said, putting finger quotes around the word, "sounds like romantic spy novel stuff. But it isn't. You know that, and I know that. On edge every minute of all the grunt work that makes you sick for how the animals are treated. Tim was there for a long time, as these things go. It's no disgrace if he couldn't take it anymore."

"That's not what happened," Jude insisted.

"If it did, he probably doesn't want to have to face you. Everybody in this movement looks up to you."

Jude shrugged him off but cringed inside. Lucas was probably her best friend and she should have told him the truth. God knows, he deserved it.

More than once she'd wondered if she needed to keep her relationship with Tim a secret because of an ego-driven need to hang onto her status as a seasoned, no-holds-barred investigator. What would her colleagues make of the fact that Jude Brannock – intrepid animal welfare luminary – was sleeping with her young male trainee? But more than that, it was nobody's business.

"You texted him?" asked Lucas.

Jude grunted a vague, semi-affirmation and said, "I gotta go. I have to pack and get Finn over to Madelyn's."

"I'd take him for you, but …."

"I understand."

Lucas had looked after Finn a couple of times when she had to go out of town, but he had his own companion animal, a rat named Habib, who wouldn't emerge from his nest of shavings when the big dog was around.

"Just one more thing," volunteered Lucas as they reached the fire door. "Tim quitting and not telling you is a way better scenario than if his cover got blown."

"Don't try to make me feel better," said Jude.

"God forbid."

Jude clattered down the industrial staircase as much to escape from Lucas as to prepare for her trip. She felt guilty for lying to him yet again about the text. But as bad as things were, Tim might still be working to document violations that the government wouldn't be able to ignore. They had to salvage something from this. She pushed off the deadline once again, hoping to buy a little more time.

# CHAPTER 4

John Harbolt wasn't easily shaken. With over forty years of medicine under his belt, there was hardly an injury, disease, or fatality he hadn't seen, and he'd treated just about everyone in the small town of Half Moon at some time or other. But on that late summer day, young Tori Lacey showed him something that baffled him. Her symptoms were inexplicable and downright scary.

She was his first patient of the day, a young woman who had battled her weight for years. In between the earaches and the sore throats, Harbolt had gently counseled her about diet and exercise. He hoped she wasn't here to ask him about diet pills again, because as far as he was concerned, they were off the table.

After removing her file from the plastic holder bolted to the outside of the examination room, he adjusted his wire rim glasses and straightened his lab coat. The younger doctors often wore khakis and a short-sleeved shirt at work, and maybe it put the kids more at ease. But Dr. Harbolt stuck with a freshly starched white coat, believing that it made his patients feel more confident in his abilities. And confidence in one's doctor was important to the healing process.

"Tori Ann Lacey," he announced jovially as he shambled into the room.

"Hi, Dr. Harbolt." The morose girl before him sat on the table. She had taken off her running shoes but left her sweatshirt and shorts on.

"I haven't seen you for a while," he said, noting with some surprise that she had slimmed considerably, her round face now leaner and more mature. "How is college life treating you?"

"Ok, I guess." Her voice and posture belied this.

"What brings you here today, my dear."

"I don't really know. But we thought you should look at these." She pushed back the sleeve of her sweatshirt and held out her arm for inspection.

There were several bruises that vandalized the translucent skin of her inner arm. Dr. Harbolt held her wrist and peering over his glasses, looked closely at the red and purple marks.

He pressed lightly on one of them. "Does that hurt?"

She shook her head no.

"What happened?"

"That's the thing. Nothing happened. They just appeared." She showed him another set of bruises on her other arm.

"Did you fall?"

"No."

"Knocked into something?"

"No," she exclaimed, as though he didn't believe her. "My mom thinks it's my diet. That I should be eating meat."

"And you're not?"

"No. I needed to lose five more pounds for the track team, which I was having a hard time doing, so I switched over to a raw food diet. And it really helped because I made my goal."

"And you were selected for the team?"

She nodded, anxiously chewing on a nail.

"Congratulations. You getting enough protein?" he asked, studying the bruising and letting her answer drift past him. This wasn't because of her diet.

She rambled for a moment about nuts and spinach, then peeled off her socks and lifted her bare feet to the end of the examination table. "And then yesterday after a run, I found this," she said. "I didn't even show my mom 'cause she'd freak out."

Dr. Harbolt caught his breath. It looked as though someone had taken a baseball bat to the soles of the girl's feet. Fiery maroon blotches screamed out some kind of violence. Three of her toes had turned a dark purple.

"Good Lord!" he blurted out. "What *happened* to you?"

"Nothing! I'm telling you nothing happened," wailed Tori. "They just ... showed up."

\* \* \*

"Are you related to him?" asked the acne-scarred teen behind the reception desk.

Jude eyed the crooked badge on the boy's shirt pocket that identified him as Steve, Assistant Manager of the Riverside Motel. "Not exactly," she replied evasively.

"Because we have a strict policy that we don't give out keys except to the occupant." He tucked a piece of floppy bangs behind his ear and tried to sound official, but the word *occupant* came out as if he wasn't quite sure what it meant.

"I can understand that," said Jude. "But I'm worried about him, and he's not answering the door."

"Probably not in then, is he?"

Jude had driven eight hours straight and was in no mood for games. The smell of fried onions and ketchup lingered in the cubbyhole that served as the motel's reception, and Jude spotted the remnants of Steve's dinner in a McDonald's takeaway container. It made her a little queasy. She took another moment to size him up: late teens, wearing a white button-down shirt with short sleeves and slacks easily ten years out of date. Probably the motel manager insisted on the uniform but at the same time hadn't been able to get the kid to cut his hair. Ergo, the manager was either Mom or Dad.

"Maybe the manager can help me, Steve," she said.

He blinked a few times. As young as he was, after seeing the variety of folks who came through, he could read people, too. But he wasn't certain about her. She was too pale for one thing, a city girl who didn't dress like one – not in those loosely-fitted jeans and a black t-shirt. Plus, her direct gaze was unsettling and not like the girls he was used to hanging with, their eyes always glancing around for something or somebody better within shooting distance.

"He's been with us for a few weeks," he noted, stalling.

"Uh-hunh. He's working nearby."

"Where?"

"Why don't you ask him?"

"Seems like a nice guy," Steve added, believing the humorless woman in front of him was an angry ex-girlfriend and he had an obligation to stand up for men in general, and for Tyler in particular, because he *was* a nice guy.

"Whaddya say?" pressed Jude. She stared him down.

Steve rolled his shoulders uncomfortably and replied, "Okay. I shouldn't do this, but I'll let you in for a quick look is all. I have to stand outside, though. Policy, you understand."

"Sure." He retrieved a key from a cabinet and led the way.

As far as Jude could tell, the Riverside Motel wasn't anywhere near a river, but it was convenient, right off the main road not far from the center of Half Moon. Situated on the upper curve of a hill, it overlooked several miles of farmland with the dark outline of mountains in the distance. A couple of wrought iron benches served as viewing spots near a gravel walk that ran from the parking lot to the motel office. The rooms themselves were in a long two-story building covered in cedar shingles. The white woodwork had been recently painted and strategically-placed barrels of colorful geraniums gave the place a homey, country feel.

Steve mounted the outdoor staircase to the second floor. At the third door, he knocked, mumbling, "Jeffries sometimes goes out at night." Nonetheless, he knocked again and waited an appropriate amount of time. Moths flickered around the low-wattage lamps mounted outside each door. Finally, he slid the key into the lock, opened the door, and flipped on the overhead light.

Jude stepped in. The room, carpeted in a resigned shade of green, lacked the charm of the motel's exterior. It was sparsely furnished with two single beds, a desk, a dresser, and one rocking chair with a sad gingham cushion.

Right away, she began a visual inventory. The bedspread was thrown haphazardly over one of the twin beds, the other hadn't been slept in. There was nothing on the chipped particle board desk except a television and its accompanying remote. No bags, no clothing strewn around. The closet door had been left wide open, revealing just a few wire hangers. She walked over to one of the wall sockets where a portable charger still dangled. With even a fleeting look, Tim would have seen it. Same with the single white sock that hadn't been able to crawl all the way under the bed.

He'd left in a hurry.

"When was the last time you saw Tyler?" Jude asked Steve.

"I guess it would have been a couple of days ago."

"Can you recall exactly?"

"Uh, yeah. It was Tuesday night, around eight, eight-thirty. I saw him going up to his room."

"You didn't see him after that?"

"No. I was behind the desk."

Jude needed to search more thoroughly. "Okay, thanks. I've got it from here." The look on the boy's face let her know that she'd been too short with him. "Hey, Steve, I really appreciate your help," she added.

"He didn't pay the bill this week," he complained.

"Don't worry. I'll take care of it."

And thinking that Tyler Jeffries wasn't such a nice guy after all, Steve left.

Jude was thinking along the same lines. Stinging irritation welled up as she pulled open dresser drawers and got down on her hands and knees to check under the bed, looking for something, anything, that could explain why he'd taken off so quickly.

Where the hell was he? It was the height of irresponsibility not to tell her what was going on – even if he had decided to quit. All he'd have to say was, *I can't do this anymore.* She would've helped with an exit strategy. They'd talked about that possibility. It occurred to her that all of this was just a way to get her attention. And of course, it had.

She moved on to the bathroom that had the plasticky smell of a new shower curtain. It, too, had been cleaned out. But for a small spider that had set up residence in the mirrored cabinet over the sink, she might have missed the blood. Needing something to help gently capture the spider and transport it outside, Jude went for a few sheets of toilet paper. It was then she saw a pile of tissues thrown carelessly on the floor near a wastebasket. They were wadded and stiff with dried blood.

Using the tips of her fingers, she lifted one of the clumps to inspect it. Seemed like a lot of blood – way more than if he had nicked himself shaving. She left the tissues where they were for the moment and went back into the room which suddenly and eerily felt as though no one had been there for years. Her frustration with Tim was replaced by a growing sense of unease.

After a moment, she pulled up his number and texted, *Dad's back in the hospital. Need you home. Emily.* This time she sent it.

# CHAPTER 5

Morning mist hovered over Kurt Buck's farm like a ghostly blanket. It was cool now, but the Half Moon weather was supposed to hit the high eighties by mid-afternoon. The elephant-eared cabbage leaves and bush beans dripped pearls of condensation into the thirsty soil.

Inside the Buck farmhouse, the routine proceeded like any other early September day. Kurt left his muddy boots outside and padded across the kitchen floor in his socks to pour himself a second cup of coffee. On the way, he deposited on the counter a half dozen ears of corn that he had just picked. Their dogs Rosie and Chipper trooped in after him and slurped noisily from their water bowl before settling under the kitchen table, which was where Kurt's wife Katherine sat, surrounded by a stack of invoices and the checkbook.

"What did you tell me you need for the spreader?" she asked Kurt.

"A hitch kit," he replied, looking to see how much was left in the pot. "You want more coffee?"

"You finish it. How much are they?"

"Probably get a new one for about three hundred."

"Want me to order one for you?" asked Katherine as she lifted sections of paperwork looking for the catalogue she'd stashed somewhere. When he didn't answer, she looked up to see him staring out the window deep in thought. "Hello?" she prompted.

"What? I'm sorry."

"Do you want me to order a hitch kit for you?" she repeated.

"I found two more crows this morning," said her husband. "Behind the barn, just lying there like ... like they'd been shot out of the sky. But not a mark on them."

"Any sign of disease?"

He chewed on his bottom lip and replied, "I don't see anything, but it makes me worry about that West Nile outbreak a few years ago. Crows are particularly susceptible. If you see one, don't pick it up without gloves. Christ, that's all we need. What were you asking? Oh yeah, no, don't order anything yet. I'm going over to Willet's and I'll see if they have somethin' used in decent shape."

He washed his hands in the sink and dried them with paper towel; too many times he'd left swaths of dirt on Katherine's just-cleaned kitchen towels. Beyond the driveway and the faded, unused swing set, he surveyed the late summer harvest through the haze. The acres of evenly plowed rows gave him a sense of contentment, the knowledge that he was providing sustenance without ruining the land, without becoming a vassal to one of the giant agrochemical companies like Monsanto. Farming was hard, and organic farming harder still. But Kurt Buck accepted the challenge.

"Where's Heather?" he asked Katherine. "The bus will be coming any minute."

"She's getting ready. I told her she could drive." His wife didn't need to see the slight stiffening of his neck to know what he was thinking. "It's fine. All of her friends drive to school."

"What's wrong with the bus?"

"She's a junior, hon. The bus is for *losers*," Katherine replied, imitating her daughter's sentiments.

Kurt sighed the sigh of a man who knew he was out-matched. And his daughter's timing couldn't have been better. She bounced into the kitchen, her long blond hair freshly washed and painstakingly blown-dry to swing loose and silky. She wore just enough make-up to compete with the other girls at school, most of whom ardently believed there were valuable things to be learned from celebrity magazines.

"Morning, Daddy," she chirped.

"Mornin' sunshine girl." Despite his endearment, she caught his reserved tone and went over to disarm him with a hug. When she wrapped her thin arms around him, he looked down at her softly freckled face and was rendered helpless. This girl was the beating heart of their lives.

Heather absently picked up one of the corn ears, pulled back some of the husk, and began to nibble on the tender white kernels.

"You want something other than uncooked corn this morning?" her mother asked.

Heather grinned. "It's the breakfast of champions."

"Well, how about lunch? Let me make you a sandwich."

"No, thanks. I'll get something at school." She dropped the corn back onto the counter and slung her backpack over her shoulder, careful to flip her hair aside so it wouldn't get caught under the strap.

Kurt wasn't ready to let her go. "You have good teachers this year?"

"Not bad," she replied. "I have Mr. Bronstein again for AP history, so I'm happy about that. The others I'm not sure yet, but I hear pretty good things." She shifted her feet, anxious to be on her way.

"Go," urged Katherine. "Or you'll be late. I don't want you rushing."

"Yes," echoed her husband. "Drive carefully."

"I will, Daddy." She offered him a sweet sideways glance. "Don't worry. I'm fine."

"Do you need gas money?" he asked.

"Nope. All set." Heather headed toward the front door, then stopped, remembering something. "Oh, is it okay if I go to the movies tonight? There's a new X-Men we want to see at the Cineplex."

Kurt cleared his throat. "Who are you going with?"

"Friends."

"Like who?" he wanted to know.

"I don't know. Rachel and a few others."

"I want to know who."

Katherine broke in, "Oh, Kurt." But she seemed unable to explain further why she was taking Heather's side.

He knew, though. "You can understand why I'm asking, right?"

"Of course, Dad," agreed Heather. "I'm fine, really. Please don't worry about me."

Kurt looked like a non-swimmer about to jump off the high dive. "Okay. Text me or your mother later and let us know your plans."

"Of course. Um … I could actually use some money 'cause maybe we'll get something to eat afterwards." When Katherine relieved the cash jar in the kitchen cupboard of a twenty-dollar bill, Heather took it gratefully. "Thanks. I'll pay you back." And with a, "Love you, guys," she was gone.

Heather headed to the car, the youthful buoyancy she'd put on to match her parents' perception of her gone from her step. She threw her backpack into the car, settled into the driver's seat, and pulled out her phone. Scrolling down the list of friends, she selected the entry marked by a single letter B. Her text to him was short and succinct – *Be there at 4. I got cash.*

When she heard the friendly whoop sound on her phone that indicated the message was successfully sent, she glanced back at the farmhouse and saw her father watching from the kitchen. She gave him a feeble wave.

\* \* \*

Jude sat at the edge of one of the molded plastic chairs in the bare reception area of Amaethon Industries, reviewing her own cover story: she was Tyler's big sister, Emily Jeffries, come to break the tragic news of their father's death – not something you did over the phone.

The woman at the front desk informed her that Tyler wasn't at the lab. She had already made that clear when Jeffries' sister was patched through from the security gate. But Emily had been persistent, demanding to see the person in charge.

Taking stock of her surroundings, Jude noted that everything Tim had described was accurate. She knew enough about testing labs to be familiar with the one-story building, a nondescript, concrete box, surrounded by an electrified fence. She'd experienced the same indoor filtration system that kept the temperature constant at 68 degrees and the humidity low as it silently inhaled and exhaled scentless, hygienic air through vents in the ceiling. Beige walls and ceilings muffled voices and swallowed any color that drifted by. In the middle of the rich, green landscape of Vermont, it felt like landing on a barren planet.

Tim had grown increasingly troubled as the weeks wore on, and she understood. It was painful to be a dog lover and see what they endured here.

They were animals with a capacity for scent forty times that of humans, able to smell fear, anxiety, and sadness in people or other animals. They could tell by a sniff of old pee which dog buddy had recently visited the park and what they'd eaten for breakfast. But here in the lab, they lived out their days surrounded by the savage bite of the disinfectant used throughout the kennels. Even for humans, it was so strong it could make your eyes sting.

"He'll see you now," said the receptionist, a woman as bland as her surroundings.

She led Jude down a hallway to meet Dr. Stuart Ostrovsky, the Chief Scientific Officer in charge of Amaethon's animal research. His office was cramped and messy. Boxes of files were stacked everywhere, monitors and hard drives spread out as though he repaired computers for a living. There was no exterior light in the office save a glimmer from a small window begrudgingly cut into the wall close to the ceiling, as if sunlight were a guest that no one wanted at the wedding but had to be invited.

The man who stood to greet her was younger than Jude had expected, with a sandy-colored, thick mustache that hid his mouth. "Hello, Miss Jeffries," he said. "Margaret told me why you're here, but I'm afraid it's a waste of your time."

Jude cleared a stack of files from a chair near his desk and sat, letting him know she had time to waste. "I hope you didn't say anything to Tyler yet. I really must be the one to do it," she said crisply.

"I thought Margaret told you, he doesn't work here anymore."

"She just said he wasn't here," Jude said, feigning surprise. "I was going to wait for him. What happened?"

Ostrovsky furrowed his brow and rubbed his mustache. His fingers twitched slightly. "He hasn't come to work since Tuesday."

"And he didn't tell you he was leaving? That doesn't sound like my brother," said Jude, twisting a button on her brown cardigan. She'd dressed in shapeless earth tones to be as unmemorable as possible.

"Perhaps he heard about your father from someone else?"

"Dad only died yesterday. I've been trying to reach him, but he hasn't returned any of my calls or texts."

"Oh." It would have been the moment for Ostrovksy to offer his condolences, but social grace didn't seem to be his forte.

"Did he work closely with anyone who might know where he is? Any of the other techs? Maybe I could talk with them."

"That would be difficult."

Jude wasn't accustomed to playing the victim, but she did her best to look as though she was on the verge of tears, even getting her voice to crack as she said, "I have to find him. He and Dad had their differences, sure. But he'd never forgive himself if he didn't make it to the funeral."

Stroking his mustache uncomfortably, Ostrovsky reconsidered. "Okay, wait here. I'll see who's around." He brushed past Jude and headed down the hall.

Jude darted up from her seat and poked her head out the door. She had maybe a minute or two. There were several piles of colored folders on the table. A quick glance inside the top folder revealed charts filled with data in the form of equations, seemingly organized by date. She moved to another set of papers and was met with more scientific data. Voices came down the corridor.

Ostrovsky entered, finding Jude in her chair. With him was a tall corporate type in his mid-to-late thirties. He wore confidence like strong cologne. "Hello, Ms. Jeffries," he said. "I'm Dillon Byer."

Right away, Jude noticed his wristwatch – a brand advertised as one you never really own, you merely look after for the next generation. He was modestly attired in khaki pants and a blue button-down with the sleeves rolled up. Even so, he carried an air of privilege which, along with strong, handsome features dominated by arched full lips, many women would find sexy.

He pulled up a seat and leaned toward Jude, resting his elbows casually on his knees. "Stuart told me why you're here. I cannot tell you how sorry I am about your father," he said earnestly. "And I'm sure Tyler will get in touch with you soon. I've asked two of the techs who worked with him to come over."

She figured Byer to be the senior official that Tim had told her about. She was dying to ask what his position was, but she folded her hands in her lap and thanked him for all his help.

The first tech was an older man named Lester, a retired veterinarian. Because he worked alternate shifts with Tyler, he was unable to say much about him. The other was a woman in her late twenties named Sylvia. She had an insolent curl to her lip and under her plastic head covering, long hair colored a rebellious shade of red.

She had more to offer about her co-worker, which still wasn't a lot. *Tyler was great to work with, super nice guy. Funny, too. He was nuts about the dogs.* Jude asked if she spent time outside work with him. *Not really.* Did that mean occasionally? *A couple of times we ran into each other at Galvey's.* What's that? *A music joint in Montpelier.* And that's all? *Like I said, we didn't really hang out.* Did she have any guess about where Tyler could be? *Nope,* uttered quickly and emphatically.

With Ostrovsky and Byer hovering nearby, Jude could hardly mount a challenge. But she was sure that Sylvia wasn't telling her everything. Not by a long shot.

# CHAPTER 6

From the lab, Jude drove around in search of Tim's car. The center of Half Moon was a blend of hopeful restoration and small-budget neglect. It had its fair share of shops, banks, and cafés on either side of the main drag. Some of them were in renovated three-story brick buildings that might once have been wool or cotton mills, and they were well-kept, the wood trim painted in antique-style hunter green or beige. Still, a mega CVS and a few fast food joints were evidence that commercial America was encroaching. Similarly, the surrounding side streets were a mix of picturesque white colonials and rundown prefab homes with junk littering the yards.

She tried to put herself in Tim's shoes. He might feel vulnerable and a little paranoid. It came with the territory. And if that were the case, thought Jude, he might have found another motel and kept the first as a decoy; drive to the Riverside Motel after work, then later, if all looked clear, slip out to get a decent night's sleep somewhere else. Maybe even at the girl's house. As

Jude cruised the residential roads, that thought was a constant sore that left her with a blurred sense of disappointment and relief each time she turned a corner and his car wasn't there.

By the afternoon, she gave up and went back to the Riverside where she had taken over his room. She got on the phone and tried the area hospitals. After that, with her heart hammering in her chest she called the morgue in Burlington. Nothing.

There were various possibilities. The first was that Lucas was right and the undercover work had become too stressful. Tim couldn't take anymore and packed up, or he believed his cover had been blown again, either of which he might have been too embarrassed to admit. There was another possibility – one that she didn't want to think about. But she did and after consulting with Gordon, went to the police.

Brenda Ramirez, a heavy-set woman in a dark blue uniform, commandeered the front desk at the Half Moon Police station, a squat, brick building next to the Community National Bank. She was eager to offer motherly advice. "You know, young men at that age do crazy things. They always turn up and with any luck, they've learned a thing or two." Her tone changed, however, when Jude got to the part about Tim working as an undercover investigator for an animal protection organization. No surprise – most people didn't immediately understand the connection between animals and undercover operations.

"What was he doing there?" demanded Ramirez.

"Documenting violations of the Animal Welfare Act."

Ramirez silently mouthed the words "Animal Welfare Act," then asked aloud, "Is that a law in Vermont? Because I've never heard of it."

"It's federal law."

"Well, that's not our jurisdiction."

Jude suddenly had an overwhelming desire to stumble back to the bench in the vestibule and go to sleep. She rubbed her eyes. "Is there a detective I could speak with?"

"There is not," replied Ramirez, with more than a hint of irritability. "We have a chief, a lieutenant, two officers, and a victim's assistance coordinator – which would be me. Besides, we don't generally handle missing persons. That's the state police. He probably wouldn't appreciate me telling you this, but Sergeant Haydon is in the back. I suppose you could talk to him." After fielding a couple of phone calls, she finally wandered off to find him.

The sergeant had chocolate skin and refined features. His light brown eyes radiated an intellect that seemed out of keeping with his heavy leather gun belt. He held a broad-brimmed campaign hat in his hands.

"My name's Hugh Haydon, Ms. Brannock. I'm with the Vermont State Police. Why don't we go to the office where we can talk?"

He led her to an empty cubicle in the back where she repeated what she had told Officer Ramirez.

"And why do you believe he's missing?" he asked.

"We stay in touch with our undercovers on a daily basis and the last spoken contact I had with him was this past Sunday. He texted me a few days ago, but I can't get him on the phone."

"Any mental health problems that you're aware of?"

"No," replied Jude adamantly.

"Personal problems?"

"He told me he'd met a girl up here, but I don't know who it is. I didn't get the feeling it was a serious relationship, in any event," she added hastily.

"Have you checked with his employer?" he asked, as if reading off a checklist.

"Yes, I went there this morning. They say he didn't show up for work on Wednesday."

Haydon looked at her. "Just curious, but how did you walk into a testing laboratory and broach the subject of Tim being an undercover investigator?"

"I used a pretext. Animal activists are not generally welcome in such places."

"That's an understatement. You folks break into labs, don't you?"

"You're thinking of another group."

"Okay. Any reason to believe they found out who he was?"

"If they had, I hardly think they would've let me waltz in there this morning, claiming to be his sister." When the corners of Haydon's mouth twitched in a near smile, a wave of irritation hit her and she said, "You know, just because we investigate animal abuse, doesn't make our undercover work any less dangerous than going deep with a bunch of white supremacists or a drug cartel. Not where there's big money involved."

It had been just shy of a year since she herself had gone undercover in Idaho, trying to ferret out fraud and deception in the secretive federal agency Wildlife Services. She'd pushed too quickly and too hard, and they'd caught on. Being outed had nearly cost her life. She knew well that operating covertly on a long-term investigation carried a much higher level of risk. It meant hanging out in the wind alone for weeks. No backup.

No one at the listening end of a body wire to hear the dreaded words, *Who the fuck are you?* Moreover, her experience taught her that once the target discovered he or she had been scammed, they harbored an intense animosity. It was often humiliating for them. They hadn't merely been hustled, they'd been stabbed in the back by someone they thought was a colleague, an employee, maybe a new friend – and that someone had been looking for the right place to thrust a knife the whole damn time. It could get ugly.

Haydon nodded his understanding. "I didn't mean to minimize your work. I was impressed with your brazenness."

"Oh, well, I ... I just notice that you're not taking notes."

Haydon looked at her levelly. "Miss Brannock, most people Tim's age go missing because of mental instability or because they're trying to escape family or relationship problems. That's probably the case here."

"I think I would know–"

"People will surprise you," he broke in. "They take a runner for reasons you can't even guess. Given that he's only been with your organization for a few months and much of that time, he's been here in Half Moon, maybe you don't know all that's been going on in his life."

Haydon had a point. She never imagined that Tim would take a lover while he was on assignment. She thought that the two of them were ... No, she didn't know what the two of them were.

Refusing to give in to the self-doubt, Jude took a new tack. "I found blood in his bathroom," she stated.

At this, the Sergeant's eyes sharpened.

"On bunches of tissues on the floor. It was *a lot*."

"You still have them?"

"I bagged them up myself."

The possibility of violence seemed to change Haydon's mind. "Okay. I'll come over and have a look." He checked his watch. "Do you have a picture of him?"

"I do." Jude rummaged through her canvas bag and handed him a photo of Tim playfully posing on a pitcher's mound at Rock Creek Park. He had the sleeves of his trademark NY Mets t-shirt rolled up, revealing muscular arms.

Haydon scrutinized the picture. "Looks like he can take care of himself."

Jude looked again at the picture, remembering that spring day.

They had walked with Finn happily off-leash down the lesser paths of an urban park until they wandered onto a deserted baseball field. Tim pulled a tennis ball from his pocket and like an excited kid, ran onto the field, taking up position on the pitcher's mound.

He dug his toe into the soft dirt, rolling the ball in his hand as if to find its seams. It had only been a few days, but he was tired of talking about laboratories and hidden cameras and how to keep your face from giving away what you were really feeling when you had to watch dogs shake with fear. It was a beautiful day in the park and he wanted to enjoy it.

"Here we go, Finn. Here we go, boy!" Adopting a pitcher's stance, he squinted toward the empty home plate. While the big dog danced in anticipation by his side, Tim shook off his imaginary catcher behind the plate, telling him, "No way, he *wants* the curve." He checked the runner on first, then looked to his catcher again. This time, he offered a slight nod and went into his wind-up. He let the ball fly and it caromed off the backstop fence. Finn deftly caught it on one bounce and ran into the outfield.

"Dang!" declared Tim with mock dismay. "He's reading my fastball." With that, he dashed after Finn to get the ball back and try again.

Jude laughed and followed at a leisurely pace, giving in to the sun's warmth and the scent of sweet viburnum coming into flower. They'd been hard at it for hours, and Finn could use the exercise.

But as she watched the two play, she reverted to mentally reviewing and prioritizing the points she wanted to convey on the next topic: living in the community. He could be friendly with co-workers and the folks in town, but he had to think of himself as a seasonal worker – he wasn't going to stick around after the testing was over, so there was no point in getting close to anyone. And in fact, it could be dangerous.

If, on the other hand, he felt it was crucial for his cover that he be sociable and go out for a beer with the guys on occasion, keep the alcohol to a minimum. You could never be sure some-thing wouldn't slip after a few too many. And rule number two: no girls. Like alcohol, sex clouded the thinking. Get used to watching the Red Sox on the hotel's cable TV.

When Finn galloped back to greet her, she realized she'd lost sight of Tim. She spotted him on his knees in the outfield.

"Is everything okay?" she asked, hurrying over.

"Shhh," he cautioned. He was holding on to a gray squirrel whose head was caught in a discarded plastic jar. The squirrel was fighting both Tim and the jar. "Come here, I need your help," said Tim.

When Jude knelt beside him, he instructed her to hold the jar firmly. With one hand he kept the squirrel from forcing himself deeper inside, and with the other, he fumbled for a swiss army knife in his back pocket. Managing to get a thin blade out with his teeth, he made an incision into the throat of the jar to widen it.

"Okay," he said. "Hold tight. I'm going to pull him out." Tim tugged the body of the squirming animal until his head came free. For a moment, the squirrel seemed stunned, unable to move. Then he promptly turned and clawed Tim's hand before running off.

With a yelp, Tim cried, "Hey, buddy, I did you a favor."

Jude stifled a grin, saying, "So much for animal gratitude. When was your last rabies shot?" She took his hand and examined the wound.

Their heads were close together and Tim leaned forward and kissed her softly on the mouth. His lips were warm and yielding. She feigned a moment of surprise but knew it had always been just a matter of time. She knew, too, despite the voices in her head berating her to get up and pretend it hadn't happened, that there was no turning back.

# CHAPTER 7

Haydon followed her back to the Riverside Motel.

"That's not your ordinary shaving cut, right?" asked Jude, pointing to the plastic bag of bloody tissues.

"I suppose," he admitted. "We'll call around to the urgent care centers to see if he came in for stitches. But the way they're folded with even blots, almost Rorschach-like, you see?" he held up the bag to look closer. "Looks like a bad bloody nose. Makes me think he broke it, or someone broke it for him. When did you say you last talked with him?"

"Sunday, but then day before yesterday he sent me this." Jude scrolled through the photos on her phone until she retrieved the ones that Tim had sent. She showed them to Haydon and asked, "You recognize the house or anything?" she asked.

Haydon shook his head. "Could be anywhere in Vermont," he replied. "Could be Montana. They mean anything to you?"

"No, but they came in an email about having something big on Amaethon."

"Big, meaning potentially damaging to Amaethon?"

Jude caught a renewed spark of interest in his eyes and said, "Sure, we're trying to document animal abuse." She held out the bloody tissues, asking hopefully, "You want to take these?"

"You hang onto them," he replied, adjusting his brimmed hat before he went back out into the heat.

Jude was disappointed that he didn't seem to be taking Tim's disappearance seriously. She trotted after him down the motel stairs and out to the parking lot, pestering him with questions about what he intended to do. In the end, Haydon only committed to take her cellphone number in the event he received any information. He asked what she planned to do, and she told him she was going to try showing Tim's photo around town.

"You could start at the farmers market in Montpelier," he suggested. "It draws a lot of locals. Maybe somebody's seen him. Good luck."

Jude took his advice and arrived at the market around lunchtime. Losing herself in the festive atmosphere, she wound through the crowd past brightly colored umbrellas and tents that filled the large parking lot behind a movie theater. Dads carried toddlers on their shoulders with a firm grasp on their pudgy ankles while Moms filled the strollers with bags of veggies, bread, and the first of the season's apples.

Montpelier was the capital city of Vermont, but with a population of less than 8,000, it was not much larger than Half Moon. It felt less like a city than a town; you could walk the entire downtown in fifteen minutes. But in that fifteen minutes, you'd pass a lot of vibrant and trendy shops and restaurants. The weekly market was more than just a place to buy local produce. Jude walked by a booth where kids were getting their faces painted.

Nearby was a play area with bales of hay for the youngsters to climb and benches for the adults to relax while they supervised.

She soaked it all in and wondered if she could live in Vermont. Flush with the community spirit of the farmers market, she thought that the people around her seemed smart about things that mattered – food, sustainability, supporting one another. She imagined having a peaceful little place with a wood burning stove and a garden. Maybe a house she and Tim could fix up together. Somewhere she would take a break from seeing or reading about the atrocities done to animals while she took long walks with Finn. And when the snow came, they would cuddle up next to the stove and–

"Ow!" cried the man.

Jude plowed directly into a man waiting on line for a cheese tasting. She apologized, explaining feebly, "I didn't see you."

"It's okay," he answered. But his expression said, "If you had your eyes open, you would have seen me."

Flustered, she moved off. She did have her eyes open. The neurologist's voice echoed in the back of her mind, *I recommend that you see somebody. Ruth Harris is very good. You'd like her.* Jude brushed away the thought as quickly as it had come and got to work, going vendor to vendor with the photo of Tim.

"Do you recall seeing him around?"

*No. What did he do?*

"Excuse me. Do you recognize him?"

*Uh, no. You the police?*

"Have you seen him before?"

*Who is he? Might have seen him around, I don't know. Why?*

It went that way until she got to one of the larger produce stands underneath a faded yellow tent promoting it as "Buck Farm

- Certified Organic." A man and woman were busy packing kale, corn, and tomatoes into customers' re-usable bags and making change from a cash box. Jude waited for a break in the activities before approaching the woman, whose face and arms were tanned from working in the sun all summer.

"Wondered if you could help me," said Jude, robotically pasting a smile on her face. She held out the photo, fully expecting the same head shake she'd gotten all morning, and asked, "Do you recall seeing him?"

Katherine Buck stared hard at Tim and then at Jude. In a voice thick with warning, she called, "Kurt. Come over here."

The man working with her rushed over. Graying sideburns protruded from his brown AGCO Tractors cap. His hands were large with awkward angles in the joints that suggested some arthritis. Katherine handed him the photo. His reaction was a sharp, sudden intake of breath. "It's about time you people came for him."

"You know him?" Jude asked in surprise, her pulse quickening.

"Damn right. What'd he do now?"

"Oh, I'm not with the police if that's what you're thinking. He's a friend of mine."

"Ah, Jesus," he muttered.

Stunned by his hostility, she stammered, "I'm not here to give you any trouble."

"Who are you?" interrupted Katherine.

"Like I said, he's a friend of mine."

"Don't care for the people you associate with," said Kurt, still fuming.

There was some mistake. They were not talking about the same person. "Would you look again?" Jude pleaded. "I don't think he's who you think he is."

Reluctantly, Katherine did as she requested, and after another quick glance, asked, "It's Tyler, right?"

Jude's stomach lurched.

"What do you want from us?"

"Do you know where I might be able to find him?"

"No. Who are you?" demanded Kurt.

Jude steadied herself. She had hoped that walking the market might elicit a simple, *Oh, sure, that's the dude I see at the library all the time*. But the Bucks had just shot that one down. She was going to have to tell them. She'd discussed with Gordon her next steps, and they decided that once she went to the police, there was no going back to a fabricated story about Tyler Jeffries. They had agreed, however, to provide as limited a version of the truth as possible.

"My name is Jude Brannock, and I work for an animal protection group," she began.

They listened warily for a few seconds before Kurt huffed, "You're with the ASPCA?"

"No."

"Lucky for them, I would have sued them for everything they're worth."

"Could you tell me what it is you think he's done?" asked Jude, becoming frustrated.

"Oh, it's not a question of *think*," Kurt countered bitterly. "I know. The sonofabitch was screwing my seventeen-year-old daughter and trying to get her addicted to heroin."

Jude could hardly believe her ears. Tim didn't do drugs. And a seventeen-year-old girl? "That's not possible," she asserted.

"Well, it's true," Katherine said.

Her husband leaned threateningly toward Jude. "I found them myself with the needle practically sticking out of her arm."

The bright colors and voices around Jude blurred into one buzz saw whine that obliterated coherent thought. Heroin? *What?*

"I'm … I don't …," she uttered haltingly.

"If my daughter hadn't begged me not to, we would've had him arrested. And you can tell that sonofabitch," continued Kurt, jabbing his finger in her direction, "that if I ever see him around Heather again, I'll kill him."

The whine inside her head played like a soundtrack, along with cinematic images of Tim fleeing Half Moon to escape criminal charges. *What in God's name did you do, Tim?*

"And don't think I won't," he added with emphasis.

But Buck had left an opening. He had not said the word *rape*. Nor, obviously, had he gotten the cops involved. There must be more to it. Jude lifted her head and met his angry glare. "In that case, maybe you *do* know where he is."

"What is that supposed to mean?"

"Just acknowledging your threat," replied Jude. She let a stunned moment elapse before asking, "Can I talk to Heather?"

"No," her parents said together.

"You can be present if you like. I'm only trying to understand what happened, because this is not the Tim that I know."

"You're not talking to her," Kurt reiterated.

His wife, however, had a better read of the woman standing in front of them, guessing that she wasn't going to simply slip away, and it would be preferable that when she did talk to Heather, one of them was around. She put a hand on her husband's arm. "Let her ask her questions. I'll go over with her."

A few customers waiting to pay for their produce had lined up at the other end of the table, and Kurt eyed them with some frustration. He licked his lips uncertainly. "I don't want her upset." Then he turned to Jude and warned, "And then you leave us alone."

Katherine walked Jude back through the market to the face painting station, where a young woman was holding up a mirror to a little boy, showing him his newly-painted tiger face.

Was this *her*? Jude felt a stinging pang of jealousy, and then of betrayal. The girl could have passed for twenty or twenty-one, but Tim must have known her true age. *Seventeen years old.* She was so delicately slim that Jude suddenly felt large-boned and awkward. Blond, sweet, young. Was this what Tim really wanted? Jude wondered if she had been a place holder all along.

"Heather, this woman would like to ask you some questions about Tyler," said Katherine.

The flash of fear in Heather's eyes was unmistakable.

"It's all right, honey," said her mother. "She works with him and just wants to ask if you know where he might be."

Heather's shoulders tightened up. It should have been a tip off, but Jude missed it, preoccupied by her growing belief that Tim had blown up the whole job for this ... cheerleader.

"Okay," said Heather cautiously. She patted the child waiting for the finishing touches to his face paint and told him, "You look ferocious. Go play with your sister."

He happily galloped off to join a few other kids in the hay bale circle of sugar-induced mania.

Katherine turned to Jude. "Tell Heather who Tyler really is," she prompted.

Jude met the girl's cornflower eyes. A part of her wanted to make this painful. "Tyler isn't his real name," she said bluntly. "His real name is Tim, and he works for our animal protection organization. He was here working in an undercover capacity." *Meaning, if he told you how beautiful you were, and he kissed your earlobes and your neck in a way that was tender and arousing, he was just playing a role. It wasn't real.*

"Are you shitting me?" The girl's jaw dropped open in genuine surprise.

"He never told you about that?"

"God, no. I mean, I knew he worked at the lab, but I didn't know he was like a spy or something."

"When was the last time you saw him?" asked Jude.

Heather flushed, and her mother answered for her. "Kurt found them last Monday night, and I'm sure that Tyler has not been in contact with Heather again. Am I right?"

"Yeah, yeah," confirmed her daughter.

"How did you two meet?" Jude asked, wanting to know but not wanting to hear it.

"At Galvey's."

"The music place?"

"Uh hunh." Heather's eyes moved back and forth between Jude and her mother, gauging their responses and trying to figure out how to skate through this one.

"We assumed they were going out with friends, to the movies and such," said Katherine.

"That's what we were doing, Mom."

Katherine sharpened her tone. "Obviously, that is not *all* you were doing."

"Do you know where he is?" asked Jude.

A high-pitched scream from the kids' play area shredded Heather's response. All three women looked over to see Tiger Boy holding his stubby fingers over his nose and mouth, his black and orange whiskers smeared with blood. Two younger children stood rooted in front of him, watching with curious horror.

Katherine glanced around to see if one of the boy's parents would respond, then clucked with disapproval. "Who is that?" she asked.

"Mrs. Healy's little guy," answered her daughter.

"Alright," sighed Katherine. "I'd better see what's going on."

She rushed off to attend to the boy, pulling tissues from her pocket. After a quick assessment, she looked back at them and gave a slight shake of her head in a way that conveyed "minor child crisis, no big deal, I've got this covered."

Grateful for the distraction that had taken Katherine out of earshot, Jude took the empty seat across from Heather to commence a real interrogation. "So, where is he?" she asked.

"I told you, I don't know. Really."

"When was the last time you saw him?"

"Monday night. It was … awkward."

"I'll say." Jude took a slow breath, then said, "I gather you two were sleeping together."

Heather looked down at the ground.

"Listen, I don't care one way or the other," declared Jude, telling herself she really believed it. "But we haven't heard from him for days, and you must know something."

"I don't, okay? I mean, yeah, we hooked up, but only a few times. We did other stuff, too, you know. We hung out at Galvey's and around."

"What about the drugs?"

"What *about* the drugs?"

"Do you use heroin?"

Heather gasped. "Jesus, no!"

"Then what were you doing shooting up?"

"It was just the one time. I was like trying it, you know? But it was a huge mistake, I get that. I really do."

"And how did it go down?"

"What do you mean?"

"Who brought smack to the party?"

"Tim."

"*Tim* convinced you to try it?"

"Yeah, he was just like I should check it out, that it would expand my horizons."

"And did it? *Expand* your horizons?" Jude felt herself becoming catty. "Never mind. I don't suppose that it crossed your mind that shooting up is stupid and dangerous."

"He said he knew what he was doing."

"Wait. You're telling me he presented you with the heroin, all the paraphernalia to shoot up, and personally gave you the injection?"

"Yes."

Jude looked over to Katherine, who was still tending to the boy, and she used the time to take in what Heather was telling her. Finally, she turned back and asked, "Where did he get it?"

"I don't know."

Jude watched carefully, looking for the smallest facial tic that might give away a lie. But the girl's expression remained authentically blank.

"You really don't know?" pressed Jude.

"I would have told my parents if I did. I am in deep shit, as you can probably imagine."

"According to your father, you didn't want to press charges. You begged him."

"Why would I press charges? I can make my own decisions about who I hook up with. The age of consent is sixteen."

"Are you *serious*?" Jude asked, her mouth dropping open. "Tim was ten years older than you."

"It doesn't matter in this state. At sixteen you can sleep with anyone you want."

From the look on Heather's face, it was apparent that her female intuition was telling her that Jude and Tim were a thing – or had been. Maybe it wasn't a guess and Tim had said something outright. Either way, Jude felt painfully exposed.

Heather went on, saying, "But I liked Tyler."

"His name is Tim."

"Whatever."

"I don't believe you," challenged Jude. "I don't believe you about the dope, and I think you know where he is."

"How many times do I have to—"

A shadow fell over them as Katherine returned. "Jarrod's alright, his mom is with him," she reported. "Just a bloody nose. You have a garbage pail?"

Heather nodded to a small plastic pail where Katherine tossed a large wad of tissues soiled with blood. Jude's eyes followed it into the waste bin.

She got to her feet and handed Heather a business card. "Thanks for your time. I appreciate you talking to me," she said woodenly, then reconsidered. It never helped to antagonize. Aiming for a genuine smile, she added, "Look, if you hear from Tim or have any information about where he might be, I'd appreciate a call."

As she left the booth, Jude glanced over her shoulder to see Katherine speaking gently to her daughter. Beyond them, a woman with round spectacles was administering to Tiger Boy, dabbing gently at his nose with a napkin. From what Jude could see, however, it was still coming away bloody. The kid must have taken quite a bump.

\* \* \*

Heather quickened her pace as she left the farmers market, forty-six dollars in tips tucked in her jeans pocket. Her parents thought she was going for a soft-serve with Rachel.

She crossed the stone bridge over the Winooski River, made a right onto Summer Street, and walked down the residential street to a three-story clapboard house. The wood window frames were rotting, and weeds sprouted up between the uneven bricks in the sidewalk. An older model blue Grand Prix with a long gouge on the front fender was parked in front. With a quick glance behind her, she climbed to the third floor. His apartment was in the back and he'd left the door open a crack.

Afternoon light came through the grimy windows and pooled on the linoleum floor of the kitchenette where some liquid had spilled and hardened. The place smelled of roach spray and cigarette smoke. Bobby Gravaux spoke from the shadows in the corner. "What took you so long?"

"I told you, I had to do the market today," said Heather. She traipsed over to the mattress on the floor where Bobby sat, ankles crossed, his back against the wall. "What happened to your car?" she asked.

"Some asshole side-swiped me." Bobby's voice was smooth and ripened. So was the way he moved and the way he looked in his trademark black leather vest. A thick lock of wavy brown hair fell across his brow and he brushed it back with long fingers.

"Guess what?" asked Heather. "Tyler is an undercover investigator. He was working undercover at the lab over on 107. Do you fucking believe that?"

Bobby pulled a half pack of Marlboros from his vest pocket, tapped out a cigarette, and flicked a disposable lighter to the tip. He drew in a lungful of smoke and exhaled lazily. "So?" he asked.

"So, isn't that like totally insane?"

"How'd you find out?"

"Some woman came looking for him today. She's with this group he works for. She said it does animal protection things, but I think only hardcore animal activists go undercover."

"What'd you tell her?"

"I told her I don't know where the fuck he is. That I haven't seen him since that night."

"You tell her what happened with Tyler?"

"Nothing more than what my parents know. Christ, my mother was standing right there. You haven't seen him, have you?"

Bobby shook his head, but Heather wasn't sure she believed him. "Isn't that crazy, though? *Under-cover*," she intoned, wiggling her fingers in front of his face. "Like a real spy."

Gazing at her through narrowed eyes, Bobby asked, "Is that a turn-on for you?"

"No, I didn't say that. I just … think it's crazy."

"Yeah, crazy," drawled Bobby with another smoky exhale. Then he held out his hand, "Come 'ere, baby."

Heather let herself be pulled down onto the mattress where, without moving from his fixed position, Bobby kissed her, thrusting his tongue slowly and luxuriously into her mouth. She responded in kind, and soon he was unzipping her jeans and pulling them off, ready to devour her. She wriggled away, saying, "I wanna do up first."

"Naw baby, then you ain't interested."

"I will be, you'll see," pleaded Heather. She sweetened the deal, leaning in to run the tip of her tongue across his lower lip.

Bobby balanced his cigarette across the top of an open soda can and reached over to get a kit from the floor. The pale hairs on Heather's neck rose in response like tiny cilia seeking nourishment. He tore the sterile cellophane wrappings from the spoon, the vial of distilled water, and the acidic solution. Bobby relied on prepackaged injection kits – his livelihood was too important to risk infection just to save a buck here and there.

He emptied some grains of heroin into the spoon and added the water. Before he began to heat it with his lighter, he tossed a rubber tube to Heather, who grabbed it and with practiced hands tied it around her upper arm. She watched with hungry anticipation. When the brown juice was ready, Bobby drew it up into a new syringe, tapping on the glass to remove any bubbles. Then he fed it into Heather's waiting vein.

Almost before he had withdrawn the needle, Heather lifted her head, a beatific expression spread across her face. She closed her eyes, feeling as though the softest, warm blanket had just been draped around her body. She was floating and everything around her was perfect.

"You good?" asked Bobby.

"Yeahhh. Good."

"Tell me about the woman asking for Tyler."

Heather responded with a quiet moan and shook her head. She couldn't be bothered now. She just wanted to be inside herself, cradled in God's arms, all the expectations and conflict vanquished.

"Don't get too used to it, baby," crooned Bobby. "You've only got a chicken shit habit now. Let's keep it that way."

He left Heather lolling on the mattress and picked up her jeans. He rifled through the pockets and found her tips, counted out twenty dollars, then reconsidered and added two fives. She owed him from last time, too. Bobby stuffed the cash into his pocket and drifted into the kitchenette to get himself a bowl of cereal.

He ate standing up, watching the first drops of rain hit the river and turn it from muddy green to black. *Tyler Jeffries was an undercover investigator for animals? Sonovabitch.*

# CHAPTER 8

That night Galvey's pulsed with energy. A band from Burlington was hammering out a cover of a hot country duo from the elevated stage, and the young crowd, a mix of wanna-be hipsters from the community college and some of the locals, were geared up to blow off steam at the end of the workweek. All were having fun, dancing and getting drunk.

Jude pushed her way up to the bar and studied the chalk board that listed the beers on tap. She tried to catch the attention of one of the bartenders. Finally, a girl with a lip piercing and a long, black braid came over.

"I'll take a Magic Hat," shouted Jude.

The bartender nodded and brought back a tall, frothy glass of the amber ale. Before Jude put her money on the counter, she thrust the photograph of Tim in front of her and asked, "You seen him around recently?"

The girl toyed with her lip ornament for a moment, giving Jude the once over.

"Not a cop," Jude read correctly. "Just a friend."

Eyes whisking over the photo, the bartender said, "Not for a few days."

"How many days?"

"I don't know. A week, maybe? I don't work every day."

Thanking her, Jude picked up her glass and held it aloft to keep from spilling while she jostled her way to a spot along the wall as far from the band as possible.

It wasn't that she minded the music. In fact, she liked country music, especially the old artists like Merle Haggard and Johnny Cash. Friends often made fun of her preference for the traditional sound, but regularly jolted by the latest cruel and capricious ways animals were abused, she was comforted by country's predictability. The same cadences and stories, music that was sure and steady, something in her life she could count on.

Tonight, however, she wasn't here to enjoy the music and needed to position herself near the entrance where she could see who was coming and going. She didn't know exactly who she was looking for and wasn't holding out hope that Tim would appear, but Galvey's had been mentioned more than once as a place he hung out. In her job, if you were patient and kept your eyes open, sometimes a lead would surface.

The band had launched into its second set and the place was rowdier than ever when Jude spotted a familiar face. Indeed, who could miss the flaming red hair that was now free of its laboratory hair covering? Sylvia, the tech from Amaethon, came through the door with two girlfriends. The three women pranced across the dance floor and up to the bar, where they ordered shots of tequila. They were soon joined by a couple of guys.

When Sylvia's pals drifted off with them onto the dance floor, Jude made her move.

She gently elbowed her way up to the bar next to Sylvia and ordered another draft beer. Then, as if running into the Amaethon tech was a surprise, she said, "Oh, hi. Remember me?"

Sylvia remembered all right. "Did you find Tyler?" she asked. "I'm sorry about your father."

"Yeah, well," hedged Jude. "You want a drink? It's on me." She pointed to Sylvia's empty glass.

"I can pay," she replied warily.

"No, let me get it." Jude motioned to the bartender to bring another round for her friend, then faced her.

Sylvia's eyes were bloodshot and there was high color in her cheeks; Jude guessed she'd been drinking before she arrived. "I know you couldn't really talk before, not with your bosses standing around. Neither could I," she added, projecting over the noise. "Here's the thing. I didn't exactly tell them the truth, which is I'm not really Tyler's sister. We both work for an animal protection organization. You probably know if you've worked at other labs that they don't always treat the animals well. So, um, Tyler – actually his name is really Tim – was there to see how Amaethon is doing in that regard."

Sylvia looked at her strangely for a moment as if she had misheard. Then she said, "We do not abuse animals at Amaethon."

"I'm not accusing you of anything," Jude replied.

After a moment to take in Jude's confession, Sylvia asked, "You're telling me Tyler was an undercover animal rights person?"

"Guess you could say that."

"Holy shit."

Their drinks arrived, and Jude tipped her glass against Sylvia's. "Cheers," she said brightly.

"It's the God's honest truth?"

"God's honest truth," said Jude.

Sylvia's face twitched and a giggle erupted from her throat. "That is sick!" she said, starting to laugh. "That is so sick." She collected herself and asked, "What is his real name again?"

"Tim."

"And your name isn't really Emily, is it?"

"No. It's Jude."

A new bout of laughter overtook Sylvia. She wiped her eyes. "I don't know why I find this funny. It's just … so weird."

"Yeah, a little weird," concurred Jude. She felt in some odd way that she was making progress. "But it gets weirder, even. Because we don't know where Tim is, and we're concerned that something's happened to him."

The tech downed her shot quickly, and while her throat adjusted to the burn, stared at the empty glass … buying time. Jude was sure she was holding back, but by now recognized that it wasn't just the alcohol; the girl was so stoned she might not be able to organize her thoughts well enough to pick and choose what to reveal.

Jude decided to help her out. She leaned in and asked, "You have any ideas? Like, for instance, you have any reason to think that the bosses at Amaethon, Dr. Ostrovsky and that other guy Mr. Byer could have known or suspected that Tim was undercover?"

"I doubt it," offered Sylvia. "If they did, he would have been out on his ass."

Robin Lamont

"And how about Tim? Did he seem his usual self or did he seem bothered about anything?"

"Well, now that you mention it, the whole last week he did seem kinda sketchy."

"Sketchy, how?"

"Oh, rushing through everything, like he kept forgetting to make notes on the humidity and temperature charts. And he got crazy about one particular dog that we called Bailey. We're not supposed to give them names, but we do."

"What was the matter with Bailey?"

"He wasn't doing well."

"What do you mean?"

"There was blood in his stool, and he wouldn't eat. We had to hand feed him so he'd get the proper dosage."

"Of the heart medication? That's what you're testing, right?"

Sylvia hesitated. "I'm not sure I should be talking to you," she said warily.

"I don't care about Amaethon," responded Jude. "The undercover thing is over. I'm only interested in Tim, and I need to understand his state of mind."

"Okay," Sylvia said cautiously. "So, what's your question?"

"What happened with Bailey?"

"He died." She swigged the last few drops of tequila.

Jude had an overwhelming urge to heave her glass against the bottles lined up behind the bar. The sudden concussion of smashing glass might have obliterated the image of Bailey, a brown and white beagle with soft, floppy ears. The patrons' shrieks might have blocked out the knowledge that he and the other dogs, most of them barely six months old, were bred to be used as living petri dishes. Bred to be dosed, then coolly monitored as they sickened, and finally to be disposed of when the experiment was over. The sense of human entitlement sometimes made Jude want to shatter things.

But tonight, she needed information. Jaw clenched, she asked, "Do you think Tim is still in the area?"

"I have no idea." Sylvia finally made eye contact now that Jude had moved on to more solid ground.

"He didn't give you any indication that he was going to quit?"

"No."

Wafting scents of sweat and perfume, Sylvia's friends breathlessly rushed back to the bar.

"Hiya," said Jude cheerily. "I was talking with Sylvia here. Either of you ladies know Tyler Jeffries?"

"Who?" asked one girl.

"What does he look like?" asked the other.

"Curly brown hair, six-two, nice looking … you know who I'm talking about?"

Both girls tittered and shook their heads. They seemed hyper and unable to focus. One of them poked Sylvia gently with her elbow and said, "Hey, you need to use the bathroom?"

The second girl jumped on the idea, "Yeah, I have to pee," she agreed, giving Sylvia a knowing look.

About as subtle as a Humvee; the eyes on both of them weren't just bright – they were ablaze, red-rimmed, pupils huge. They were miles high on something, probably coke, and aiming to snort a couple more lines in a bathroom stall.

Sylvia was good with that and said to Jude, "Well, sorry I can't be of more help, but … I do have to use the ladies' room, so …"

"Hold on," said Jude, putting her hand on Sylvia's arm. "Before you all go hit up, I gotta ask you something."

"Don't know what you're—"

"Spare me, okay? I'm not a cop," she said, for what felt like the umpteenth time that day. "Listen, I got word that Tim was involved with some heroin. I don't know if he was or not. But if he was, where around here would he get something like that?"

The women checked in with one another before shaking their heads.

"Come on," chastised Jude. "You ladies have been around, you know what I'm talking about. Just give me a clue, if not a name, a coffee shop, a street corner, I'll make my own inquiries. No one will know it came from you."

"No, we don't know about that," said Sylvia.

"Unless, maybe, Tim was getting his smack from you," said Jude, louder than was necessary.

One of her friends leaned in and said, "You could ask around for Bobby G." She said his name with a smile that made Jude think she was smitten.

"Shut *up!*" cried Sylvia, smacking the girl on the arm.

"Where might I find this ... individual?" asked Jude.

"Jesus Christ," barked Sylvia to her friend. "Uh, we're done here."

"Okay, okay," Jude said, holding up her hands in surrender. "Listen, if you think of anything or hear anything about Tim, I'm staying at the Riverside Motel, room 210."

Sylvia scooped up her pals and steered them away.

Watching them blend into the dancing crowd, Jude wondered what Sylvia was hiding. It would make sense that she didn't want to name her drug supplier, but she'd been uncomfortable even before that.

The space occupied by Sylvia and friends was soon taken by a couple of flushed young men who eyed Jude admiringly and appeared poised to strike up a conversation.

Muttering an excuse, she put her half-finished beer on the bar and headed out. At the door, she looked back over her shoulder. Maybe I'm reading too much into it, she thought. Who wouldn't be defensive talking about force-feeding dogs just to see how sick they'd get? Who wouldn't want to smoke something or pop a pill that could make you forget what you did all day?

She watched Sylvia – head thrown back, red hair dancing wildly to the music, not caring if she had a partner – and had the feeling that the dogs weren't the only ones who were suffering.

* * *

Four months earlier on a warm evening in May, Jude kicked off the damp sheet on her bed and arranged the pillows behind her for better back support. For a moment, a distant siren crowded out the chirping of urban crickets outside. She wore nothing except one of Tim's old denim shirts. It was soft with the color bleached out from a hundred washings and it smelled of him: earthy and sweaty underneath the "fresh scent" of laundry detergent.

She settled herself cross-legged and ran her finger down the list she'd prepared on a legal pad. "Come back," she hollered. "We still have a lot to go over."

From the kitchen, she heard the refrigerator door open and close several times. "What are you doing?" she called impatiently.

Tim wandered into the bedroom, buck naked, holding a dish piled high with broccoli and carrots. "Getting something to eat," he said. "Want?" He held out the dish.

She shook her head. "Let's go over the video systems again."

"Let's not." Tim stretched out next to her and continued crunching on his snack. Finn padded in and dutifully sat next to him, hoping he would share.

Jude looked over with mild disapproval and asked, "How can you eat broccoli *raw* like that?"

"I like it raw."

"I don't understand how you digest it."

"When I was a kid growing up on my uncle's farm, I ate raw veggies all the time. Guess my system is used to it."

"The other day you ate brussels sprouts right out of the bag. Really? Why not just chew on a branch?"

"You ran out of 'em," said Tim. He fed a carrot stick to Finn before popping another floret into his mouth.

"Let's talk about the video," sighed Jude.

"We've been over it a thousand times. I know, I know, 'verifiable, solid evidence to connect the animals with the laboratory.'"

"And how do you do that?"

"By keeping objects and personnel unique to Amaethon in the continuous footage," he intoned.

"Is this so dull for you?" accused Jude. "I hope not, because there's no point taking this risk if all you come away with is generic video of animals being tossed into cages. They'll just call it fake, doctored footage. And then we're in a we-said-they-said situation which we always lose. It has to be specific to Amaethon."

"Don't worry," soothed Tim, reaching over to sweep her loose hair over her shoulder. "I'm going to get you a lot of good stuff."

"We don't need *a lot*," she countered. "What we need is irrefutable evidence that the USDA cannot sweep under the rug."

"You worry too much." Tim put the half-eaten vegetable plate on the bedside table and plucked the pad out of her hands. He tossed it aside as he climbed over to straddle her thighs.

Jude tried to gather her concentration and press on. "And don't do it for *me*. There are animals suffering, and I presume you took this job to make a difference."

Tim kissed her neck. "Are you going to come up and visit me?"

"I … no, probably not."

"Why not?" He slowly undid two of the buttons on her shirt and kissed her bare shoulder.

"Because if anyone is keeping tabs on you and sees us together, it would raise questions."

"I won't make it three months without you."

At this, Jude pushed him roughly back. "Of course, you will."

He grabbed hold of her hands and said, "I need you."

"Well, don't."

"I can't help how I feel."

"Oh God, Tim, let's not get into this again. We've only got two more days to–"

"No, let's talk about it. I'm crazy about you, and I'm tired of having to keep us a secret."

"I never promised you–"

"I never promised to hide like a criminal. Why do you think Gordon and everyone wouldn't understand? We're on the same team, remember?"

"It wouldn't look good."

"Screw that. We're both grown-ups, we both want this."

"It's unprofessional."

"Not if you're doing your job and I'm doing my job. I don't want to just assume this is temporary."

"Oh, Tim. You don't know what you want."

"That's insulting. Of course, I do."

Jude wrested her hands away from his grasp and said, "It cannot work with us long term. I care about you, but I don't do long term."

"Because you're older than me?"

"No, because the animals will always come first."

Hurt flashed in his eyes and then was gone. As easy as breathing, he leaned down to take her ear lobe in the tip of his teeth. Using his tongue, he swept down her neck, while his hands pulled up her shirt and cupped her breasts.

Jude didn't resist. She couldn't. Even knowing this was his way of exerting control, his tenderness was so rich, so arousing, it took her will away. He touched and kissed in places he knew excited her, hesitating at just the right moments to make her ache for more. When she beggingly arched her hips toward his, he was ready.

He looked deep into her eyes, and said, "I'm going to make you proud of me, you'll see." Then slowly, he slipped inside her and Jude came with a strangled cry.

# CHAPTER 9

The image of Sylvia's fierce, defiant dancing was still with her as Jude drove back to the Riverside Motel. If nothing panned out with Bobby G, the girl would be worth contacting again, hopefully next time when she wasn't wrecked.

Jude eased her old Subaru station wagon into the first open parking slot, surprised that the place was so full. When she got out, she could hear the thudding of heavy bass coming from one of the rooms and even at this late hour smelled barbeque smoke.

She stepped along the pathway from the parking lot, her feet crunching on the gravel. The knee-high solar lights shone on the surrounding grass, and in the glow, lingering raindrops looked like tiny jewels. They made her think of second grade when she'd been desperately and hopelessly enthralled with fairies, headstrong maidens, and powerful dragons who fought for good. She'd point out twinkling dew in the early morning sun, telling anyone who'd listen, and many who didn't, that the sparkling droplets were fairy money – valuable, but fleeting.

One day, her teacher tried to disavow her of her fantasies. "You know, Jude, that fairies are just made up, right?"

"They're real!" insisted Jude.

"No, dear, they're not."

"Oh, yeah?" challenged Jude, small chin thrust forward. She pointed to the windows of the classroom that were dusted with overnight frost, creating impossibly intricate crystal patterns that winked in the sun. "Then how do you explain that?" She tromped off, having proved her point.

There was a childlike part of her that still wanted to believe in fairies. On early morning runs with Finn when the grass shimmered with dew and her running shoes became sodden with their currency, she imagined they might exist in the places where the land and sky still belonged to the animals.

But not tonight. And not here in Half Moon where dogs and mice were kept in cages from the moment of their birth until they were euthanized and necropsied. Here there was no magic or wonder in the beating hearts of animals – they were just useful statistics on a graph.

A man stepped out of the shadows in front of her and Jude quickly jumped back.

"Ms. Brannock."

"Sergeant Haydon." It took a moment before she relaxed the grip on her keys she'd instinctively fashioned into a weapon.

"Sorry to startle you. Thought I'd catch you here when I couldn't reach you by phone," he said.

Her chest constricted so tightly she could hardly breathe. Police officers didn't usually come around in person unless they had bad news. "Did you find anything?" she managed to get out.

"No, I just wanted to let you know that I put out a BOLO, a be-on-the-lookout, for Tim and his car. Nothing back yet."

The air came out of her lungs in a rush. And then she wondered why, if Haydon hadn't come to tell her they'd found Tim's body, he'd sought her out at this hour. To report that he'd been doing what a missing persons investigator did as a matter of routine? No, there was something else behind it.

"You work long hours, Sergeant," she noted dryly.

"I wanted you to know, that's all."

"Thanks, but come on, it's nearly midnight." Then it hit her. "Oh, right, I get it. I'm an animal activist and you have to keep tabs on extremists like me."

Haydon didn't offer a denial, nor did he seem in any way defensive that she'd seen behind his pretext. "Goodnight, Ms. Brannock," he said, nodded curtly, and stepped around her.

"What are you afraid I'm going to do? Burn down the lab?" she called after him.

He stopped and turned. "Are you?"

"Jesus! Of course not. I told you, we don't do that sort of thing."

"We? You didn't tell me you have colleagues here."

"I don't. I meant, we ... as in my organization."

"And you can't see that an organization like yours might be on our radar screen?" he shot back. "I'm supposed to take your word for your good intentions? I'd like to, but here I am wondering how you got Tim into the laboratory and what lines you folks might have crossed to do that."

Jude didn't like where this was headed. "Sergeant, I'm just here looking for my friend. That's the truth. Yes, he was working undercover, but that's not illegal. Not in Vermont, anyway. If you had a co-worker undercover and he suddenly disappeared, I bet the state would pull out all the stops to find them. We're not on opposite sides."

"Maybe not."

"And I could use your help."

"I'll do what I can, so long as you stay on the right side of the law."

"It's a deal. We might even be able to help each other."

Haydon walked a little closer. "Did you learn something?"

"As a matter of fact, I did. Tim was sleeping with a girl named Heather Buck, and she claims he introduced her to heroin. She's only seventeen and her father found out. He was livid. I saw him today at the farmers market, like you suggested, and he's still very angry. He said, and I quote, 'If I ever see him around Heather again, I'll kill him.'"

"Not an unusual reaction from a father, I'd say."

"It'd put him on *my* suspect list," Jude replied.

"Suspect for what, exactly? There's been no crime committed. Until I file my report, you don't even have an official missing persons case. All you have is an animal activist that you can't find and for all we know, is sipping a piña colada in the Bahamas right now."

"Well, something doesn't add up. Tim was not a user, I'd stake my life on it."

"There's a first time for everything. We happen to have a big heroin problem in the northeast."

"You ever hear of a dealer named Bobby G?"

If he had, Haydon didn't let on. He just said, "If I was you, I would just go home. We have your contact info and will call you if we come across something. Should your guy turn up, maybe you let me know."

But Jude wasn't going anywhere. "If I were looking for someone *like* Bobby G, where might I find him?"

Haydon squinted at her and sighed, "Lady, you are looking for trouble."

"No, I'm looking for information."

"Go home, Brannock. That's the best information I can give you."

As Jude was opening her door, her cellphone began to chirp. It was Lucas. "Where have you been?" he asked. "I've been trying to reach you all night."

"Sorry, I was busy."

"Anything develop after we talked?"

"I might have a lead on where Tim allegedly got his heroin," she said, letting herself in and tossing her shoulder bag on the bed.

"Allegedly?"

"I don't believe this drug thing. Hell, I never even saw him smoke a joint. Maybe he was forced into it or maybe he was so stressed he was looking for a moment of escape."

"Listen to yourself, Jude. You told me that he and the girl got caught *shooting up*. That's no beginner stage. Usually, people start by snorting it. Injecting heroin is a whole other thing, okay? You have to cook it with water and a solvent. You have to filter it, and you have to know how to get it in without blowing a vein."

"Straight from the horse's mouth."

Silence.

"I'm sorry," said Jude. "That was unfair."

"It was a long time ago."

"I know. I know that, Lucas. It's just that Tim wasn't a junkie."

"A lot of people who shoot up say the same thing."

Jude kicked off her shoes and sat heavily on the bed. Damn, Lucas could be annoying. He questioned everything. What was wrong with going with your gut once in a while? For all his hang-loose, drowsy demeanor, he approached every investigation as if he was building a Lego tower, one tiny brick at a time. She wondered if his inability to occasionally tap into instinct was a coping mechanism he'd adopted from his wartime experiences. Sometimes she wished she'd known him before his time in the military, sure that three tours in Afghanistan – the last one disastrous – had changed him. How could it not?

They'd met at an animal rights conference where he was searching for some way to channel his anger. The people and the places that abused animals were a good start. Even though he was reserved, she recognized a powerful hunger in him. He walked the conference with a cautious, watchful gate, like a big cat searching for prey. In some ways he looked like a starving lion – all ribs and tawny, shaggy mane. She took a seat next to him at one of the panel discussions and asked him what had brought him to the conference. He told her that he wanted justice for the animals, but after she got to know him better, she thought that what he was really yearning for was truth and fairness for himself. So far, life hadn't given him much of that.

She found herself drawn to his opaque wariness, keen to solve him like a puzzle, and she believed there was a mutual sexual attraction. On the last night, he invited her to his hotel room, but it didn't go the way she had imagined. Physical intimacy was not what he needed just then.

Lucas tossed the plastic room key on the dresser and took the single chair by the window, leaving Jude to sit uncertainly on the edge of the bed. She was wondering whether to make the first move when suddenly, a white rat scurried out from under the bed between her feet. She screeched and drew her legs up. To her horror, the rat leapt onto Lucas's lap.

"Meet Habib," he said.

"What?"

"He's my rat."

"You can't be serious. You brought a rat into the Hyatt?"

"We're very close."

By now, the rodent had crept up to Lucas's shoulder and was nuzzling his hair. "If the cleaning staff finds him, they'll call an exterminator," Jude pointed out. "Try explaining to them how close you two are."

"You want to pet him?" asked Lucas.

"No thanks." She didn't even want to step on the floor. She had nothing against rats and mice, just preferred they keep their distance.

"Rats are very intelligent, you know," said Lucas, stroking Habib with his finger. "They communicate with each other using high-frequency sounds we can't hear. And they like to play. I don't keep him in a cage much. He doesn't like it. If I have to put him in, as soon as I open the door, he's like, boom! I'm outta here."

"Why do you call him Habib?" asked Jude, feeling only slightly more comfortable since the rat showed no signs of bounding in her direction.

Lucas gazed out the window at the lights spread out below and didn't say anything. His face had all but closed down.

"Habib's an unusual name ... for a rat," prodded Jude gently. Finally, he looked back at her. "Do you really want to know?"

"Yes, I want to know."

"I've never told anybody this, but I'll tell you because I think you're as damaged as I am, and you'll understand."

"Thanks," replied Jude, not entirely sure what she was thanking him for.

As he absently stroked Habib, he recounted, "My last tour in Diyala, I was a squad commander. One night when we were stationed away from the base, a bunch of Sunnis took us on. It was quick. Two of my men were killed and I was taken alive. Turned out they weren't really Sunnis. They might have been Shi'a, who the fuck knows – religious affiliations are pretty strict over there, but allegiances run a whole lot looser. Either way, they thought they could get a decent price for an American squad commander.

"They moved me around some, but finally I ended up in a village in the mountains. They kept me in a room with no windows. Four months. They tossed me food in the afternoon and beat the crap out of me once a week for fun. Anyway, there was a rat that used to come visit me. At first, he came for the food, whatever crumbs I dropped. But then he started to hang around. He took food from my hand and after a while, he let me pet him. He was my friend and I named him Habib. The only thing that kept me from losing my mind was looking forward to his visits.

"One day, a guard saw him and crushed him with his rifle butt. After that, I didn't care what happened to me and I sort of wished they'd just shoot me. But about a week later, out of the blue, I was traded for some prisoners in Baghdad. That's it."

Jude allowed the painful memories to wash over them for a moment before asking, "So, obviously, that's not the same Habib."

"No, even if they hadn't killed him, rats in the wild don't generally live for more than a year or two. I've had several since I've been home. I name each one Habib." He looked at her with mournful eyes. "To me, they're all Habib."

That night, Lucas and Jude talked until the sun began to brighten the horizon.

Back in the present, Jude settled more comfortably on the bed and put her phone on speaker. "Okay, Lucas. Let's just say Tim thought he could woo Miss Heather by introducing her to heroin, as she claims. What if he really liked it? Do you think he could have OD'd someplace?"

"Possible. But look at this rationally. If he was new to drugs, he wouldn't be going off to shoot up by himself. He wasn't stupid. It's much more likely that he's alive and well. If he left the lab outright or if he somehow got made and had to run, he's made a choice that doesn't include phoning in to you and having to face your disappointment. For all we know, he's in California having a grand old time."

Annoyed that both Haydon and Lucas were so quick to place Tim in a palm-treed paradise, implying a lazy indulgence in him, Jude pushed back. "I don't think so. I think something happened to him."

"Like what? If Amaethon made him as an undercover, they never would've bought your story about being his sister."

"What about Heather's father? He's out there broadcasting that if he ever saw Tim again, he'd kill him. Maybe he already did and that's just an act."

"Mmmn," demurred Lucas.

"Don't be so quick to dismiss the idea. I get the feeling that Heather was his princess." Not that Jude knew anything about being a father's princess, not in any of the foster homes she had lived. But she did know something about domestic violence and what an angry, drunken man was capable of. "Kurt Buck is convinced that Tim is the evil boyfriend who's despoiled his daughter and turned her into a junkie."

Lucas still wasn't buying. "I can guarantee you that if she's telling her folks she *never* tried it before Tim came along, she's lying. Like I said, shooting up ain't a rookie play."

"Okay. If she is lying, how much money would a habit like that cost?"

"Depends on how much she's using. Can get very expensive."

"The girl is in high school," exclaimed Jude. "How could she afford it?"

"Funny you should bring that up. That's partly why I'm calling." There was a you're-not-going-to-like-this warning in Lucas's voice. "I talked to Tim's roommate Chris today. He told me that Tim had gotten behind in his rent payments. And then just before Tim left for Vermont, he paid up in one lump sum, including three months advance. Six thousand dollars."

For a moment Jude couldn't speak. Tim had never said a word about debt problems or coming into a considerable sum of money, and they'd been together until the day he left.

"Kind of a red flag, wouldn't you say? Kinship salary barely pays the rent, much less a hardcore drug habit. So, where did the money come from? And why would he pay up in advance?"

"He was going undercover for twelve weeks," Jude tried. "He probably felt he should pay Chris up front for the time he was gone."

"Cash? He could've done a money transfer or sent a check when the rent came due. That's how it's usually done."

"Well, maybe he didn't want to alert Chris to where he was with a postmark or …." she knew damn well Tim did his banking online.

"Or maybe he paid up front because he knew he wasn't coming back," suggested Lucas.

They both let that possibility hang in the air.

"Anyway," he finally continued, "Gordon wants me to explore the money thing further, see what I can dig up. Unless you have any ideas."

*Unless you have any ideas.* An artificial lightness had crept into his voice, which she knew was his way of disguising his feelings. Was he trying to ask if she and Tim were involved?

Ever since the night he'd confided in her about his capture, she'd known that if she let him, Lucas would fall in love with her. Often, she thought that if she was smart and perhaps not as "damaged" as he suspected, she'd feel the same way. But he had never pushed, and Jude left it there, offering what she could: the honesty and fairness he needed from a friend. Only now, she wasn't giving him either.

"No ideas," replied Jude, her lips suddenly parched. "Haven't a clue."

Before getting undressed, she went over to the window to pull the curtains closed. She stared out and listened to moth wings beating against the light, the leaden weight of betrayal settling into her chest. Hers in withholding the truth from Lucas and

Tim's in withholding the truth from her. He'd been screwing a seventeen-year-old, doing major league drugs, and who knew what else, all the while playing the committed animal activist. All the while telling her how much he missed her and how he wanted to do such a great job. Screw him. And now this thing with the money. Who the *hell* was Tim Mains?

Jude looked down at the pathway, hoping to see the sparkle of fairy dust on the wet lawn, but all she could see was artificial light shining on barren patches of grass.

# CHAPTER 10

"Thanks for the quick turnaround. Send them over and I'll take a closer look," said Dr. Harbolt.

He hung up the phone, leaned back in his chair, and stared out his office window while he reviewed the information he'd just heard. Tori Lacey's platelet count was very low, which could explain the young woman's excessive bruising, although the word "bruise" didn't accurately describe the bottoms of her feet. They showed classic signs of thrombocytopenia — leaking capillaries under the skin's surface. Why? He knew her history; she wasn't a hemophiliac. What with her weight loss, his first worry was leukemia. But she had no fever and her heart sounded fine. There were other possibilities: Cushing's syndrome, liver disease, HIV. But each of these would present additional symptoms which she did not exhibit.

His assistant poked her head through the door and announced, "Your wife is on two."

The receiver was barely to his ear when he was accused. "John Harbolt, did you put out rat poison around the barn?"

"Hello, dear."

"I found two dead rats in back of the barn."

"Oh, my." With his free hand, the doctor pulled up his email to see if the specifics on Tori's lab results had come through. They had.

"And I think a few of the hens might be sick. They've stopped laying."

"Darling, you know I wouldn't put out poison anywhere near the hens. Maybe there's a fox in the neighborhood and they're edgy."

"Mmmn. I think I'll bring them in early tonight."

"That's a good idea, dear." He clicked on the attachment to see the full CBC on Tori.

"What do you want for dinner?"

He mumbled a vague response while he enlarged the document.

"Well, I can hear you're busy," said his wife.

Dr. Harbolt leaned in to read the numbers. Looking for an answer. He didn't find one, but he did see enough to prompt a call to Tori and let her know that she had to stop running and forego all other track activities until they figured out what was wrong. It would only take one bad fall to precipitate internal bleeding that might well be fatal.

* * *

Stuart Ostrovsky picked up a lab rat by its tail and peered at the number tattooed on a shaved patch of skin. He read it aloud, then weighed his test subject, while Lester made notes.

After depositing the animal back in its cage, Ostrovsky swiftly moved on to another. This one was harder to grab. Several were showing signs of increased agitation. It wouldn't be long before they stopped eating regularly. Not surprising, but it meant that his team might have to begin oral gavage. The scientist felt a surge of irritation; force feeding took time, restraining the animal and inserting the feeding tube. And it was no easy procedure with rats. It meant liquifying the nutrients and making sure you got it into the esophagus and not the trachea — a sure way to drown the animal.

The lab door swung open and Dillon Byer poked his head in. "Hi Lester," he said to the tech. "How're you doing today?" He didn't wait for an answer. "I need a couple of minutes with Stu, okay?"

Ostrovsky looked up, displeased. "We're in the middle of something."

"It'll only take a minute."

Byer waited until Lester left the room before stepping in cautiously. Ostrovsky continued with his task, making one last grab at the rodent, this time successful. Dangling the animal by the tail, he brushed past Byer, who instantly recoiled as the rodent came within inches of his face. This was only the second time he'd been in room B19, the rodent housing and procedure room, and it was two times too many. At one end, the bleached walls were lined with white counters and stainless-steel cabinets much like the other procedure rooms. But this one was different. The opposite end was also stocked with tall moveable racks holding up to fifty clear storage bins, each the size of a large shoebox. They pulled out like drawers and easily opened with a quick flip of the latch on the cover. Too easily, in Byer's opinion. Each bin held one or two rats. The sight of them was uncomfortable enough, but the sound of hundreds of tiny feet scrabbling in the paper shavings made him want to scream.

"What is it?" asked Ostrovsky with a general wave at the cages. "I have a lot of work to do."

"That tech you hired? Jeffries? He's an animal rights investigator."

Ostrovsky froze. "What? How do you know?"

"Sylvia Hoerenburg just told me."

"How did she find out?"

"Jeffries' sister … the alleged sister. The one who came around with a sob story about their father dying? Apparently, she works for the same organization. She told Sylvia at a bar last night."

"So, her father didn't die?"

"Bullshit. All a lie. Supposedly, Jeffries has gone missing – only that isn't his real name."

"Goddammit!" Ostrovsky exploded. "Who's he working for? PETA? Animal Liberation? Why can't they leave us alone?" He marched back over to one of the bins and tossed the rat inside. "We're on the brink of something major, something that will benefit all of society. But do these crazy people care? No. They'd like to see science shut down for good."

"Don't take it personally, Stu."

"How can I not? He stole one of my animals." He turned in a frustrated circle, pulling at his mustache. "Now it all makes sense. All his damn questions about what drug we're testing and how it works. I knew he'd gotten too emotionally involved, but I never saw *this*."

"Take it easy. It doesn't affect the protocol."

"Like hell it doesn't affect the protocol! We bought twenty-four dogs, I have to account for twenty-four dogs."

"You said yourself it wouldn't survive. So, we stick to the story: you found it and did the necropsy. You can extrapolate the data based on the others. It's just one small piece of data, it doesn't change the overall study."

"You don't understand."

"Here's what I understand, Stuart. We're close to the finish line. I talked with Bob Harrington again yesterday. He's very interested, after the Monsanto merger. Thirty-five million dollars worth of interested."

"What if Jeffries goes to the USDA?"

"Did he see any animal cruelty in your lab?"

Ostrovsky chewed on his lip. Finally, he said, "I can't be watching my techs every minute, but they know the rules."

"Has anybody *reported* abuse to you?" Byer clarified impatiently.

"No. God, no."

"Then as far as the USDA is concerned, if one of the techs did something wrong and Jeffries got video, the worst they can do is slap a fine on us. That happens, we'll pay it and move on, like before. But it probably won't even go that far. The government is as sick of these animal watchdogs as we are, especially with this administration. Besides, by the time it goes through all the red tape, we'll have our deal with Harrington and you'll be the lead article in the *Molecular Cell Journal*. You keep doing what you're doing. I just thought you should know about Jeffries."

Ostrovksy pulled at his mustache hard enough to remove a few hairs. Then he straightened his lab coat and moved toward the cages.

"One last thing," said Byer. "Probably best if we keep this information about Jeffries to ourselves. I mentioned that to Sylvia, and I think she understands."

The Chief Scientific Officer of Amaethon had already switched gears. He pulled out a white rat to weigh and said, "Send Lester back in."

Keeping his eyes on the rodent, Byer backed into a tray of instruments. The clatter of metal on metal caused increased activity in the cages. He couldn't get out of there fast enough.

# CHAPTER 11

Through the classroom window, Heather watched the wavy lines rising from the hot asphalt parking lot, her forehead creased with an involuntary glower. This morning, she'd sounded off about the government abrogating its environmental responsibilities, and she heard that punk Lonnie McGrath whistle softly from the back and mimic her use of "abrogating." She wanted to smack him.

And then, as they were leaving class, Kevin Fleuette walked up behind her and said slyly, "Impressive vocabulary, Buck."

She gave him the finger. "Look *this* up, asshole."

He just grinned. "You coming to the game Wednesday?"

"Not if you're playing."

He seemed oddly flattered and said, "Stick around afterwards. We'll grab some pizza." Then he touched her lightly on the arm before sauntering off with a sing-song, "See ya later, abrogator."

Heather wondered if Kevin really meant the invitation. Sounded like he did, and it might have been fun. But it was way too late for that. Last year, she'd had an all-consuming crush on him, but back then she was a different person. Summer happened. A friend from Burlington got hold of some heroin. Bored out of her mind and feeling Half Moon closing in on her, Heather smoked some. The rush was so intense, so freeing, that she tried it again the next week. Twice turned into three, four times, and then she met Bobby, who gave her the needle. The summer turned into a time of wild exploration, going after what she wanted, when she wanted it: Tyler, Bobby, the ultimate high.

And here she was, breathing in the diesel fumes that spewed from the long, yellow school bus growling past the window. If she knew anything, it was this: going to Kevin's basketball games, hanging out at parties, sleepovers with friends, those things were long gone. She pretended to her parents that she was still their sunshine girl, and they wanted to believe it so much, it was easy. But underneath the clean hair and the Cover Girl face, she knew that she'd become someone else – someone uglier, more twisted. The heavenly sting of the needle had dulled and dirtied her, and she couldn't see any way back. Recently, she'd been having the same nightmare in which she was in a field with her dad and she was trying to call out for him. He'd get close, but then he'd walk right by her like she was a rotting husk of corn.

Heather tugged the cuffs of her long-sleeved shirt to cover her hands and shivered with cold.

* * *

The final period bell echoed through the halls of Half Moon Union High School, resonating with freedom. A moment later, the front doors opened and there was a mass exodus of back-packed teens in clusters. Only the boys showed a sense of individual style. The girls went with one look: short, flouncy skirts and sleeveless tops, with long, straight hair as part of the uniform. All but Heather Buck, who finally emerged wearing jeans and a ribbed-knit shirt. She made a bee-line through the lot. Jude sprung from her parked car and trotted after her, calling her name.

When Heather turned and saw who it was, she quickened her pace. "What do you want from me?" she groaned.

"The truth, for starters," answered Jude.

"I don't know what you're talking about." Heather re-slung her backpack and continued walking.

"Come on, your parents may be clueless, but I'm not. Rookie heroin users don't start with the needle."

"What are you, my social worker?"

"Maybe you need one."

They had reached Heather's car and she dug around in her backpack for keys.

"Tim didn't use drugs," Jude insisted.

Heather snorted, "Oh my God, you must be his mother. For your information, your little boy *did* use drugs." Unable to find her keys, she dropped the backpack on the ground and began to open one zippered pocket after another.

"I think *you* turned Tim on to heroin, not the other way around."

"Yeah, right." Heather drew up her sleeves to rifle through her backpack, revealing what looked to be a large rash on her inner arm.

"What's that?" asked Jude.

The girl jumped up and self-consciously pulled her sleeves back down. "It's nothing," she snapped. "Why don't you just leave me alone."

Jude made a time-out sign with her hands. "Let's start over, okay? Much as I believe drugs – even experimenting with them – is really dangerous, what you do with your body is your business. My concern is Tim. He's disappeared, and I need to find him."

"I told you, I haven't seen him, and he hasn't called or texted."

"Tell me about the last time you saw him."

"Get lost."

"I will. But then I'd have to tell your folks how worried I am about your continuing drug use."

"Fuck." Heather rolled her eyes. "It was last Monday. He came over around seven and said he had something to show me."

"What was it?"

"A heroin kit, duh."

"Come on, Heather. Tell me something that has the remotest chance of being true."

A pack of laughing teens raced past them and Heather turned her head away. When they were out of earshot, she said quietly, "We drove out to a place on our farm."

"What place?"

"Behind the barn. There's a dirt road that goes out into the orchard."

"And that's where you shot up?"

"Yes. Can I go now?"

"How long had you been dating?"

As soon as the words left her mouth, Jude wanted to kick herself. The question was a dead giveaway, and Heather jumped on it. Her eyes flicked across Jude's face and down her body, assessing the competition before replying, "Uh, nobody *dates* anymore, but yeah, about a month, I guess."

*A month?* He had told Jude he loved her just two weeks ago. He pressured her to come up to Vermont, and they'd argued on the phone when she refused. And all that time, he was screwing the farmer's daughter, and for all Jude knew, he was telling Heather he loved her, too.

For a moment, Jude felt like slinking back to her car and having a good cry. Lucas and Haydon were right – Tim wasn't who she thought he was. She should just go back to Washington and put the whole sordid affair behind her. But retreat was not in Jude's DNA. She thrust her feelings aside and crowded in on Heather. "Did he seem upset about anything recently?" she asked, letting the teenager know she was going to keep asking questions until she got the answers she needed.

"I don't know, he never said anything."

"Was it just the two of you?"

"What do you mean?"

"When you drove out into the field to shoot up?"

"Of course," answered Heather blithely.

"No one else was there?"

"No, I just said."

"Do you know a guy named Bobby G?"

Heather's sneer was suddenly replaced with the practiced vacant expression she'd adopted at the farmers market, only this time Jude recognized it for what it was: *show nothing while you figure out how to lie your way out of this.* But the girl shook her head adamantly and resumed searching for her car keys. She found them. "I really got to go," she said. "Are you going to say anything to my folks?"

"Not unless you give me reason to."

Heather eyed Jude uncertainly, then unlocked the car and slid into the driver's seat.

Jude blocked her from shutting the door. "Was Tim getting his heroin from Bobby?" she pressed.

"How should I know?" She slid the key into the ignition and the car rumbled to life. Before pulling out, she added, "I don't even know who you're talking about."

Jude was left inhaling the car's noxious exhaust, but a spark of discovery had been lit. Heather was caught off guard by Bobby's name and had given herself away. She knew who Bobby was, all right. Same with Sylvia, who nearly had a fit when her friend mentioned him. Maybe they denied knowing who he was because he had a reputation for being dangerous. Or maybe it was just bad form to talk about your dealer. Either way Jude was sure that Heather had some grand secrets all her own and was lying through her perfect white teeth. That put finding Bobby G at the top of the list.

# CHAPTER 12

"Tell me how it happened," said Dr. Harbolt.

Jarrod Healy's mother smoothed her son's bangs away from his face. "We were at the farmers market a couple of days ago," she replied. "He took a tumble. You fell down, right, honey?" she amended, wanting to empower her five-year-old by letting him speak for himself. But he clamped his mouth shut, eyeing the doctor suspiciously, so she continued. "He didn't seem to have any other injuries, but his nose just wouldn't stop bleeding for the longest time. And I thought we had it under control, but that night it started again for no reason. The same thing yesterday. I mean, he's had bloody noses before, but this is ridiculous." She turned her face away from her son and silently mouthed to the doctor, "And there's *so* much blood!"

Harbolt gave the boy a pat on the shoulder and said, "How about we have a look."

"Am I getting a shot?" asked Jarrod with a frown.

"No shots," answered the doctor. "We're just going to take a little peek." He retrieved his otoscope to examine the boy's ears. Then he gently lifted the tip of his nose and peered briefly into his nostrils. He moved on to check the boy's eyes. Finally, he felt the glands along the side of his neck and listened to his lungs and heart.

Harbolt let his stethoscope dangle. "You must have hit the ground pretty hard, young man," he said. "Okay, you can get down now. Why don't you go out to the waiting room and find a lollipop while I talk to your mom?"

The boy slid off the examination table and bolted. Harbolt began to ask the questions foremost on his mind: had Jarrod lost consciousness when he fell? Had he complained of headaches afterwards? Had he seemed disoriented in any way? Any vomiting? Change in appetite? The answer to all of these was no.

"Alright, that's good. I don't think he sustained a concussion but keep an eye on him for a day or two, and if anything changes, let me know."

Jarrod's mother let out a tentative sigh of relief, then asked, "What about his nosebleeds? Why aren't they stopping?"

"Could be allergies, could be a broken blood vessel and he's picking at it and aggravating it. I wouldn't worry. But call me with an update in a couple of days."

When Harbolt passed his nurse in the hallway, she motioned that a patient was waiting in the second examination room. "One minute," he said. He went straight to his office and closed the door. At his desk, he opened Jarrod's chart and wrote, "playground fall, vitals good, no signs of concussion ... mother states nosebleed resumes at slightest provocation. No evident reason for epistaxis. Continue to monitor." After putting his pen back in its holder, he opened the desk drawer and pulled out two more charts, one of which belonged to Tori Lacey. He reread his notes on her unexplained bruising. Then he opened the chart belonging to a worker at a limestone and gravel quarry who had sliced himself with a box cutter. It wasn't a particularly long or deep cut, but he'd come in for stitches with his entire sleeve blood-soaked.

The doctor stared again at the charts in front of him. Then he put them in his desk and locked the drawer.

* * *

That night the humidity hit seventy percent, making the warm air feel thick and oppressive. Jude had taken up her post on a bench in a small park down the street from Galvey's. She found it curious that the local illicit drug exchange was directly across from the town courthouse, a white-columned Greek Revival building that looked sober and dignified, oblivious to the activities across the street.

After a few inquiries at Galvey's, she'd been directed to this plaza which was dotted with unhealthy trees, a few benches, and an overflowing garbage can. The music venue/bar was the main hang-out, but apparently management there took a dim view of on-site drug deals. The patrons looking to get high came here. Should the cops roll by, they'd see a gaggle of young people congregating near the ice cream truck on the corner or just grabbing a smoke, and if they knew what was really going on, it seemed they'd decided to pick other battles.

Prepared to wait, Jude sipped on an iced-decaf from Starbucks, wishing she'd worn more than a tank top so she'd have a sleeve to wipe the sweat from her forehead. So far, she hadn't found anyone willing to talk about Bobby G. Twice, she was approached and asked if she was looking for something. "Yeah," she replied, "but I'm waiting on Bobby."

"He don't have nothin' I don't have," said one with a leer.

"He may not come by tonight," warned the other. "He doesn't always."

Jude shook her head. Both potential sellers looked her up and down. It might have been the small tattoo of a dog on her bare shoulder that reassured them she wasn't a cop, but then again, no one seemed too worried about the police. Her biggest problem was that she didn't know what Bobby G looked like. She had to count on what she did know: if he wasn't admired, he was respected, and from the awestruck way Sylvia's friend had breathed his name, he was probably a turn-on for some of the ladies.

Buyers came and went, but there were a few who appeared to be waiting for something special. Jude mimicked them, scrolling through texts and making short calls. She used the time to touch base with Madelyn, who often took Finn when Jude had to leave town. "Hey, Madelyn, how's my big boy?" she asked.

"He's great," replied the shelter director. "He misses you, though."

"I miss him, too. Not causing too much trouble?"

"This big brute? Never. Any word on Tim?"

Lucas must have cruised by the shelter to ask if they knew anything.

"Not yet. But I'm hoping to be home in a day or two. How about Rocky?"

"Who?"

"Rocky! The hard-case tied to the fire hydrant."

"Oh, him. He's coming around, I guess. One of the volunteers seems to be making some headway – as long as she brings food."

"Food works."

As she rang off, Bobby G strolled onto the scene. She knew it was him immediately, and not just because female heads turned, but because the very air became charged. Simmering below the aloof crushing of a cigarette under a heel or the casual readjustment of a ponytail, muscles twitched and heartbeats quickened. Bobby G was *the man*. He worked the group like a politician, bumping fists and occasionally throwing his arm around a pretty girl. His black leather vest gleamed in the streetlights. He was smooth, she had to give him that – the exchange of bills for glassine envelopes was barely noticeable.

At one point, he looked around and their eyes met. Instantly, Jude understood the hesitancy when she brought up his name – this was someone you did not want to cross. There was an arrogance in the way he carried himself, and Carly Simon's song played in the back of her mind … *You walked into the party* … But he was more than vain, he was cold-blooded. There was also something in their brief visual contact that made her think he knew who she was, and it sent a shiver up the back of her neck.

A few minutes later, she rallied herself and approached him.

"Are you Bobby?" she asked.

One corner of his mouth quivered in an almost smile. "Depends," he said.

"Depends on what?"

"On who wants to know."

"I'm looking for someone." His eyes flicked over her, and Jude felt that in some odd way he'd been expecting her. "A friend of mine named Tim – he was going by Tyler Jeffries."

Bobby took her arm and said, "How about we take a walk?"

His touch was light, but coercive, as he led her down a side street away from the park. Brick apartment buildings loomed on either side and only one streetlamp in the middle of the block was working. Increasingly apprehensive, Jude stopped and extricated her arm. "Is there something you want to tell me that you don't want anyone to hear?" she asked.

"I want to know who you are."

"My name is Jude Brannock, and I work with Tyler Jeffries. We're with an animal protection organization. He was working at the Amaethon laboratory until a few days ago when he disappeared. I need to find him."

Bobby examined a thumbnail before asking, "Why would you think I know your friend?"

"I was told that he was involved in some drug use."

"Not my thing."

"I was led to believe differently."

"Oh? Who told you that?"

"I'd rather not say."

"You'd rather not say, hunh?" He reached out and traced the outline of her tattoo with his finger. "If you want my help, you're gonna have to be a little more cooperative."

Shrugging off his hand roughly, she demanded, "Did you sell Tyler heroin?"

He began to walk away, dismissing her.

Jude's frustration was building; it felt like hot lava about to spill over. Why did this have to be so hard? All she wanted was a little information. First Sylvia, then Heather, and now this smarmy drug dealer. Nobody would give her squat. "Hey," she yelled. "What are you hiding?"

She ran after him and as she did, everything around her seemed to grow hazy in the mist. It swirled in front of her face, softening the edges of the parked cars and muddying the light from the lone streetlamp. With each step, the darkness congealed and seemed to clog her throat, making the heavy air even harder to breathe.

Jude caught up with Bobby near the corner. She reached out to grab his sleeve, but he wrenched it away and stepped off the curb into the street, his body a diffuse shadow. Determined to get answers, she went after him.

Suddenly, there was a shrieking flash of light and the frantic squeal of brakes, metal hitting asphalt. A hand grabbed her and pulled her backward. She landed hard on her backside and her elbow skidded along the pavement. Jude fought the hands that held her until they finally let go. She scrambled to her knees as voices pummeled her.

"Jesus, fuckin' Christ! Are you okay?"

"She just ran out!"

"Are you okay?"

She didn't recognize any of them. She opened her eyes to see who they were, but they seemed out of range somehow.

Then came a voice she did recognize, right next to her. "Yeah, yeah, we're cool." It was Bobby. He lifted her to her feet and she stumbled, feeling bruised and clumsy. She smelled cigarette smoke embedded in his leather vest. But she could barely make him out.

"Okay, man. As long as she's alright."

"You sure you don't want us to call someone?"

Then Bobby, "No, it's fine. I got it from here."

The sound of doors slamming, a car driving away. Jude stood shakily, opening and closing her eyes, trying to make sense of the charcoal shapes that swam before her. The husky country music from Galvey's a few blocks away sounded loud in her ears.

"You better sit down," said Bobby, not unkindly.

"What ... what happened?" she stammered, allowing herself to be led up the curb and a few steps further.

"Here, sit."

*Sit where?*

"What's the matter with your eyes?"

"Nothing, I–"

"Can you see?"

*Not really.* Weak pulses of light flashed behind her eyes, but they didn't illuminate anything. "I just need a minute," she said.

"Well, sit," he said impatiently, turning her around and pushing on her shoulders.

She felt a stone step behind her and collapsed on the stoop. Putting her head between her knees, she drew in deep breaths. It had helped before when the vision thing happened that other time. Other times. She thought she was going to throw up.

"What the fuck did you think you were doing? Trying to kill yourself?" Bobby was asking.

"What happened?" came her muffled voice.

"You jumped in front of a car is what happened. Didn't you *see* it?"

Jude lifted her head. She detected the outline of Bobby's boots and his tight jeans. There was some vague light to her left. She blinked a few times and the light sharpened. Her vision seemed to be returning and it gave her courage. "I was following you. Why'd you cross right in front of it?" she demanded.

"Hey, you're the one who ran out. If I hadn't grabbed you, you'd be road kill now. I'm lucky you didn't get me killed, too. Shit, girl! There is somethin' seriously fucked up with your eyes."

The mist was clearing; Bobby's face came into view. "No, it was just like … for a second," protested Jude. "I'm okay now. Thanks, I guess."

"I *guess*." Bobby sat down on the stoop next to her and offered up a pack of Marlboros. "You smoke?"

"Not since I was fifteen."

He shook out a cigarette, stretched out his legs, and smoked in silence. Jude listened to the distant music, feeling the sting of scraped skin on her arm and the throbbing spot on her hip she knew would be black and blue by tomorrow.

After a while, Bobby asked unexpectedly, "Animal *protection*? Is that a euphemism for animal *rights*? You actually believe that animals should have the same rights as people?"

She'd been asked this question a hundred times and found that there were no easy answers. "I generally leave the theorizing to the academics," she replied truthfully.

"Yeah, but you must have a mind-set that drives you."

"I believe that animals who cannot speak for themselves should not be tortured, abused, or otherwise mistreated by us."

"So do I."

"Then the only difference between you and me is that I'm willing to do something about it."

"Ooh, aren't we righteous?"

"Given your line of work, you're in no position to get morally snarky." When he didn't respond, she let another few beats pass before saying, "Thank you. I mean it."

"Okay," he blew out in an exhale of smoke.

"So, tell me about Tyler."

At this, Bobby let out a guttural laugh.

"Just tell me if–"

"Get one thing straight, you suicidal maniac, I don't talk about nobody and nobody talks about me." He got to his feet and retrieved his car keys from a vest pocket.

This time he stepped into the street and continued. He got into a car, pulled out of the space and drove away. Jude remained on the stoop, pressing her hands between her knees to keep them from shaking. Bobby was right: there was something seriously wrong with her eyes – and tonight it could have gotten her killed.

The truth tightened around her chest like a straitjacket. This is not dehydration. It's not anything I ate. I think I'm going blind. For a moment, she wished she'd kept her mouth shut and not driven Bobby away. He was a smug, maybe dangerous, drug dealer but right then he would have stood between her and the crushing feeling of being totally alone. Tim was gone. And she couldn't tell anyone at The Kinship about her eyes or she'd be out of a job. Sure, they'd be genuinely concerned, but their fight for animals depended on being able to see what most of the world couldn't or wouldn't. There was no place for her if she couldn't see what was right in front of her face.

As she fought the sickening dread of what a lifetime of blindness would mean, she found she was able to identify more details. There in the light of an upper window, a woman walked back and forth to calm her baby. Here was a laughing couple, weaving a little and stopping halfway down the block to kiss. The edges that defined them were sharpening, the colors becoming clearer. Hell, she'd even been able to make out Bobby's car when he drove off. She hadn't thought to look at his license plate, but she'd caught a couple of details, the flash of a Red Sox sticker in the back window and a nasty gash along the fender. Her sight had come back – for now.

When she felt ready, Jude pushed herself up from the stoop and headed back to her empty hotel room.

# CHAPTER 13

Late morning light spilled into the kitchen as Katherine filled the sink with warm, soapy water to clean the breakfast dishes that she'd let sit for too long. Her husband wandered in for the third time in the last twenty minutes.

"Anything I can help you with?" Katherine asked him.

"No, just procrastinating," replied Kurt.

"Then here," she handed him a towel to dry the dishes that she was rinsing and putting into the dish rack. "I forgot to tell you, I ran into that woman from the animal organization in the supermarket yesterday," she said.

"Did you talk to her?"

"A little. I was already on the checkout line."

"What did you talk about?"

"She wanted to know if I'd met Tyler."

"And what did you say?"

"That I'd only met him once."

"You never told me."

Katherine shrugged. "It was very brief. He was over to pick up Heather. The weekend before the ... incident. I was out back grinding cornmeal." She caught her husband staring at her as if she'd done something wrong. "What he did, Kurt, was unforgiveable. But at the time, he seemed like a nice enough young man. We just chatted for a minute. He told me he grew up on a farm where his grandmother used to grind their own cornmeal. He took a real interest in it."

"And that was it?"

"That was it. Heather came out and they left."

"What the hell is that woman doing hanging around and asking questions?"

"I suppose she thinks that he's still here in Half Moon."

A bowl slipped from Kurt Buck's wet fingers and shattered on the floor. The sudden noise frightened the older dog so badly that she hit her head on the table scrambling to get up and out of there. The younger one, Chipper, sensing unseen, imminent danger, began to bark.

"Goddammit," cried Kurt angrily. He turned to Chipper and yelled, "Quiet! Quiet!"

Chipper did no such thing. Clearly the threat had intensified, and he had a duty to protect the household.

Katherine wiped her soapy hands on the seat of her jeans and went over to the excited dog to make him stop barking. He gave one more preemptive bark before falling silent.

"It's just a bowl, Kurt," admonished his wife. "No big deal. Go see if Rosie's okay while I clean it up."

He tossed the dishtowel on the counter, stepped over the mess on the floor, and disappeared into the living room. When he returned, Katherine was sweeping the pieces from a dustpan into the garbage. He sat on a kitchen chair and glowered as she went over the floor one more time for fragments she had missed.

She returned the dustpan to its hook on the back of the cellar door. "Is it bothering you that the police came out here about Tyler?"

"Sergeant Haydon's a state trooper."

"Okay. He's investigating Tyler as a missing persons case, right?"

Kurt shrugged. "Why should it bother me? I told him what I knew."

"Of course. But he did ask you about what you said at the farmers market. That if you saw Tyler again, you'd kill him."

"For God's sake, Katherine. I didn't mean it in the literal sense. Sergeant Haydon understood that."

"I'm sure he did. But maybe it bothers you that he might consider you a suspect or something."

"They can suspect me all they want. I didn't do anything."

"Well, honey, it's not like you didn't do *anything*."

"Okay, I punched the guy. Any man in my situation would've done that." In fact, the scene played out in his mind over and over again: Heather half-conscious with a gauzy smile on her face, buttons on her blouse undone. And Jeffries, that scumbag drug pusher, stumbling around in Davidson's field like he didn't know where he was.

"Did you tell Sergeant Haydon about that?"

"It's irrelevant, Kath. I punched him in the nose. That's it. He walked away. I didn't kill him."

"Why are you being so snippy? You've been wandering around like a lost soul for the past two hours, coincidentally, from the time Sergeant Haydon left. And all I'm trying to do is find out what's going on in your head. Maybe you'd feel better if you'd told him and gotten it off your chest."

"Yeah, maybe," he reluctantly acknowledged. Rosie padded in warily and thrust her head between Kurt's knees. Absently, he began to stroke her ears. Finally, he said, "There's something else. I'm worried about Heather. I think she might be doing drugs again."

"What makes you say that?" asked Katherine sharply.

"She's always up there on the computer."

"And what seventeen-year-old isn't?"

"Plus, she's started wearing long sleeves. It's too hot for that. Maybe it's to hide track marks or something."

Katherine came over to sit with her husband. "Oh, Kurt," she consoled him. "I went up to see her before bed last night. She's got poison ivy on her arms and doesn't want the kids at school to see it. That's why she's wearing long sleeves."

Her reassurances, however, rang hollow in her own ears. More than once, the same thought had crossed her mind. Twice in the last week, she found the farmers market cash box short. It wasn't something she could swear to. It was just a feeling and a vague sense that Heather had taken money. She would have asked Kurt if he'd dipped into the box, but she didn't want to hear him say no. There were other things she wasn't sure she wanted to know either. Like why Kurt had withheld information from Sergeant Haydon. Perhaps a single punch wasn't such a big deal. But she remembered the blood on his hands after he got Heather back into the house. Could one punch have done that?

\* \* \*

"It's not looking good," Lucas said, drawing a deep breath.

Gordon steeled himself. "Shut the door."

The lanky investigator elbowed the office door closed and took a seat across from his boss. "I went to see Tim's roommate Chris again. Turns out he hasn't really known Tim for all that long. They met last December through some mutual friends, and when he said he was looking for a roommate, Tim jumped at the chance."

"Does Chris know what he's doing with us?"

"Only that we're into animal protection. He didn't know Tim was undercover. But now with all the questions, I thought I should tell him."

"What did he say?"

"He seemed surprised, a little worried. But I don't know if it's because he's upset about Tim so much as he's wondering if he needs to find a new roommate."

"Go on."

"I tracked down one of their mutual buddies, a guy named Patrick who works for an accounting firm here in D.C. He knew Tim from New York a couple of years ago. They used to work out together. He said he hadn't heard much from Tim recently; he thought he was out in Minnesota."

"He was," Gordon confirmed. "That's where he did the dairy job."

"Where he got burned, right? They ever find out how?"

"Not as far as I know."

Lucas pressed his lips together. "Well, Patrick told me that Tim was working as a paralegal in New York.

Gordon opened a manila file that was sitting on his desk and said, "Yes, that's what he has on his resume. A law firm in Manhattan called Cromwell, Slate, and Bruckhaus."

"Right," Lucas affirmed. "So, I contacted them and talked to somebody in HR who confirmed that Tim was there as a paralegal. But she wouldn't answer any more questions, said I'd have to talk to her supervisor who's on vacation until the end of next week. To round things off, I decided to do a little digging. The firm does white collar crime and corporate merger stuff, big mergers. As a matter of fact, they were one of the firms that represented Monsanto in its merger with Bayer Pharmaceuticals. And by itself it may not mean anything, but then I found this." Lucas pulled a folded piece of paper from his hip pocket and shot it across the desk. Gordon picked it up and read as Lucas continued, "It's from a business journal about the merger and some of the companies that Bayer-Monsanto is interested in, in terms of *expanding* their capabilities. Paragraph three."

Gordon's eyes moved down the paper until he saw it. He looked up and said, "Amaethon."

"It could be coincidence," Lucas said in half-hearted defense of his fellow investigator.

"That Amaethon is the subject of a take-over bid possibly being handled by Tim's former employer?" Gordon asked skeptically. "I would say that's quite a coincidence. And it makes me wonder about his sudden influx of cash before he went undercover."

"You think the money came from Monsanto? Why would they pay Tim?"

"They've been known to hire people to infiltrate animal rights groups, keep tabs on them."

Lucas looked at his boss with growing concern. "Nah, he wouldn't do that."

"Maybe not at first. But as we've seen, money is an issue for Tim, especially if he's got a drug habit. It's possible that when he got the job at Amaethon, he saw an opportunity. They'd pay him a lot more money than we can to make sure if there *was* any animal abuse going on, neither we nor the USDA would find out about it. Bad publicity that could scuttle an important take-over bid."

"That's kinda hard to swallow," replied Lucas in disbelief. "I mean, I thought Tim was a solid guy, genuine, you know? Maybe a little reckless and immature, but acting as what? A double agent or something?"

"Like I said, it's happened before. And I'm just speculating, but if you put it together with the fact that Jude hasn't gotten anything definitive from Tim, just promises to send video …."

"Then why would he just up and disappear? They'd have to know that we'd be done with him. You'd think Monsanto would want to keep him embedded with us as an undercover."

"No doubt they would. But Jude seemed to think that Tim was unraveling – the heroin, the young girlfriend. He might have been legitimately rattled over the testing or was feeling too isolated. There's nothing to say that he didn't cut out on us *and* Monsanto."

Lucas scratched his head as if trying to scrape the idea from his brain. "Jude thinks the girl's father might have something to do with this," he finally offered.

"Like what?"

"Supposedly he threatened to kill Tim."

"Murder? Because Tim was sleeping with his daughter?"

"Well, the smack, too."

"You yourself said that she's not a rookie user. On some level, her father has to know that."

Lucas had run out of defenses and gave a little shrug.

"Jude doesn't want to see the possibilities here," said Gordon, shutting Tim's file. "She doesn't want to face up to the fact that he's run out on us and might have been using her. After all, they were sleeping together."

"Oh?" Lucas breathed. "How do you know?"

Gordon's phone rang, and he picked it up. "Sure, put him through." He hit the hold button, indicating with an eyebrow that he wanted to take the call in private. When Lucas got to the door, Gordon stopped him short, saying, "I've seen them together, and I know what Jude looks like after sex."

Lucas closed the door behind him softly, hoping his boss hadn't seen him recoil as if he'd been sucker-punched.

# CHAPTER 14

When Heather left the school parking lot and turned off towards town, her mother stayed at least four cars behind. Guilt made Katherine feel twitchy, as though something were gnawing at her from inside. Hovering like this was exactly what they *weren't* supposed to be doing. At their family session, the school psychologist suggested that as an only child, conceived after years of trying, their daughter might feel the pressure of being the "golden" girl. Her AP classes, her athletics. It's a lot for a kid to handle, he said, and maybe she acted out with a foray into heroin as a way of testing the depth of their love if she were a "bad" girl. At this, Heather burst into hot, remorseful tears.

And after the heroin incident, she had seemed genuinely chastened. She was trying to be more helpful than usual around the house and at dinner would make perky small talk. But Katherine felt it all a bit fake. She'd reassured Kurt that the long sleeves didn't mean anything, but she wasn't entirely sure. There were a few afternoons when Heather had come home late, insisting that she had to stay and work on a group project, and on those days, her eyes looked dulled.

Then there was the money. Katherine could have miscounted what was in the cash box. God knows, she desperately wanted to believe that Heather recognized how dangerous heroin was and would never go down that road again. But after Heather left for school this morning, Katherine found she was missing a twenty from her wallet. It put her over the edge. That their daughter might be stealing and lying to them made her feel physically sick.

Which was why Katherine found herself tailing her daughter like some kind of private investigator. Heather had texted about grabbing a slice of pizza after school with her friends, and Katherine had texted back *Okay*. She loved her daughter with every breath of her being, but she had to know.

Her daughter drove like a solid citizen, obeying the speed limit, the stop signs, and signaling in plenty of time. And to Katherine's chagrin, she went directly to town and found a parking place across from the kids' favorite pizza place, even remembering to put money in the meter. She trotted across the street and went right in.

Katherine drove past and pulled over to the curb, feeling a rush of relief so intense it made her laugh out loud. Heather had told her the truth. *I must be getting senile*, she thought. *Imagining things ... going through my own midlife crisis watching my daughter grow up, soon to leave and begin her own life.* With a mental apology to her daughter, Katherine took a last glance at the pizza parlor.

Suddenly, she froze.

*Oh my God, was that him? Was that Tyler Jeffries?*

She squinted at the young man who entered the pizza shop. She couldn't be sure from here. She'd only met him face to face that one time, and before that from afar when the two of them were out in the cornfield, sampling the young ears. The person she just saw, he was the right height, curly brown hair. But would she swear in court that it was Jeffries?

If Heather was lying about not seeing him or knowing where he was, they were probably still doing drugs together. Katherine was so stunned she didn't know what to do. Of all the possibilities that crossed her mind as she surveilled her daughter, connecting with Tyler Jeffries wasn't one of them. She knew that she ought to march right in there and confront them both. But she couldn't seem to move.

Finally, she pulled out into the street and continued driving, her mind reeling, her body taking her back home.

* * *

"That's insane!" shouted Jude into the phone.

"Think about it," said Lucas. "Do you remember how he used to ask so many questions about what operations we'd done and how we managed them. So bloody curious about how we got undercovers into places?"

"He was new. He wanted to learn." She paced the hotel room, her hair still wet from the shower. It had soaked her t-shirt and in the air conditioning, made her back feel like ice. "Dammit, Lucas, he was going deep. We would have been put off if he *hadn't* asked questions."

"And what about the money?"

"I don't know. There's probably a rational explanation other than he was getting paid by Monsanto! What does Gordon say?"

Jude jabbed at the buttons on the cooling system trying to turn it off; two days and she still couldn't figure out how to work it.

"He's the one who put this all together."

"Put it *together*? What, do you both think this is some detective show?"

"Calm down."

"You never liked Tim."

"Oh my God, listen to yourself. You want a rational explanation? Here are the facts: Tim worked for a big law firm that does work for Monsanto, which is interested in Amaethon as an acquisition. He comes to The Kinship and volunteers – pushes hard as I recall – to go undercover at the lab. Just before he leaves, he comes into a chunk of cash. Then the whole time he's in Vermont he never really gives you anything usable; he only says he's *going* to get video. He keeps you at arm's length with, 'Oh, I've got something big,' but all he sends you are some inane pictures of a house he wants to fix up. And then just before the job is over, poof! He disappears."

Jude pressed her fingers into her temples to stop the understanding that, like quickly-dividing, malignant cells, was growing with each breath. To no avail.

The tables had turned. The scammer had been scammed. The Kinship's seasoned undercover investigator out-hustled. If it didn't hurt so much, she would have laughed at the incredible irony that *she* was Tim's mark all along. She wasn't his handler, she was his means to install himself inside The Kinship and then see if Amaethon was on the up-and-up. Two birds with one stone. He made love to her, told her how important she was to him, he'd even pressed her for a more committed relationship. Worst of all, despite her protestations that she didn't "do long term," she had begun to consider it. *You didn't have to go that far*, she wanted to scream at him. *It wasn't enough to get me in bed? Did you have to see me humiliated?* At once, the hurt turned into a burning rage.

"You still there?" asked Lucas.

"I'm here," she replied quietly.

"I'm sorry, Jude."

"Sorry for what?" But the way he said it, she guessed. "Oh, so you know."

"Yeah."

"It was never going anyplace," she insisted, more to defend herself against the shame eating at her than to convince Lucas. "It didn't mean anything. Not really. It's … it's not what you think."

"It doesn't matter what I think."

Of course, it did matter to Jude what Lucas thought, but she was too deflated to correct him. "Does Gordon know?" she asked.

"Yeah."

"Shit. What did he say?" That Lucas didn't immediately respond told Jude she shouldn't press. But she did. "What did he say, Lucas? How did he know?"

"He said that he'd seen you and Tim together," reported Lucas haltingly, "and that he knew what you looked like after sex."

She let the coarseness of Gordon's comment rip into her as she knew it had likely ripped into Lucas. *Damn Gordon! What was his fucking problem?*

"What are you going to do?" Lucas asked.

"I'm going to find Tim," she replied. "And I'm going to finish what he was supposed to do."

"Let it go, Jude."

"I can't. Not now."

Suddenly, the whirring of the air conditioner stopped and there was a dead silence around her. She heard Lucas's pained sigh before he said, "Gordon wants you back. And I think you should come back, too."

"Are you aware that the Amaethon protocol is over in a few days and all the animals will be euthanized?" she asked angrily. "I am not going to let their deaths be for nothing. It's bad enough animals get tested on, but I refuse to let yet another laboratory get away with abusing them in the process."

"Don't do this."

"You know what? You can both go to hell."

Immediately, she regretted lashing out at him. But it felt like even her most trusted colleagues were leaving her, giving up on her. And she couldn't admit even to Lucas that her emotional life was falling apart, her body was falling apart. All she had left was what she did – being a fighter for animals, for the voiceless beings that were trod on, abused, and slaughtered every minute of every day. This was the life she bought into and the game in which she'd given so much skin. She was flayed to the core and there was no turning back now.

She took a breath to try to explain, but he'd already hung up and there was a new incoming call. She didn't immediately recognize the number and answered with a curt, "What?"

"Jude?" came a woman's voice, calm and low. "This is Ruth Harris. I'm sorry I couldn't take your call before. I was with a patient. Do you have a moment now?"

\* \* \*

Lonnie McGrath was having a shit day. It started before he'd even gotten out of bed when his mom stormed into his room and got on his case about not taking the garbage out the night before. Then it was the red D on his last history test and Mr. Bronstein's holier-than-thou, "I think you can do better, Lonnie." Fuck that, he never wanted to take AP History in the first place. And now he had the after-school job at the Buck farm when all his friends were going to mess around at the miniature golf place that just opened.

"You're late," said Kurt when Lonnie pulled up to the barn.

"Sorry Mr. Buck, I had to stay after school," he replied. He went over to the back of the pickup and began helping the farmer load empty milk crates.

"Hop up and I'll hand 'em to you," said Kurt. "How come?"

"How come what?"

"You had to stay after. You in trouble?"

"No, I just didn't do so well on a history test."

Buck grunted as he hoisted a 10-gallon bucket filled with a dark, syrupy liquid. "You're a smart guy. You can probably do better."

"Yeah, probably, Mr. Buck." Lonnie took the bucket and set it down at the front of the flatbed, mouthing under his breath, "And probably fuck you, too, Mr. Buck."

When they'd finished loading the crates, the farmer drove to the apple orchard with Lonnie riding in the flatbed. After they'd parked, Buck handed the teen his tools and instructed him on replacing the homemade traps for the codling moth pest. On each apple tree hung a can holding a few inches of the molasses-based liquid. The moths flew into the bait and died before they could lay their eggs that would, in turn, become larvae that infected the apples. Lonnie's job was to pour out the old goopy stuff into an empty pail and replace it with fresh slop from the 10-gallon container.

"Got it," he told the farmer, demonstrating far more enthusiasm than he felt with a hearty thumbs-up.

When Buck left, Lonnie tied a bandana around his forehead and got to work. Even shoveling compost wasn't as sickening as this job. Just the sight of the brown liquidy shit filled with dead bugs made him want to heave. The trick was not to get any on his hands or clothing.

He had gone about halfway down the first row when he heard the ca-ca-cah of crows over his head. There were two of them sitting atop the young apple tree he was working on. The branches were bent low with their weight.

"Scram!" Lonnie shouted. He didn't know if crows ate apples, but they probably did or else why put scarecrows all over? The big black birds continued their squawking.

Lonnie turned back to his task, figuring that if he put a little extra bait in each trap, he could get through the big bucket a lot sooner. Just then something struck his head and there was a wild flutter of feathers against his face. He dropped the bait bucket and flailed his arms to fend off what he believed was an assault by one of the crows. The bird fell to the ground.

"What the fuck!" exclaimed Lonnie as he leapt back. He peered at the ground and saw the crow twitching in the grass. One wing trembled and then the bird lay still. As he waited to see if it moved, the second crow fell from the tree and landed with a thud about ten feet from the first. This one didn't move a muscle. A fly insolently lit on the crow's head, and another joined him.

Lonnie stood rooted, trying to process what had just happened. Since when did two birds fall out of a tree like that? The teenager scanned the sky above to see if there were any more friggin' crows that might drop on his head. When he felt safe, he wiped a hand across his forehead, smearing the codling moth bait across his face. Then he looked down and saw that he'd spilled the bucket's revolting contents all over his pants. He promptly lost the bologna and cheese sandwich he'd had for lunch.

# CHAPTER 15

Trooper Willison stood on the side of the road overlooking a shallow ravine. He turned his head when he heard Haydon's patrol car pull in behind his. "Hey, Sarge," he called out affably. In his mid-twenties, Willison had been on the force for two years and was in love with his job. He'd grown up in Half Moon and knew everyone in town, most of whom still saw him as Janice and Bud Willison's kid. Someday, they'd know him only as Senior Sergeant Willison – the officer that no one dared to mess with.

"Thanks for the heads up, Seth," replied Haydon.

"Sure thing. I knew you initiated a BOLO on this as a possible missing person, so I told dispatch to get hold of you." He pointed down to the fragments of silver and glass that glinted through the tall shrubbery. "That's the car all right. The VIN traces back to Timothy Mains, with a New York address. No one inside, of course, but it looks like the driver was hurt."

"Okay," said Haydon grimly.

First, he scanned up and down Loop Turnpike, inexplicably named since it was just a forgotten country road. Its four-mile stretch was hemmed in by forest on either side, and hardly anyone used it after the Interstate was built. The cracked asphalt needed attention as did the single faded yellow stripe down the middle.

The two officers didn't have to remind each other not to scramble down the embankment where the car had gone over, thereby disturbing evidence of the accident scene. They walked several yards ahead of the vehicle where Willison had initially tackled the slope. As Haydon descended, he took in more details. There was no guardrail despite the drop off; it wasn't a state road and probably the town had no money to install one. Highway maintenance hadn't been around for ages to clear the embankment where weeds and saplings now filled the space. A rough swath of the thicket was disturbed where the car went over, but not enough for passing motorists to have noticed.

"What tipped you?" asked Haydon, picking his way through the thorny brush.

"The power company was up this way working on a utility pole. Must have seen it from the bucket," Willison answered over his shoulder. "I've been by here a half dozen times, never caught my eye."

They stepped the last few feet down to a dry stream bed where a dirty silver sedan had come to rest, tilted on its side. The front end was partially crumpled against a sturdy maple growing out of the ditch. The windshield was cracked, but the roof didn't appear damaged.

"Come look at this," said the junior trooper. He led Haydon to the driver's side window and shined his flashlight inside.

The now deflated airbags, including the steering wheel, side, and seat belt bags, had done what they were supposed to. Haydon concluded that the accident was most likely survivable. Yet, there was a significant amount of dried blood on the driver's bag.

"Head injury, you think?" asked Willison.

Reflexively, Haydon removed a pair of latex gloves from his pocket and put them on before prying open the driver's side door. He asked for the flashlight and shone it around the interior of the car, looking for a hard or sharp object that the driver might have struck to cause such an injury. Finally, he backed out.

"I don't see anything," he said. "If he was wearing the belt, the bags would've stopped him from hitting the windshield. If he wasn't wearing it, he probably would have gone right through." Haydon pointed to a section of bent frame around the windshield. "Pressure on the frame broke the glass, not anything hitting it from the inside."

"Unless the steering wheel bag didn't fully inflate," suggested Willison.

Haydon remembered the cluster of bloodied tissues Jude had pointed out in Tim's hotel room and offered, "Or maybe he was bleeding before the accident."

"Could explain why he went off the road."

"Could."

"Whatever happened, it looks like he was able to walk away," said Willison.

As he moved around the perimeter, Haydon noted, "Someone took the plates off." He continued to scan for footprints or broken brush that would tell him how Tim had gotten out of the car and where he might have gone. Most likely he would have tried to get up to the road for help. But if he'd been injured in some manner, he could easily have been disoriented. He might have wandered into the woods, not knowing in what direction he was stumbling.

Reading the sergeant's mind, Willison tailed after him. "He probably would have tried to climb back up."

"And no one saw him?" questioned Haydon. "And if he was hurt, wouldn't he try to flag someone down, get help?"

"Not many folks come this way. Maybe he'd been drinking and was afraid someone would call the cops."

Haydon murmured an encouraging response but was thinking along different lines. "What kind of search did you do in the car?" he asked.

"Just a prelim to make sure no one was inside and no bodies in the trunk. With the plates gone, at first, I thought maybe it was stolen and got dumped here. But then I saw the blood. And when I ran the VIN, it came back to this guy Mains. I didn't know why you flagged it, but just in case the car had been used in a crime, I thought …."

"You did right, Seth," Haydon assured him. "Let's take a closer look. Use gloves and be careful of needles." Given what Jude had told him about Tim using heroin, he didn't want either of them getting stuck with a semi-hidden hypodermic.

Willison's eyes widened. "Junkie?"

"I don't know. Just in case."

Haydon took the trunk, which was empty but for a plastic ice scraper. He lifted the loose carpeting and removed the spare tire. Nothing. Then he turned his attention to the exterior. Willison, meanwhile, examined the front and back seats. It didn't add up. By all accounts, Mains had cleared out of his hotel room in a hurry. But he hadn't left his things there. So where was his suitcase? A knapsack? Where was all the stuff like a change of shoes or an umbrella that guys leave in their cars? Haydon couldn't easily visualize Mains, bleeding from a head wound, grabbing his suitcase before he took off.

"Glove compartment's empty, Sarge," Willison called out. "Somebody stripped this baby. You sure no one reported it stolen? No plates, no registration … sure looks like it was dumped."

He found Haydon squatting by the front wheel on the driver's side examining a gouge that tailed off into a scrape running lengthways to the door.

"Yeah, I saw that," said Willison. "He's got a couple of dings in the rear bumper, too. Guess he wasn't winning any safe driver awards."

"How long do you think the car has been here?" asked Haydon, running his finger along the wound.

"A few days, maybe a week. Not much longer or we'd see debris from the trees."

"Un hunh," Haydon concurred. "This damage hasn't been here long, though. Not like the dings in the back."

"He must'a hit something on his way down, a rock, maybe."

Haydon examined his finger which had come away with tiny particles. "Not unless it was a rock painted blue." He stood up and instructed, "Put something over this and tape it down. Then call a tow for impound."

He squinted into the thick coppice of northern hardwoods and calculated that they bordered the Roxbury State Forest. No one would knowingly drift off in that direction, would they? Because if they did, they'd walk a long, long way over difficult terrain before finding help.

\* \* \*

"They might have missed something," said Jude.

"It's certainly possible," came Dr. Harris's reassuring voice. "But I've known Dr. Amin from our Columbia-Presbyterian days in New York. He's about the best there is, and my understanding is that his testing was pretty extensive."

"Doctors make mistakes."

"They do."

Holding the phone to her ear, Jude rolled her shoulders to ease the tension that ran up her spine and into the back of her neck and jaw.

"Let me ask you something, Jude," Dr. Harris continued. "Since you reached out to me, do you think that what you're experiencing may not solely have a physical explanation?"

"How would I know?"

"What's your sense of it?"

"If it's not physical, what could it be?"

"First of all," said Dr. Harris, ignoring Jude's testy tone, "losing your sight for periods of time is certainly a physical symptom, and it must be very frightening. But just as our bodies respond to disease or injury, they can also respond in similar ways to intense stress or trauma."

Jude cleared her throat, which she was surprised to find had closed up with emotion. "Like what?" she asked.

"Like events in your past that sensitized you to the suffering of others. Past events and relationships also can have an imprint on the coping strategies you've developed for what I imagine must be a stressful job."

"I have that covered really," said Jude, going for casual breeziness. "I go for runs with my dog which relieve a lot of tension."

"How about friends and family?"

Jude flashed on her conversation with Lucas minutes earlier. *Oh yeah, my coping strategy is to blow off my friends, sabotage relationships that might go anywhere ... and family? I don't need one, I don't want one.* But she asked instead, "You've seen this kind of thing before?"

"A few times. It can take various forms, unexplained pain or paralysis, and one patient I had whose vision failed completely. It's called conversion disorder and it's more common than you would imagine."

Feeling slightly nauseous, Jude wandered over to the hotel window and cracked it wider for some fresh air. "Did, uh, your patient's vision return?" she asked.

"It did."

"And you think that's what this is?"

"I don't know. But given that your physical tests have come back negative, I think it's worth exploring."

"Maybe Dr. Amin told you, but I investigate animal abuse. And, sure, I see things done to animals that are incredibly disturbing. But it can't be that, because I've been doing this job for years and the eyesight thing has only just been in the last few months. Besides," she hastily continued, "everyone I work with comes face-to-face with animal suffering as much as I do, and they're not going blind."

"Dr. Amin did tell me a little. But there may be other factors that come into play that are unique to you. We can talk about it. Would you like to make an appointment?"

"I can't right now, I'm in Vermont. And I have to stay until this whole business with my investigator is sorted out."

"I think it would be helpful if we could meet as soon as possible."

Pushed off balance by her sense of urgency, Jude shot back, "Sure, so I'll call and make an appointment when I get back to D.C."

There was a pause at the other end of the line, but then Dr. Harris said reassuringly, "Okay, Jude. In the meantime, you should give some thought to whether or not you should be driving or doing anything that might result in harm if you suddenly had an episode. Does that make sense?"

In the parking lot, a state police car rolled in, its tires crunching on the gravel. A fresh-faced, young trooper emerged from the car and looked up toward her room on the second floor. Jude's limbs suddenly felt heavy and rigid. "I'll ... I'll call you," she said, breaking the connection.

Clutching the phone against her stomach, she started toward the door, bracing for another in-person visit by the cops. But with the first step, her knees buckled and not sure she could make it all the way, Jude collapsed on the bed. There she sat, listening to the trooper's footsteps on the wooden staircase. Waiting for the bad news.

* * *

But it wasn't that they'd found Tim's body. The officer, a kid really, had come to tell her they'd found Tim's car and towed it to the police pound. He introduced himself as Trooper Willison and said that Sergeant Haydon had asked if she would come down and make a visual identification.

Haydon met them at the state police impound lot which was surrounded by a chain link fence topped with scrolled barbed wire. He nodded but said little as he led her onto the dusty property where a few dozen cars were randomly parked. They ranged from junk heaps to brand new luxury models. At the end sat Tim's silver-gray Toyota which had accumulated even more miles than Jude's tired station wagon.

When Jude saw the crumpled hood, she gasped, "Oh my God, what happened?"

"We're not exactly sure," replied Haydon. "If he was driving, he went off the road near Roxbury, it's about ten miles southeast of here. You have any idea what he was doing down there?"

Jude barely heard him. "Where is he? Is Tim all right?"

"He was not with the vehicle."

"Well, where *is* he?"

"Don't know, Ms. Brannock. It looks like he was able to leave the scene, but we don't have any indication at this point of where he went. Again … that's *if* he was driving the car."

"But that's crazy," said Jude, ignoring any hypothesis that Tim was not the driver. "He must have been hurt."

"The air bags inflated and likely protected him from major injury, but we did find some blood in the vehicle. Could be from the impact, although of course, there were the bloody tissues you saw in his hotel room which make me think he might have sustained an injury before the crash."

"Did you call the hospitals?" she wanted to know.

"Yes, and no one fitting his description has been admitted."

"Then where could he have gone?" With each question, Jude was becoming more alarmed.

Haydon tried to calm her by focusing on why he had her brought to the impound. "I understand your concern. Let's get through the formality of identification first, Ms. Brannock. Do you recognize this vehicle as belonging to Tim Mains?"

"Yes, it's definitely his car."

"And what about that?" asked Haydon, pointing to the scrape in the fender.

"No, that wasn't there when he left. Is it from the accident?"

"We don't know."

Jude took a step closer to examine the lacerations of blue dug into the silver paint. "Wait a minute," she said. "That looks like somebody hit him. Do you think he could have been pushed off the road?"

"It's hard to know when exactly the fender was damaged, but I'm sending some of the paint chips out for analysis."

Jude walked around the car. "Why did you take the plates off?" she asked.

"We didn't. They were gone when we found the car. And there was no registration or insurance card found in the glove compartment."

"That's so bizarre. How did you even know it was Tim's car?"

"The VIN number. It's possible someone saw the car and stripped the plates. Short term they can be a valuable commodity."

"What about his things? His suitcase or his computer? There was nothing at the hotel."

The Sergeant and Willison exchanged glances at the brass of this civilian now conducting her own interrogation.

"Car was empty."

"His phone?"

"No phone."

Jude's frown deepened. "I don't get it. Somebody must have seen him."

"Maybe somebody did." She was asking all the same questions he had, but Haydon didn't have answers, only speculation. He thought it was time to tell her. "I looked up The Kinship and spoke with Gordon Silverman." Surprised when Jude's head whipped around, he asked, "Is that a problem for you?"

"No, of course not," replied Jude, flustered. "It's just ... I could have told you anything you needed to know."

"I wanted to get another perspective on Tim."

"What did Gordon say?"

"He told me something that you haven't mentioned. Namely, that Mains might have been working not for you people, but for Monsanto."

"Gordon told you *that*?" asked Jude affronted. "He doesn't know for sure. And even if it's true, how is that relevant?"

"It does add to the mystery."

"There's no mystery here," snapped Jude. "Somebody ran Tim off the road."

"It could have been an accident, a hit and run."

Jude rebuffed that idea with a quiet grunt. But Haydon remained unruffled, saying, "Your boss also told me that you were Tim's mentor, his teacher, so to speak."

Jude felt a rush of anger and betrayal. *What else had Gordon told Haydon — a state trooper he didn't know from Adam? That she and Tim were lovers?*

"He said you were a good investigator," Haydon continued, "but thought you might have lost some objectivity when it comes to Tim."

"Well, he's right about that," Jude flared. "I'm not objective about a friend who's been in an unexplained car accident. And I'm sure as hell not objective about an undercover investigator who suddenly vanishes off the face of the earth."

Putting up his hands defensively, Haydon said, "There are some things that don't add up, I grant you. But if your boss is right and Tim was, in fact, working both sides, he might not *want* to be found and certainly not by you. Now, maybe some kids took the plates and cleaned out the car, but it was not easily visible from the road. I have to consider the possibility that Tim took those things himself to slow the process of identifying his vehicle."

"I don't know what you're getting at. Are you suggesting that Tim crashed his car deliberately? He may be a lot of things, but he is not stupid."

"No, I'm not saying that. But like I said, the car was hard to spot from the road."

Jude took a moment to collect herself. She didn't want to get on Haydon's wrong side and wondered if Gordon had found something else about Tim that he relayed to the officer. Still, she really couldn't see where he was going with this. "I'm sorry, but I can't see it: bleeding profusely, Tim climbs out of a wrecked car, unscrews the plates, grabs his suitcase and then trots off to Monsanto headquarters in St. Louis?"

"He might have called someone to pick him up," offered Haydon.

Buying herself some time, Jude stepped up to the car and peered into a side window. "Can I look inside?" she asked.

Haydon hesitated, then handed her a pair of surgical gloves. Maybe she would see something they'd missed.

Snapping on the gloves, she had to admit that Haydon's scenario didn't seem out of the realm of possibility, certainly not if Tim was, as they feared, some kind of double agent. On the other hand, it said a lot that Haydon had chosen to send paint chips out for analysis – it meant he hadn't ruled out Tim as a crime victim. And when she peered inside, she could see why. The dead air bags smeared with blood looked as much a crime scene as anything. She could picture Tim, flying down the road in the dead of night. A car coming up behind him, then alongside, ramming him hard. Losing control and careening into the guardrail or a tree. Tim thrown forward at impact, smashing against the bags, the seatbelt wrenching tight against his chest and cutting off his breathing. A symbiotic pain seared across her chest as she visualized it.

Jude turned her attention to the car. She leaned her hands on the back seat to examine the floor. There were crumbs and granola bar wrappers strewn on the floor; when it came to his car, Tim hadn't been a model of cleanliness. But she didn't see anything that told her what happened or why.

She stepped back and stripped off her gloves. She was about to hand them back to Haydon when she saw something stuck to one of them. A few pale, thin filaments that moved slightly in the breeze. Picking one of them from the glove, she turned it around in her fingers, feeling its texture. Then she leaned into the car again and sniffed the seat and cushioned backrest.

"Dog hairs," she announced.

"Tim had a dog?" asked Haydon.

"No, he did not."

"Could have been somebody else's dog."

"Maybe. But these are white, some with a little brown edge." She scraped a few more hairs from the seat and offered them to Haydon. "And they're short. If I had to take a guess, I'd say they're from one of the beagles."

"What beagles?"

"The beagles they're testing on at Amaethon."

The sergeant regarded her oddly for a moment, then asked, "They test on *beagles*?"

"Yeah. They're small, docile, friendly ... easy to handle."

"I know," replied Haydon, his eyes softening and making him look vulnerable for the first time since Jude had met him. "I have one. A beagle. Well, it's really my kids' dog."

"What's his name?"

"It's a she. Her name is Molly." He cleared his throat. "Well, Tim was working with the dogs, wasn't he? Probably got hairs on his clothing."

"I doubt it. He would naturally have gotten dog hair on his *lab uniform*," said Jude. "But the uniforms don't leave the lab. They go out at the end of the day for cleaning. They're pretty strict about that." She challenged Haydon with her gaze. "I think he had one of the Amaethon dogs in his car."

"Are they allowed to leave the facility?"

"Absolutely not. If he took a dog out, that would be totally against protocol."

"Why?"

"Because those dogs are test subjects," she replied sorrowfully. "They're born and raised in a hygienic environment. No grass, no dirt, no chasing squirrels. And no playing with kids. They're bred to be live sanitary vessels in order to test Amaethon's drug. If Tim had the dog outside the lab, even once, it necessarily meant the animal was exposed to germs, which would then make him worthless as a test subject."

"What would the lab do?"

"Euthanize him," said Jude, then added with a wan smile, "The dog, that is."

# CHAPTER 16

Jude asked to see where Tim had gone off the road and found herself in the passenger seat of Willison's patrol car speeding down Interstate 89. Her gut told her that the hairs in the back of Tim's car were important, but she couldn't put a scenario together that made any sense. How could he get a dog out of the lab with no one seeing him or raising a red flag about the beagle's disappearance? And if he was working for Monsanto, why would he do that and risk Amaethon's trials? For God's sake, where was the *dog*? As questions plagued her, Willison rocketed off the highway, heading west. Then he turned onto Loop Turnpike, where they drove for nearly a mile without seeing a house.

He drew to a stop as far onto the shoulder as gravity would allow. Jude got out and was hit with the heat rising from the asphalt. Even the birds had taken cover; the only sounds were the fluttering of yellow police tape in the feeble breeze and the squawking of Willison's radio. The scene was almost peaceful. Until Willison pointed out the spot where the car had gone over.

"The car ended up all the way down *there*?" she asked in alarm. "You didn't tell me it was that bad."

Willison winced, he didn't know what to say.

With her hand clamped across her mouth, Jude stood at the edge looking down at a few pieces of glass reflecting sunlight through the broken thicket. Just then, from the corner of her eye, she spotted the shimmer of bright orange and blue deep in the woods and the flash of a human figure.

"Tim!" she cried as she lurched forward.

\* \* \*

It had been nearly three days since they'd last spoken.

"Where are you?" demanded Jude.

"In the car," Tim replied.

"I was just about to go to sleep. Where are you going?"

"Into town." He sounded drunk.

Jude exhaled a suffering sigh. "You're supposed to call in every day."

"I know."

"And you promised to send me footage a week ago. Gordon is all over my ass."

"Wish I was him."

"Come on, what's going on? I really need something."

"I really need you," said Tim plaintively.

Hearing a vulnerability in his voice that spelled danger, she softened, saying, "I'm here, okay?"

"I need you *next* to me, not at the other end of a stupid phone."

"What's the matter?"

"I'm coming apart."

*Oh, please, not now.* "You're almost at the finish line," she urged. "Another ten days, then you're out."

"I'm not going to make it." He slurred a little on his consonants. "They just look at me with the saddest eyes, and I can't do a damn thing for them."

"But you *are* doing something for them ... and for all the dogs that'll come after them."

"They think I'm betraying them."

"Are you drunk?"

"Nothing I can't handle."

Jude swiveled her legs from her bed to the floor and switched her cell to the other ear in an attempt to start over. "You can do it, Tim. Listen, I've been there. You gotta try and push through this. The animals need you. And you're doing an amazing job."

"No, I'm not," he laughed harshly. "You've been bitching at me to get more, get more, get video, send video, we need proof, we need pro—"

"Okay, I know I've been on your case, but there's not much time left."

Jude pressed the cellphone to her ear, but all she could hear was his breathing and cars passing in the background. "You still there?"

"I love you."

"Oh, come on, Tim," she pleaded. "Now is not the time."

"Screw you, Brannock. When *is* the time? It wasn't before I left, and it won't be when I get back. You're just jealous 'cause I have a new girlfriend. And she is so cute!"

"Stop it."

"And hot …."

"Shut up."

"Then come here, dammit."

Jude fingered the bedsheet as she contemplated the idea. Maybe she could calm him down, get him through the end of the assignment.

"We don't have to meet in Half Moon," he argued. "I'll get us a room in Montpelier or in fucking Canada if that's what you want."

*Would it be so hard to meet him somewhere?* Jude was torn. She could help get him through this, but it irked her that he was extorting her with this alleged girlfriend.

He misread her silence for caving to his need. "How about Sunday?" he asked.

"I can't Sunday. That's my shelter day."

"Then Monday."

"I can't. I have a doctor's appointment." She would be in New York to meet with Dr. Amin who would have the test results from her MRI.

"Cancel it."

"No, it's important."

"Why?" he pushed. "Is there anything wrong?"

"Nothing's wrong."

"Then for Christ's sake, cancel the fucking thing!" he yelled.

Jude bit her tongue to keep from jumping down his throat. She hadn't told Tim about her eyes or what it was like to wait and hear if you had a brain tumor. She'd kept it all to herself. He had to focus on his job and shouldn't have to deal with her anxiety. But he was such a child sometimes – always thinking about what he needed, what *he* wanted.

She heard him fumble with the phone. He cursed softly to himself and she thought he would come up with an apology but got instead, "My nose is bleeding. Shit."

With an eyeroll, Jude asked, "Can you pull over?"

"I'm getting them all the time now," he mumbled.

Another attempt to get her to travel to Vermont and take care of him? She didn't respond.

"I'll call you later," he sulked.

"Hey, Tim. You can't stand to see the dogs suffer? Get it on video and we can do something about it."

\* \* \*

Willison grabbed Jude's arm to keep her from falling into the ditch. "Hey, hey! Careful now."

She craned her neck to look again, but the colors she had seen blinking in the light were actually a few early autumn leaves, and the shape of a man was just a shadow burrowing in the underbrush.

"Are you alright, ma'am?" asked Willison. "Do you need to sit down?"

"I thought I saw him."

"Saw who?"

"I thought I saw Tim. But ... it wasn't."

"Mmmn. Well, this heat can get to you."

Jude's uncertainty was more suffocating than the heat. She was seeing things that weren't there and not seeing things that were. It was like living in an Alice in Wonderland world where men in Mets t-shirts suddenly ran through the woods, colleagues turned against her, and nothing made sense. I'm not just losing my vision, she thought, I'm losing my mind, too.

She struggled to marshal her sanity and squared her shoulders, saying, "That must be it."

"I've got some water in the car. You ready to go?"

"Not yet." Jude looked up and down the road. "Where does Loop Turnpike go?"

"No place, really," replied Willison. "It runs into Route 12, which takes you down to Randolph."

"What's in Randolph?"

"Not much. There's a golf course and the Amtrak station. Beats me why they put a station in Randolph. Nothing happens, except for maybe the technical college. It's got a pretty good reputation. My brother-in-law graduated from there."

"Sergeant Haydon said the car went off near Roxbury."

"We're technically in Roxbury, but the town center is a couple of miles up the road."

"Why do think he would take this road?" Jude asked.

"Must'a had some reason."

Jude heard her cell phone and checked the caller. It was Gordon; she'd been expecting him to call. She was still angry about what he'd said to Lucas and that he'd shared his suspicion with a police officer about Tim working for Monsanto. More than that, she felt too vulnerable to speak to him right then. But the ring persisted. Jude sighed and hit the green button. "Hullo, Gordon."

There was static at the other end.

"Hello? Gordon, is that you?"

The static went on for another second and then the call was dropped. Her phone rang again, but when she picked up, there was dead air at the other end.

Walking towards his squad car, Trooper Willison threw over his shoulder, "There's no cell service here. If you wait 'til we get back on the highway, you can make your call then."

Jude stood for a moment, doing a last reconnaissance of the woods. She could feel the edges of her psyche unraveling, her mind fraying like the ends of an old scarf. Yet, through the mist, one thing emerged – a thought lodged in the back of her throat, like a horse pill she couldn't swallow. Haydon was wrong to think Tim called somebody to pick him up after the crash. He couldn't have. No cell service. And unless her eyes were playing tricks on her again, there weren't any phone booths around.

* * *

Gordon directed her back to Washington. Immediately.

"I haven't found Tim yet," she said, scuffing the hotel carpet with her toe like a defiant eleven-year-old.

"Have you thought about the possibility that he doesn't want to be found?"

Jude answered with her own question, "What if you're wrong about him? You talked with Sergeant Haydon, so you know there was a huge gash in Tim's car, as if someone had rammed into him and pushed him off the road. And by the way, I saw where he went off, and it wasn't onto any shoulder. Someone drove him into a very deep ditch. Whoever did that was trying to hurt him – bad."

"The sergeant told me about the damage to the car. But he also said that it's possible Tim wasn't driving. It could have been somebody else. And the damage could have occurred any time within the last few weeks. You haven't seen Tim in two months."

"Haydon's sending out paint chips for analysis. He wouldn't do that if he thought the damage was old or if he was sure there was no connection."

Gordon's chair creaked in the background, and she knew he was leaning back, the way he did, to try and ease his frustration. "I'm sure he's covering all his bases."

"Well, there's something else," offered Jude in a last-gasp effort to defend Tim. "I found what I think are beagle hairs in the back of Tim's car, and I think they're from one of the lab dogs. What was Tim doing taking one of the dogs? If they got wind of it, his job is toast and the whole undercover is blown."

"He blew up the undercover anyway, Jude. In fact, he probably took the job to find out what The Kinship is doing and how we operate."

"You don't really buy that, do you?"

"What about the six thousand dollars? The job with the law firm representing Monsanto? And the fact that he hid all of that from us." Gordon's voice sharpened. "At least, I'm presuming he never told you."

"Of course not." There was a doubt-heavy silence at the other end to which Jude, stung by his comment, asked, "Are you accusing me of *knowing* Tim was on the wrong side?"

"I'm not accusing you of anything. But it's time to let the state cops do what they do, and you get back to your own work."

"You're giving up on Tim, is that it?"

"You have lost perspective," he barked back. "He has jeopardized our undercover operations, our credibility, and our entire organization. Even if all he did was quit because he couldn't handle it, he screwed up big time. I would hate to see you go down that same path."

Jude bit hard on her lower lip while she let his words sink in. Finally, he said more gently, "Come on back, Jude."

She had no choice. As she told Tim, the animals would always come first. Fighting for them was the only thing she knew how to do, the only thing that kept her going, even if the finish line kept slipping farther away, day after day, year after year.

It didn't take long to throw her clothes in her duffel bag. She did a last check of the hotel room and was shouldering her gear when she realized that there was something that she'd neglected to do. It was a call that should have been made days ago. She'd only met Tim's older sister once – he did, in fact, have a sister – but Jude didn't want Haydon to be the one to tell her about Tim's car.

She was too late.

Lisa was understandably upset. "I'm freaking out," she fretted. "What are the police doing to find him? Should I come to Vermont? The trooper said there wasn't anything I could do, but what if they find Timmy and he's hurt? I should be there."

Jude could hear Lisa's eight-month-old crying in the background. "I agree with Sergeant Haydon," she replied. "I don't see what you can do right now. Try not to worry. They said that the air bags inflated, and the trooper was pretty sure that he was able to walk away from the accident."

"Hang on a sec." The wailing became louder as Lisa went into another room and picked up the baby. The crying subsided. "Sorry about that. But the sergeant is missing the point, which is why hasn't Tim called?"

Jude wanted to be gentle with her, spare her any of The Kinship's suspicions. "I don't know," she said feebly. "I think he may need some time to re-boot."

"What are you talking about *re-boot*? From what?"

"I think the job was stressing him out."

"No shit. You people pay crap wages."

"A lot less than he was making in New York, I'll grant you. Did you know about his money problems?"

"Yeah, but some of it was his own fault, if you really want to know. He never should have invested in that stupid comedy club."

"What comedy club?"

"Oh, some friend of his in New York was putting it together. He emptied all his savings, and then something happened with the zoning or permits. He lost practically everything. I had to loan Timmy money just to pay his rent."

"You loaned him money?"

"Yeah, six grand."

Jude's breath caught. "When was this?"

"Beginning of the summer. June, maybe?"

Jude felt as though she were watching a film clip running backwards, the worst of their doubts about Tim unwinding. She suppressed a relieved laugh. "Are you sure?"

"Of course, I'm sure. My husband was super pissed even though it was from my own account."

Six thousand dollars – the supposed "payoff" from Monsanto. It came from his own sister, rescuing him from a bad investment. Jude was beginning to feel blood moving in her veins again and asked, "Was Tim working as a paralegal in New York?"

He got his certificate and was with a big firm in the city, but all they had him do was research and organize files. Anyway, he thought the whole paralegal thing was a mistake. He never planned to stay."

"Did he ever talk to you about doing stuff for Monsanto?"

"Mon-insanto? That's what he calls them. He gets all over me about feeding the kids GMO's and glyphosate and other shit that they make. He despises them."

"He … he never said anything to me about that." The clip was running backwards even faster.

"Wouldn't surprise me. He doesn't like to talk about it," Lisa was saying. "I think it embarrasses him, and why wouldn't it? Nowadays, who wants to advertise that they're aiding and abetting Monsanto? I mean, that's why Timmy quit when he did. He told me that every day he worked for them, he felt like he was flushing a piece of his soul down the toilet."

Jude released the breath that she'd been holding since Lucas first told her about the money. She wasn't ready to forgive Tim. He'd been a jerk about Heather – worse than a jerk – he had put the organization in jeopardy. Gordon was right about that. But Tim wasn't a damn spy. And he hadn't scammed her. Maybe the only scam was the one he'd played on himself, believing that he had the nerve and the commitment to be an effective undercover. And she had to take some responsibility. She should have come up to Vermont to visit, should've eased up on the pressure to send her "usable evidence." And if she couldn't tell him that she loved him – because she didn't know what loving someone was or how exactly you did that – she should have told him that he was important to her. Because he was.

"Hello, Jude, are you there?" asked Lisa.

"I'm here."

"What can I do?"

"Nothing right now."

"What about you? Are you going back to Washington?"

"No, no I'm not. I'm going to stay here until I find him."

# CHAPTER 17

Stuart Ostrovsky arrived at the Byer home clutching a bouquet of flowers he'd brought for Dillon's mother. It had been a longer drive than he'd anticipated to this wealthy enclave an hour outside of Boston, and his back was still stiff as he gaped at the expansive front hall, its marble tiles, cream-colored brocade walls, and the sparkling chandelier that hovered over him like a spaceship. He knew that Dillon's family was financially *comfortable*, but he hadn't expected this: the ten-foot iron gate, the mansion, the valet parking.

A uniformed maid approached with a smile. "I'll take those for you," she said, holding out her hand for the flowers. He was reluctant to part with them, having envisioned handing them to Dillon's mother himself. "They're for Mrs. Byer," he said.

"Of course," replied the maid. "I'll make sure she gets them."

Feeling as though he had no choice, he let her take the bouquet and lead him through a richly upholstered living room, then a game room with a pool table and oiled mahogany bar, and finally through French doors to the patio. He hesitated at the threshold. His PhD in molecular developmental biology and genetics was not adequate preparation for the social skills necessary to navigate the Gatsby-like garden party spread out before him. A grand white tent had been erected near the tennis court, the stone patio hosted two separate bars, and there seemed to be more catering staff than guests.

When Dillon had first invited him, he'd mumbled something about a party at his family's place in the country, but the scientist had gotten it into his head that he was going to a backyard barbeque. He'd imagined a pool and a badminton set. Remembering he'd almost worn shorts, he broke out in a sweat. A buff, young waiter found him immediately and asked if he'd like a drink.

Ostrovksy sucked in his stomach. "I'll take a beer."

The waiter rattled off a few exotic brands he'd never heard of, so Ostrovksy nodded at the last choice. "That one sounds fine."

Moments later, it appeared in a flared beer glass, ice cold and delicious. He went in search of his business partner, praying that he would not have to talk to anyone else. Finally, he spotted Dillon inside the tent at a table with three men. Luncheon not yet served, they were the only ones seated and had pushed aside the carefully laid place settings to set up shop. Like most of the other men at the party, they wore sport coats – all but one who was more casually dressed in tangerine pants and a blindingly-white polo shirt.

"Stu, m'boy!" cried Dillon when he saw Ostrovksy walk over. He jumped up to clap his partner on the shoulder. "Dad, this is the guy I've been talking about. Brilliant, nothing less."

The man in brightly-colored pants half rose to greet him. He was, of course, Dillon's father. They had the same Germanic cheekbones and wide jaw. Only his silver hair and weathered skin, deeply tanned after a summer of golf, set them apart. "Nice to meet you, Stuart," he said. "This is Ted Carruthers from Wells Fargo, and meet Marvin McCutcheon of McCutcheon and Dean. Pull up a chair for Stuart," he instructed his son.

Hands were shaken while Dillon dutifully pulled over another folding chair. The senior Byer was clearly in charge and comfortable in the role; and if the foursome had been talking business before, they weren't going to anymore. Byer made sure that they never got past banter involving boats and golf, neither of which interested Stuart in the least. He laughed at their jokes all the same.

With heroic joviality, Dillon tried to put himself in the center of the conversation, but more than once, his father found a way to deflect him. And the harder his son asserted himself, the quicker it reminded the elder Byer of a story that changed the subject. About fifteen minutes later, he announced that luncheon was soon to be served and shooed the bankers off to help themselves. Then he turned to his son and said, "Let's take a walk." He pointed to Stuart, adding, "Join us, please."

Holding drinks, they wandered below the tennis court toward a par three expanse of lawn. All repartee aside, Byer addressed Stuart directly. "How's the project coming?"

"Very well, sir. I would say ... quite well."

Dillon jumped in. "We have most of the animal test results in. They look good. On target."

"I'm asking the brilliant scientist," said his father gruffly.

His discomfort growing, Ostrovksy replied, "Well, yes, the effects of the drug modification are as predicted. In fact, better than I had anticipated."

"Any problems getting it through the FDA that you foresee? Any wrinkles that I should know about?"

Stuart risked a glance at his partner who warned him off with a twitch of his lip. "No, sir," he said.

"Good," announced Byer. "Because I've put my reputation on the line – not to mention five million dollars of my own money to fund yet another start-up for my son." A cruel edge had crept into his voice. "You see, my good friend Marvin McCutcheon is the one who brought Monsanto to the table. And I have assured him that Dillon has found himself a venture that will be extremely profitable. Naturally, I didn't tell him that my son has fucked up just about everything else he's touched."

"Dad …" Dillon's hands were clenched.

"Have to be honest here, boy," said Byer. "You seem to have a singular direction toward failure. Almost like a calling. Real estate. Internet security. I could go on.

"This is the real thing, Dad, I swear."

Byer ignored him, remaining focused on Ostrovsky. "You married, Stuart?"

"No, sir."

"Well, if you ever do marry, take my advice and don't have children. You'll sink a shitload of money into them, and they'll end up disappointing you."

Something snapped for Dillon. He narrowed his eyes and threw back, "Oh, poor Father! Life has been so unkind to you. A good-for-nothing son *and* a wife who sleeps around."

The elder Byer's fingers tightened around his gin and tonic; he looked ready to throw it, glass and all, into Dillon's face. He turned to Ostrovsky and said sourly, "You see what I'm talking about." Then he wheeled around and marched back toward the house.

As if he'd won this round, Dillon draped his arm around his partner and said, "Welcome to our happy home, Stu." But he was quiet as they walked back up the hill, and after knocking back a quick drink, he disappeared.

The scientist waited around and ate hors d'oeuvres that the servers brought around. When most of the guests began to amble toward the tent for the sit-down meal and Dillon had not reappeared, Ostrovsky left the party. He made a wrong turn inside the house, passing through a room where dozens of gift orchids and beribboned wine bottles were heaped on a sideboard. His bouquet, still wrapped in its floral tissue, was among the bounty. But next to the rest, it looked cheap and sad.

* * *

That night the country sound at Galvey's grated on Jude. Far from being comforting, its predictable melodies and lyrics – big trucks, short skirts, cold beer and broken hearts – were getting under her skin.

She didn't know if her target would show, but Jude had few options. She got a break when Sylvia came in and strode up to another girl waiting at the bar. After a quick word, the two of them left Galvey's.

Jude followed at a distance. As she thought they might, the girls walked briskly up the street toward the "drug park." When they got there, they mingled with a half dozen others looking to score. Jude hung back on the opposite side of the street, concealing herself in the shadows of the courthouse. She didn't have to wait long. Even without Bobby G on the scene, money exchanged hands and small glassine envelopes were thrust deep into jeans pockets. Her friend hurried off, and Sylvia returned to Galvey's.

Elbowing her way through the crowd, Jude stayed on the redhead's heels. The tech made a beeline for the ladies' room and anxious for her fix, was oblivious to anything and anyone around her. Just as she reached the short hallway where the bathrooms were located, a girl with freshly painted lipstick emerged. Sylvia wasted no time.

Bounding after her, Jude pushed against the door.

"Hey, someone's in here," cried the tech.

The move, however, so surprised Sylvia that she offered little resistance. And once inside, Jude locked the two of them in. She found herself in a small one-room affair with a toilet nestled in an alcove and a wash basin on the opposite wall. Jude put her back to the door to keep Sylvia from reaching around to undo the lock.

"What the fuck!" cried Sylvia.

"We need to talk," Jude replied.

"I have to take a piss, do you mind?"

"Not at all, go right ahead."

"You're a pervert," said Sylvia bitterly. "I'm gonna have you thrown out of Galvey's."

"Try it. I'll tell them about the coke – or whatever – in your pocket and how you and your friends come in here to snort up. Have you ever been arrested for possession?"

Sylvia scowled, put the seat down on the toilet and sat, crossing her arms and legs. Jude leaned against the sink. "I want you to tell me about Tim … Tyler to you. He was no junkie and you know it."

"I don't have to tell you fucking squat," Sylvia protested.

"Yeah, you do. Because if you don't, I'm going to Amaethon and inform them that you're a drug addict. You think you'll still have a job?"

"You can't prove anything."

"Oh, really?" replied Jude cheerily. She pulled out her cell-phone and scrolled through a few photos. "Not bad, considering the light," she noted. "What do you think?" She held the phone out to Sylvia still perched on the john and forwarded through two or three pictures. The photos were murky, but Sylvia's red hair and pale complexion at the moments she happened to turn in Jude's direction made her instantly identifiable.

"So? I'm with a few friends," said Sylvia dismissively.

Using her fingertips, Jude zoomed in, enlarging a grainy image of Sylvia holding out cash, and then in the next photo, a small bag containing a white substance being pushed into Sylvia's hand. "Un hunh. Just a few girlfriends hanging out and buying heroin."

"What do you want?" Sylvia demanded.

"I want the truth. Was Tim using heroin regularly?"

Sylvia maintained her scowl, but Jude seemed to have gotten through because she finally replied, "No, I don't think so."

"Do you know Heather Buck?"

A roll of her eyes said yes.

"Was Tim supplying Heather?"

"God, no. It was the other way around."

Jude nodded. She thought as much. "Heather's the junkie, right? And she got her stuff from Bobby G."

"Still does, as far as I know. None of this better get back to Bobby," Sylvia warned.

"It won't. So, where did Tim fit in?"

"I told you the truth before, we weren't close or anything. We'd see each other here once in a while and sometimes we'd shoot the breeze at work. I got the feeling Tim had a girl since he didn't seem to be on the prowl. But then, Heather showed up. One night a few weeks ago, we were all here, he had a few beers and started putting the moves on her. I tried to warn him. I mean, everybody knows that Heather and Bobby are a thing. But she seemed pretty hot for Tim. Of course, I have no doubt that she was still sleeping with Bobby. Big mistake in my book."

"Did Bobby know about Tim?"

"He had to – he was here with them a couple of times. But he'd never let on that he was jealous. He was all joking around and like that, but underneath ... he didn't like it one bit. He sees Heather as his property."

A different picture was beginning to form in Jude's mind. "Was there a fight or confrontation between Bobby and Tim?"

"Not that I saw."

"Any reason to think that Bobby might have hurt him?"

"Wouldn't put it past him."

Jude thought back to the previous evening when Bobby had kept her from getting run over. The event was a chaotic mess in her memory – the world going suddenly and inexplicably black, the screech of tires, the nausea as he sat her down on the stoop. But she remembered a few things: Bobby's dismissive laugh as he jingled his keys, his car as he pulled away ... and the damage to the fender. Jude gave Sylvia a hard look and said, "The police found Tim's car in Roxbury today. It looks like someone might have run him off the road."

"No shit," said Sylvia, her eyes wide.

"No shit," echoed Jude. "And somebody stripped everything out of his car to make it look like Tim didn't exist."

She waited to see if the tech had anything to say about that, but there was a knock at the door and an irritated voice, "Are you almost done in there?"

"Yeah, yeah," answered Jude. Then back to Sylvia, "What's Bobby's last name?"

"Gravaux."

"Where does he live?"

"Aw, come on. Please don't ask me that."

Jude held up her cell phone and waved it at Sylvia, who rubbed her face with her hands and sighed, "He's got a place on Summer Street in Montpelier. That's all I know."

"You'd better be telling me everything."

"I swear. Go ask Heather. She can tell you more than me."

"One more thing. You told me about one of the lab dogs that Tim had gotten attached to."

"Yeah, Bailey."

"And you said that Bailey died as a result of the drug dosage." When Sylvia looked down, Jude queried her further. "What did they do with him? Necropsy?"

"I assume so."

"You don't *know*?"

"Well, I never saw it. Dr. Ostrovsky told us Bailey had died in the night. He said he'd taken care of it, so I assume he did the necropsy and disposed of the body."

"Where *do* you dispose of the carcasses?" asked Jude.

"There's a freezer in the basement. A company comes a couple times a week to pick them up."

"Lovely."

Sylvia got up. "Are we done?"

"Not quite," said Jude, moving between her and the door. "Was Tim at the lab when Ostrovsky told you about Bailey?"

Sylvia thought back, and said, "Uh, no. I think that's the day he didn't show up to work."

"What day was that?"

"Wednesday."

"So, he did come to work on Tuesday?"

"He came in."

"And did he leave with everyone else at the end of the day?"

"Yeah. But I saw him after that. I was on the closing shift, cleaning up, and Tim came back to the lab. Said he'd left his cellphone in his locker."

"And then he took off again?"

"He offered to close for me."

Jude looked at the girl incredulously. "They let *you* lock up the lab at the end of the day?"

"Not the actual lock up. We just notify Dr. Ostrovsky or Mr. Beyer, and they do it."

"So, who locked up that night?"

"Mr. Byer. He was the last one out."

After a moment's thought, Jude asked, "It didn't strike you as a little odd?"

"I think I already told you. The last few days before he left, he seemed a bit off, so it made sense that he forgot his phone. And I thought maybe he just wanted to check in with Bailey who was pretty sick by that time. I've seen stuff like that before and

I'm kind of used to it – not that I'm proud of that or anything. But Tim wore his heart on his sleeve, especially when it came to the animals."

"Anything wrong with that?"

"Give me a break. No one thinks it's fun seeing the animals get sick. But you people think you're so high and mighty."

"Why? Because we don't want to see animals abused?"

"How many times do I have to tell you? We don't abuse our animals at Amaethon."

"Well, somebody there is treating them badly. Just before Tim disappeared, he told me he had evidence of major violations of the Animal Welfare Act."

Sylvia's eyes darkened with concern and she seemed to lose her footing for a moment. "I haven't seen that," she said haltingly.

"Maybe because you're not looking for it."

"That's not true. I care about those animals," she parried, and in an effort to retaliate said, "Anyway, I got news for you. A few more days and the protocol is done. And when it is, every single animal in there will get euthanized and dumped in the freezer. Just like Bailey."

When she left Galvey's, Jude wandered through town, trying to shake off the overwhelming feeling of helplessness. *A few more days.* There wasn't enough time to save the lab animals. There might have been if Tim had gotten her the evidence he promised. There might have been enough time to get it to the USDA or leak it to the media, shut down the testing, and maybe get them released. She clung to a sliver of hope that Tim had made a video and she could find him in time. Even if Sylvia was telling the truth and she had never seen any abuse, Tim felt that he had something big – and then he disappeared. Jude wasn't much of an optimist, but it didn't stop her from being tenacious. She had to find him.

She went through what she knew. Sylvia had just provided a motive for Bobby G to get rid of Tim: Heather was his property, and Tim had stolen her. There was the damage to Bobby's car. How far would the drug dealer have gone to enact payback?

On the other hand, she was almost certain that Bailey had not died as Ostrovsky claimed. Too convenient a story. No, Tim had taken Bailey. It would explain the hairs on the back seat of the car. How he had gotten him out was anyone's guess. But Ostrovsky knew, of course he knew. He comes into the lab the next morning, finds one of his dogs missing, and the new tech – the one who had such a fondness for dogs – doesn't show up for work. Yet Ostrovsky lies to his staff to cover up what Tim had done. And where in God's name was Bailey?

Jude thought that if she could find the beagle, she could find Tim … or at least some answers.

\* \* \*

Later that night Jude rummaged through her duffel bag, holding up one t-shirt after another and sniffing each one to see which was the least gross. She hadn't expected to be gone this long. When she got to the bottom of the bag, she gave up, promising herself that she'd wash out a few by hand and hang them over the shower rail. In the morning. Now, however, she was ravenous, not having had a real meal since … had it been breakfast? Did she even eat yesterday? Luckily, she'd packed a bag of trail mix for an emergency like this; she tore it open with her teeth and brought it over to the bed. Dinner, while she made some calls.

She dialed the number she knew by heart. As soon as she heard, *Hello,* Jude rushed into, "Hi, Maddy, it's Jude. Sorry to call so late, just had to see how my Finn dog is doing? I miss him so much, I–" The answering machine was still going. *I'm not here to answer your call right now, but please leave a message at the tone. The shelter hours are Monday through Sun—*

Jude ended the call and whispered into the empty room as close to a prayer as she could, "Please take care of my boy. Thanks, Maddy."

She tried Lucas and got another recording, this one a succinct, *Leave a message.*

This time, she did. "It's me. I just wanted to tell you that I'm sorry about what I said before. I didn't mean it. But I guess you know that. I hope you know that. Anyway … it's late. You don't have to call me back tonight. I'll try you again tomorrow. I know it looks crazy that I'm still here, but I think I'm getting somewhere. And the six thousand dollars … it's not what you think. Look, I can't get into details now, but … I'll talk to you."

Jude ate trail mix until her stomach rebelled. Then she threw today's t-shirt onto the pile on the floor and got under the sheet, listening to the yips and howls of a nearby pack of coyotes. The pack might have been scrounging garbage cans in the neighborhood or on the hunt for a wounded deer, and for many, the feral sounds could be frightening. But Jude found them oddly comforting, knowing the animals were free.

# CHAPTER 18

Jude spotted Haydon with an older uniformed officer at the last booth in the diner. As she navigated past the busy waitresses, she surmised that based on the number of chevrons on his sleeve, Haydon's booth-mate was of superior rank. So, she thought it not wise to interrupt. There was a free table across the aisle from the officers, and she took up her position there instead. The sergeant's eyes flickered in her direction, but he refused to make eye contact.

The men had finished their meals, and the captain – or whatever he was – tossed his ketchup-stained napkin on the table and said he'd be right back. As soon as he was out of earshot, Jude leaned forward to catch the trooper's attention. "Hey, Haydon," she said.

He stared straight ahead, his jaw muscles working overtime.

"I have some information you need to hear."

"I'm having lunch," he said under his breath.

"But you're done, right? Can I come over and sit down?"

"No," he hissed.

Jude moved her chair an inch closer. "Your office said I'd find you here. It's really important that I talk to you. Your theory that Tim called somebody to pick him up from the crash site doesn't hold water. There's no cell service on Loop Turnpike. Ask Willison."

Haydon signaled for the check.

"Secondly, I learned that Heather Buck and Bobby G were an item before Tim came along, and Heather hooking up with Tim did not make your local heroin dealer too happy. I met with Bobby a couple of days ago and–"

"I told you to stay away from him."

"And I saw the car he drives – it's *blue* – and it has a huge gash on the side." When Haydon didn't appear impressed with her sleuthing skills, Jude asked, "Did you get the results from the paint chips?"

Haydon lifted his head at the returning figure of the captain. "Not yet," he said.

"When do they come back?"

"When they do," he answered tersely.

"I think we should get a sample from Bobby's car to see if the paint matches."

"A couple of days ago, you thought it was Kurt Buck."

"I didn't know about Heather and Bobby then."

His eyes on the captain, Haydon said out of the corner of his mouth, "Not now, Brannock. I'll call you if anything comes up."

The captain eased his way onto the slick, green leather seat. If he'd caught any exchange between them, he didn't comment. "I got this," Haydon said as the waitress slapped the check on the table.

The officers rose from their booth and headed to the register at the front. Jude jumped up from her seat. "There's something else," she said, trailing after Haydon. "The dog hair in Tim's car? From one of the test dogs? His name is Bailey, and I'm positive that Tim took him." Haydon's straight back and broad shoulders kept moving away from her. She knew that she hadn't gotten the sergeant at an opportune time, but she couldn't understand why he wasn't listening to her. Persevering, she said, "But then, at the lab, Dr. Ostrovsky told the other techs that Bailey died in the night and he took care of the body. Why would he lie like that?"

Haydon paid the check while the captain eyed Jude as though she were a curiously amusing, but unfamiliar species. The sergeant had had enough. He wheeled around and barked, "Go home, Ms. Brannock. You're not supposed to be here, according to your boss."

"But what about–"

He leaned in close to her and said, "Get some help."

Grabbing his sleeve, she pleaded her case, "That's why I'm talking to you."

"I mean *personal* help," he said, firmly removing her hand from his uniform. "You look like hell."

Back in the car, Jude examined herself in the rearview mirror. Haydon was right, she did look like hell. There were dark purplish bags underneath her eyes and her hair was a stringy mess. A few pimples had broken out on her forehead. She touched them gingerly to make sure they weren't an optical illusion. She was a vegan, for Chrissake – she never had skin problems.

Damn Haydon. She thought he was on her side. He saw the bloody tissues in Tim's motel room, he saw what happened to

Tim's car. And he must suspect foul play if he sent paint chips out for analysis. But now, suddenly he was acting like she was a nuisance. Until she remembered. *Oh, yeah.* She was an animal rights activist, presumptively unbalanced, militant, and rudely intolerant of well-established social norms. Law enforcement did not take people like that seriously – not unless they were the target of an investigation. And of course, Tim was in the same category. If there was no solid evidence of a crime, what was one less animal activist?

"Screw you, Haydon," said Jude out loud.

She snapped the rearview mirror back into place and headed to Summer Street in Montpelier. If Haydon wouldn't do it, she would – find Bobby Gravaux's car, take pictures, and try to get some paint samples. With the evidence in hand, she'd make another run at Haydon.

Summer Street originated in the middle of Montpelier not far from Galvey's and wound through several blocks of two and three-story houses, each separated by shared gravel or dirt drive-ways and plots of green. Many of the houses had been adapted to multiple residences with separate entrances.

Jude drove the length of the street before she spotted a blue car that looked like the Grand Prix that Bobby had driven off. She couldn't be sure; it was dark that night and right on the heels of her vision episode. She made a U-turn and went by again. It was parked in front of a three-story clapboard house. Believing it merited a closer look, she pulled to the curb farther down the block and went back on foot. At first glance, she concluded that she'd been mistaken. There was no damage anywhere she could see, so it couldn't have been Bobby's car. But then, she noticed a

Boston Red Sox sticker on the back windshield and a memory bubbled to the surface.

Wait a minute.

Jude bent down to inspect the wheel guard over the right front tire. It bore none of the underside rust that was visible on the door frame. In fact, it looked brand new, as did the headlight. The replacement fender would have been unnoticeable but for the fact that the paint job wasn't an exact match to the rest of the car. Close, but not perfect. *Dammit.* Bobby had gotten the car repaired.

Overcome with frustration, Jude had a good mind to pick up a stray brick, heave it through the windshield, and send Bobby back to the auto body shop. And as if her criminal fantasy summoned them, two officers in a town police car cruised slowly down the street. Jude rose from her crouch, pretending to have "found" her car keys. The driver of the squad car gave her a brief nod and she smiled back. When they disappeared around the corner, she quickly lost the smile. The thought of doing damage to Bobby's car had given her an idea.

\* \* \*

Auto body shops.

The mechanic wiped his grease-stained hands on his coveralls and went into the office to take the call. "Service," he yelled to get over the thumping of the air compressor.

The woman at the other end sounded upset.

"Hold on," he said, reaching behind him to shut the door and close off the worst of the sound.

"I know this is a strange request," the woman was saying. "But I don't know what else to do. My ex is crazy. He gets real mean when he's drunk. He rammed my car about a week ago. But when the cops finally came out to interview him, he'd already gotten it fixed. 'Oh, look,' he says. 'Not a scratch on it!' Bastard. It was him," she went on hurriedly, "I saw through the window. But look, I don't want to bore you with my sob story. I just want to try and find out where that sonofabitch got his car fixed."

"Why do you think he brought it here?"

"I don't know where he took it. I'm calling everybody."

"This is probably a police matter, don't you think?" asked the mechanic hesitantly. He was starting to wish he'd let the answering machine take the call.

"His brother is on the force. They're all standing behind him," answered the woman, breaking into a sob. "I'm sorry, I shouldn't have called. I just ... oh, God."

The mechanic scratched his head. Shit, he hated it when women cried. "No, no. It's okay," he said. "Uh ... uh, what kind of car is it?"

"A blue Grand Prix," she sniffed. "It would have been the whole right fender."

"I don't remember it," he replied. "But maybe one of the other guys worked on it. I could check with them and get back to you."

"You're a life saver. What's your name?"

"Charlie."

"Oh, thank you, Charlie. Here, let me give you my cell number."

He slid a crumpled napkin over and jotted it with a pencil. "Got it," he said. "Well, best of luck, ma'am."

"Charlie, thank you. You make me think there *are* good men in the world."

He couldn't think of anything else to say and went back into the garage.

Jude checked another shop off her list. It was tedious business. An internet search had given her a long list of body shops within a thirty-mile radius. And after a couple of hours, she'd developed a headache from the whine of sandblasters and air compressors that sounded in the background while mechanics shuffled paperwork or flipped through their calendars. One guy, trying to be extra helpful and perhaps thinking she didn't know her car models very well, disclosed that he'd worked on a dark blue Honda. The owner was named Greg Dunne and had come all the way across Lake Champlain from Plattsburgh to get the work done. No, not him.

Toward the bottom of the list, she got a hit. Fellow had brought in a blue Pontiac Grand Prix owned by one Robert Gravaux. And the shop owner, who'd recently been pulled over for speeding and wasn't feeling too kindly about cops, had offered up an address on Summer Street in Montpelier.

\* \* \*

"You skedaddle," Dr. Harbolt told his assistant. "I'll lock up. There's some paperwork I have to get to."

He waited until he was sure she was gone, then he went outside to his car and dragged a beer cooler out from the trunk. He lugged it to one of the examination rooms and wiped down the counter with alcohol. Donning a pair of latex gloves, he opened the cooler and withdrew a ziplock bag he'd kept on ice. Inside was a dead rat. It was the third one his wife had found in the barn. There was no outward sign of injury, so he concluded that it hadn't died at the claws of a hawk or a wood owl. The doctor thought a necropsy might give him some clues.

After pinning the animal on a piece of cardboard, he cut away the fur along its belly. Then he made an incision lengthwise down the body to reveal the organs. No need to proceed further. He'd suspected this is what he'd find. A significant amount of blood had pooled underneath the rat's skin and around the joints. Rat poison. Had to be. Some type of "superwarfarin" like brodifacoum or difenacoum – a blood thinner. Tasteless, odorless, and commonly used as a rodenticide since rats were unable to vomit. The drug caused hemorrhaging throughout the body, and death was certain within a few days.

The *why* seemed fairly clear; the *how* was still a mystery. Neither he nor his wife would ever have put out rat poison, not with the dogs and hens around. For a brief panic-filled second, Harbolt wondered if someone with a grudge had snuck onto his property and dusted the barn. He couldn't come up with anyone or any motive. Then he remembered that a few days ago he'd noticed that animals had been digging around in the compost pile. It could have been rats. But how could poison have gotten into the compost? Only he and his wife had access to it.

A strange, crawling sensation began at the base of his neck and his mouth suddenly went dry. He disposed of the rat and stripped off his gloves, washing his hands in water as hot as he could stand. Then he went into his office and unlocked his desk drawer. The files had grown to five. Tori Lacey. Young Jarrod Healy. A farmer who'd come in with blood in his urine; preliminary tests for kidney or urinary tract problems were negative. And there were two others – all of them unexplained hemorrhaging.

Harbolt stacked the files, absently making sure the edges lined up perfectly while he thought about what he should do. Five cases, not all exactly alike, but all with similar symptoms and no confirmable diagnoses. Did he have any liability if he didn't call the Center for Disease Control? He didn't believe any of them fell into the category of communicable diseases that would mandate a report. And he surely did not want the CDC or the state health department coming down and combing through his patients' medical charts.

He made his decision and locked the files back in the drawer.

# CHAPTER 19

Katherine knocked softly on her daughter's bedroom door. It never used to be so permanently closed, such an impregnable barricade. These days Heather was talking less, listening hardly at all, adding one or two bricks a day to the wall between them. And Katherine wasn't helping; she felt herself closing off, sure that her daughter was lying about knowing where Tyler was. And each day Katherine had taken one more step to infringe upon her teenage daughter's unspoken request for privacy. Earlier, she'd searched Heather's bedroom, tentatively fingering dresser drawers open as if something horrible might jump out. Something that would validate the feeling that she was living with a stranger.

It was time to reintroduce herself and end the stalemate. She knocked again, and Heather finally said, "Come in."

"Hi," said Katherine.

"Hey, Mom. What's up?"

"I thought you were kind of quiet at dinner, and I wanted to see if you're okay."

Heather sat on her bed with her back against the headboard. She had a textbook in her hands open to clean, conspicuously unmarked pages. She adjusted the pillows on her bed to sit up a little straighter. "I'm fine."

"You think you might be coming down with something?"

"No, why? Do I look sick?"

"Yeah, a little pale to me. And you haven't been yourself lately."

"I'm right in the middle of my period, and it's really heavy this month."

Her brow furrowed, Katherine said, "Still? I thought you started about a week ago."

Heather shrugged, then waited for her mother to question her further or leave.

"How's the poison ivy?"

"Better." She held out her arm where the red blotches did appear somewhat faded.

"Okay, good."

"Anything else?" Heather asked, clearly hoping it was a no.

Uncomfortable, Katherine replied, "Well, I need to ask you something. I was in town yesterday afternoon and I happened to see you go into the pizza shop."

Heather stared at her blinking.

"I had some shopping," her mother added.

"Shopping?"

Katherine didn't feel like she had to explain herself. "Yes. And ... I thought I saw Tyler."

"What?" Heather let the book fall from her lap. "Where did you see him?"

"You told us that you didn't know where he was."

"I don't know where he is. And I have no idea what you're talking about."

"I saw him walk into Angelo's while you were there."

"You're bugging, Mom. He didn't come into Angelo's."

"Right after you walked in? Tall, thin, curly hair?"

Heather's mouth dropped open, incredulous. "Do you mean Jerry Holman? Jesus, he looks nothing like Tyler or Tim, or whatever his name is. Jerry wears glasses, for one thing."

"The boy I saw wasn't wearing glasses," countered Katherine.

"He wears them for *reading*."

"And you're telling me the boy who walked in right after you wasn't Tyler?"

"No, Mom." Heather rolled her eyes dramatically. "It was Jerry Holman."

Katherine felt her confidence slipping. "Oh," she said.

But Heather had gained some, demanding, "Were you spying on me?" And when her mother couldn't think of a response fast enough, said, "I can't believe it! Why would you do that?"

"Honey, I ... I'm worried that maybe you're doing drugs again."

"I'm not, okay?"

"You seem so distant."

"Well, following me around is not going to bring us closer."

"I just want you to be safe. I love you."

"I know, Mom," said Heather, softening. "Love you, too."

"You can tell me anything, you know."

Heather gave her a weak smile, feeling the sting of tears behind her eyes. She was scared. The spots on her arm had faded, but there were a ton of them now on her legs. If she told her mom, she would take her to Dr. Harbolt, and he might say the spots were from heroin use or see the needle marks on her arm. Heather suspected she was having a reaction to the dope and told Bobby she wasn't coming back. "I'm done with all that," she informed him. He nodded and replied, "Sure, babe."

Now what she wanted more than anything was for her mother to rock her in her arms like she was a little girl and tell her it would all be okay. But she waited until Katherine left before letting the tears fall. Suddenly, she doubled over. The cramp was a bad one. And it was so unfair that on top of this stupid rash, she had a bitch of a period that felt like it would never end.

* * *

Jude parked across the street from Bobby Gravaux's apartment house and watched his front door. She sat for an hour and saw a total of four people come and go. They ranged in age and manner of dress, yet all appeared on the furtive side; Jude made them as clients. Each person used the uppermost doorbell and spoke into the intercom before being let in. About five minutes later they left – just enough time to make a transaction. Bobby G was open for business.

Jude convinced herself that she was waiting for the right moment to make her move. But since she had no clue what the right moment felt like, it never came. Besides, she didn't even know what she was going to say. Bobby could be a murderer. And how did she imagine that would that go? It played out in her mind like a bad thriller. *You ran Tim off the road, didn't you? You killed him and got rid of his body? Answer me, you ... you ...* She shook her head, realizing that it was cowardice that kept her in her seat.

Oddly, it was her fear, as familiar as an old sweater, that mobilized her. She'd spent her whole life pushing through fear. And patterns, even self-destructive ones – particularly self-destructive ones – were something she fell into easily. Jude wiped her clammy hands on her jeans and got out of the car.

As she approached the house, a stringy twenty-year-old with a cap pulled down over his eyes stepped out, letting the front door slam behind him. The kid barely glanced at her, probably assuming she was just another junkie. She could understand why; she hadn't washed her hair in days, and she'd lost enough weight in the last week to make her tug at her jeans to keep them from slipping down her hips. Jude stabbed at the top doorbell.

"Yep," came from the intercom.

"Jude Brannock," she said.

"Who?"

"Jude. The *blind* lady, remember?"

"Whaddya want?"

"Talk to you."

Bobby grunted his displeasure, but after what felt like an eternity, buzzed her in.

Slightly breathless after the three-story walk up, Jude pushed open the door to Bobby's lair. The close, smoky room nearly gagged her.

"Don't you want to open a window?" she asked.

"No."

Jude had second thoughts now that she was in the same room with him. Her heart beat hard in her chest. Bobby emitted a kind of darkness that felt not exactly evil but suffocating. She needed air. She also needed to assert herself, so she walked over to the window by the kitchenette and pushed on the frame. It was stiff but lifted a few inches, enough to allow in a stream of night breeze.

"That's better," she said, taking a seat at the table, as in, *I'm here now and nothing you can do about it.* She tried to project a boldness she didn't feel.

"How'd you find out where I lived?" he asked.

"I'm resourceful."

Bobby came slowly toward her and drawled, "You want to talk? So, talk."

"I'd rather you," replied Jude. "Because you've been lying to me. You and Heather Buck are a thing – at least you were until Tyler came along."

As he stared down at her, he casually pushed back his leather vest to reveal a gun parked in the waistband of his pants.

"Okay, got it," she said brightly over her thudding heart. "You have a gun."

"Just establishing the parameters."

"And do the parameters include shooting me like you shot Tim?"

He laughed, a low, greasy laugh. "Is that what you think?"

"I don't know what to think, to be honest. I might. I *might* know what to think if anyone told the truth. But apparently, around here truth is a limited commodity."

"More like a luxury."

"I've got money."

"Let's have it."

Jude glanced around the room, searching for a quick exit if needed. But the door to the apartment was the only way out and Bobby was standing in her path. If she showed her hand, he might hurt her. If she didn't, nothing would come of this risky confrontation.

Licking her dry lips, she said, "Okay, here's what I know." It was the only currency she had. "I know that Heather is an addict and that you're supplying her, along with half the town. I know that she was your girl until Tim ... I mean Tyler ... came along, which didn't sit well with you. I know that Tyler was forced off the road down near Roxbury by a blue car and that you own a blue Grand Prix. Moreover, quite coincidentally, that very same car has gotten a new fender and paint job. The work was done by an auto body shop that has your name on record."

He picked at something stuck between his teeth, then asked, "That's it?"

"Mmmn, let me see .... Oh, and I know that the state police have paint chips that will match a blue car. Possibly yours?"

Bobby moved closer to her, so close she could smell the tangy sweat seeping from his pores. He put his hand around her throat and lifted her chin so that she had no other place to look but his eyes. He wasn't afraid, he was angry. "You're quite the detective, aren't you?" he asked softly.

Feeling like a coyote caught in a snare, Jude thought that if she moved at all, the noose would tighten. She held her ground, meeting his burning gaze.

All at once, he let go. "Pretty flimsy evidence, Blind Lady, but I've come to like you in a strange kind of way, and I don't need you messing with my business. So, I'll deal. But then, I never want to see you again. First off, I never lied to you. You didn't ask me about Heather. Secondly, I already knew your boy was named Tim Mains."

"How did you find out?"

"I'm resourceful." He smiled, his teeth flashing white in the darkness. "And no, I didn't like the way he was all over Heather. But he was never any serious competition. If she wanted to fuck him, that was up to her. I knew she'd always come back to me. In fact, for a while I thought he was hanging around not because of *her*, but because he was tryin' to get to *me*. I figured him for an undercover with the cops or DEA, and when you showed up, I thought you were, too. Only now, I'm beginning to believe that you kooks really are animal rights people." He shook his head in disbelief.

"Do you know what happened to him?" asked Jude.

"No, and that's the gold-plated truth. The last I saw of him was the night Heather's daddy found them together. She'd been dying to turn Tim on, and he was fine with that. We went out to the back of Buck's place, Heather and Tim in her car, and I took mine."

"Wait a minute," interrupted Jude. "You were there?"

"For a little while. She wanted the needle, but Tim didn't. I don't think he'd ever done it before, but he was happy enough to snort some. For me? I don't partake with my customers. I stay long enough to make sure they're breathing."

"Big of you," commented Jude.

He smiled. "I was going to leave the stoned love birds when Tim starts freaking out. Heather's gone, she's totally smacked. But Tim is getting real agitated. At first, I think it's because of his first time using, you know? But far from being mellow, he's jacked ... pointing into the field and spouting some truly weird shit."

"Like what?"

"Like 'there he is ... he who walks behind the rows.'"

"Who was he talking about?"

"One of them was Jim Davidson."

"Who's Jim Davidson?"

"He has the place next to the Bucks. I tried telling Tim that Davidson is just another Half Moon farmer on the verge of bankruptcy."

"What did he mean about 'he who walks behind the rows?'"

"You never saw that movie? *Children of the Corn.* Scared the shit out of me when I was kid. 'He who walks behind the rows' is the evil entity who gets all these kids to kill people as a sacrifice, so they'll have a good harvest."

Frowning with confusion, Jude asked, "What did Tim mean?"

"No freakin' idea."

"Did Davidson see you?"

"I don't think so. It was getting dark and they were too far away."

"Who was the other?"

"Never saw him before. Maybe that's who Tim was buggin' about. It was all I could do to keep him from running over there, which I did not want. And by that time, I thought maybe your friend had dropped acid 'cause he kept repeating some Russian name. Assanov, Dostoyevsky, something like that."

Jude felt like she was looking at a Rubik's Cube in motion: along one plane, colors were snapping into a pattern, but when she turned it over to look from another side, there was no sense of order. She took a stab. "Ostrovsky?"

"Yeah, that might have been it."

# CHAPTER 20

S leep, like the truth in Half Moon, was hard to come by. A few fitful hours were all she could manage. Just before dawn, Jude slipped on a thin hooded sweatshirt, hoping to get onto the Davidson farm before everyone woke. Tim might have been "jacked" as Bobby put it, but the drug dealer admitted that actual hallucinations on heroin were rare. Maybe Tim really had seen Ostrovsky with the farmer. But why would he refer to him as 'he who walks behind the rows'? Tim had never described him to Jude as evil or abusive, in fact he'd said Ostrovsky seemed detached and clinical to a fault.

She had sketched out a timeline, adding the little that Bobby had told her: Kurt Buck found Heather and Tim on Monday night, when Tim became alarmed at possibly seeing Ostrovsky – or someone he *thought* was Ostrovsky. He went to work the next day and left at the end of his shift. He later returned to the lab, telling Sylvia he'd left his phone – which probably wasn't true since he had sent Jude the photographs in the interim. Jude believed he'd come back to the lab for Bailey. It was the last anyone had heard of him, over a week ago.

In the half-light, she saw the outline of Jim Davidson's house set back from the road. Across the way was an old barn with an attached pen where a dozen cows were standing knee-deep in manure. Nearby, a pickup truck missing a wheel had been left to rust. Something about the place tugged at her, but Jude didn't stop to analyze it. She drove another two hundred yards where she found a line of beech and cottonwood trees and a barbed wire fence that separated the two farmers' properties. There was a tractor path on the Buck side running parallel to the fence.

Jude pulled her car onto the shoulder at the tree line and began to follow the path. The horizon was beginning to brighten but footing was difficult because of the rutted tire tracks. More than once, she slipped on a cow patty.

She smelled the apples before she saw the smaller, well-spaced trees. Bobby said that they'd parked in the orchard at the end of the tractor path, and that's where Tim had seen Ostrovsky. "Don't know what it is you think you'll find," he'd said, "but knock yourself out."

When the track ended, she stopped and stared out at Davidson's empty field. It was brown and barren. What was Ostrovsky – if it really was him – doing here? Carefully, she climbed over the wire fencing where it sagged. Rows of something had grown and since been harvested. Picking her way over the furrows, she walked deeper into the cultivated area. It was a cornfield – an ex-cornfield to be exact. Pale, yellowed stalks stuck up from the ground in six-inch spikes and dried corn husks were strewn everywhere. Just a field, no different from the other harvested cornfields that stretched for miles in this part of the world. She wondered if Tim *had* been hallucinating. Flooded with disappointment, Jude kicked at a worm-eaten cob missed by the combine.

An angry tractor's growl broke into her frustration. Snapping her head up, she saw someone at the far end of the field driving a tractor purposefully in her direction. For a moment, she thought to meet him and ask if he knew Ostrovsky. But something felt wrong. She didn't like the way the tractor was driving directly at her and the driver's head was lowered in anger. A primal instinct kicked in.

Jude turned and began to trot back toward the road. The tractor driver was over fifty yards away and she thought she could easily outpace him. But behind her she could hear the engine gears shift as it ramped up speed. She started to run, yet the sound kept getting closer and closer. *How fast can a frickin' tractor go?* she thought as she leapt over the rows. Pretty fast it turned out. Up ahead she could see the road but didn't think she could get to her car before being overtaken.

Veering to her right, she ran to the wire fence between the properties. She pushed down on the wire to swing her leg over the barrier. One of the barbs dug into her palm. Able to get her right leg over, she let go, trying to balance on one leg and lift her other leg over. But her jeans caught on the fence and she fell backwards. The tractor was still coming toward her as she tugged on the fabric.

Finally, with a rip, her jeans came loose. She could see the man's face, his features twisted in fury. He was still yelling at her. Jude scrambled onto all fours, got to her feet, and stumbled into the line of trees on Buck's side.

Once she was safely out of sight, she stopped and caught her breath. Behind her, the man she now believed was Davidson hauled the tractor around and made a beeline toward his house. Through the branches, she watched him stop at the barn, jump off the tractor, and jog into his house – probably to call the cops. Only then did she make a dash for her car.

A short time later, she circled back and risked driving past his house. To her relief, there were no police cars in the driveway. Didn't mean he hadn't called them, but if he had, it meant they hadn't deemed a solo female trespasser an imminent danger to the farmer or to the community. There was a car in the driveway, however – a BMW. It looked brand new, very expensive, and out of place on the run-down property. As she went by, the clouds parted, and the car's shiny blue finish flashed in the early morning sun. For a moment she cast about for the name of the color ... sapphire ... marine?

Until something else hit her like a thunderclap. She'd gotten a better look at Davidson's house. A yellow house. The same house in the photograph Tim had sent – the fixer-upper he had his eye on, or so Jude assumed. But she'd misunderstood. Tim had taken the photo to alert her to something about Davidson and his field.

Holy shit, Tim *was* trying to document the big thing that would bring Amaethon down. But it wasn't about the Animal Welfare Act and it wasn't inside the lab. It was here. *What is it, Tim? What were you trying to tell me?*

* * *

At the motel, Jude brought out the file that months ago they'd put together on Amaethon, even before Tim came to them. They'd known it was a small company. The big guys – the Pfizers and the GlaxoSmithKlines – had thousands of employees and were very careful to vet those they hired. The Kinship had a much better chance of getting an undercover in place with a startup like Amaethon. Still, its website was thin – the usual drivel about being *poised for the future* and *translating vision into reality*. Executive officers were listed as Dillon Byer (CEO) and Stuart Ostrovsky (Chief Scientific Officer), but information on their products was only available "on request."

Jude turned her attention again to web searches, surprised anew at how little information she could find. Lucas had forwarded the journal article concerning Monsanto's interest in a take-over bid of Amaethon, but it didn't tell her anything about what the company actually did.

It took an hour of searching, clicking on links that directed her to other links that sent her to scientific journals to which she didn't have access or to unintelligible technical articles, until finally, she found a year-old reference in an online blog which itself didn't appear to be active any longer. It read: *Amaethon Industries – a private biotechnology company pioneering the use of recombinant proteins for large-scale production in the pharmaceutical, animal health and industrial protein markets.*

Okaaay … what the hell were recombinant proteins? Jude dug in again. And with every new piece of information she gathered, more colors in the Rubik's Cube snapped in line and her horror grew. It wasn't just Amaethon, there were others. They were part of a growing industry that sought big profits with little thought to environmental impacts or unintended consequences. Jude sat back from her computer, barely breathing. She couldn't be a hundred percent sure not yet – but if Amaethon was doing what she thought it was, she suspected something had gone horribly wrong. And Tim had found out what it was.

* * *

Dillon Byer was reaching into a lower file drawer in Ostrovsky's office when out of the corner of his eye, he saw a flash of white on the floor. He whipped around so fast that he banged his knuckles on the upper drawer, believing he'd seen one of Stu's rats scurrying out of a floor vent. But it was just a white disposable shoe cover that skittered toward him in the draft created when the door opened.

"Oh, sorry," exclaimed Sylvia. "I thought Dr. Ostrovsky—"

"Don't you knock?" Byer accused, rubbing his hand.

She flushed. "He doesn't always hear."

Byer regained his equilibrium and offered up a conspiratorial grin. "Scientists! What can I do for you, Sylvia?"

She wrinkled her nose, pretending to be charmed. But she didn't like Byer. It wasn't only that he tried to look all country-casual. Everything about him seemed calibrated to make people think he was just a plain ole' Vermont boy. He wore mismatched socks and a creased sport coat, as if his wardrobe was an afterthought. But one time, he left his blazer on a chair and she looked at the label ... some fancy Italian name. And his car? Yeah, right. She wasn't fooled; everyone knew he came from old money in Boston. Old, *big* money. But what spooked her more was that behind his façade, she sensed something dangerous. A dangerousness that drove a hundred miles an hour, do not pass go, all the way from the home state of desperation. She saw it all the time in the kids waiting on Bobby Gravaux, trying to act like it was all chill, when they knew that if he didn't show, the bugs under their skin would try to claw their way out. Sylvia didn't like what she saw in Byer because she saw it in herself.

Nevertheless, an opportunity had presented itself and she thought she could buy herself a little insurance. "I came up to tell him about a couple of the dogs, but I'll find him later," she said. Then, as if she'd just thought of it, added, "You know that woman with the animal rights group? She's still around, asking a lot of questions."

"Oh, what kind of questions?" asked Byer, lightly brushing the bangs from his forehead.

"I don't know what's she saying to other people, but she told me that she thinks something happened to her pal Jeffries, which isn't even his real name. I guess the cops found his car, but she's like obsessed with this idea that somebody ran him off the road and maybe killed him, I don't know."

Byer made a face. "That's crazy."

"Yeah, right? I seriously think this woman is off her rocker."

"What ... why is she talking to you?"

"She saw me at Galvey's and got right in my face. Supposedly, Jeffries was caught with one of the locals using heroin, and she wanted to know where he got it ... like I would know."

"He was using heroin?"

"It's what I heard, yeah."

"Why does she think he was run off the road?"

"Supposedly the girl Jeffries was doing heroin with is the girlfriend of some drug dealer. Maybe the guy found out and came after Jeffries."

"Wow. Sounds like a drug deal gone bad."

"I couldn't tell you. But I do think this woman is not right in the head. She's like fixated on the drug thing, not to mention obsessed with Jeffries himself. She was even accusing me and my friends of using drugs."

"I'm sorry. That must have been distressing."

"It really was. Anyway ... I just thought you should know, what with animal rights people trying to shut down labs and all. They can be very aggressive. So, when she started asking about the dogs here and them getting sick, I just turned around and walked away."

"She was asking about the lab?"

"Like I said, I walked away."

"That's good," Byer assured her. "That's precisely what you should do. And Sylvia, let me know if she bothers you again." When the tech turned to depart, Byer stopped her. "Where is this woman staying, anyway?"

"I think she said the Riverside Motel."

Byer winked. "Got to keep an eye on these crazy animal activists. Never know what they might do."

When Sylvia left, he brought his sore knuckles up to his mouth and pressed them hard against his teeth.

# CHAPTER 21

From across the road it looked like any other Vermont farmhouse – a cedar wood shingle house with a steeply pitched roof. A child's swing set peeked around the corner from the rear of the house. Nearby was a faded red barn with a few horses grazing in the meadow out back. Only the sign at the bottom of the driveway - Dana Packer DVM, Integrative Veterinary Services – gave away that this was, in fact, a business.

Jude was bone tired. She had spent much of the afternoon tracking down vets in the area, working her way in ever-widening concentric circles around Half Moon. All the while she thought about Tim. He wasn't working for Monsanto and he hadn't abandoned his mission, she believed that now. Rather, he had learned something about Amaethon – something more than the all-too-common abuse of animals that might net them a government fine. And if he uncovered what she was beginning to suspect, he would have tried to get back to her, to give her the evidence he found. Isn't that what she kept pressing him to do? *Stop whining about what they're doing and get proof.*

When she first surmised that Tim had taken Bailey, she believed it was because he was sickened by the dog's suffering and wanted to save him. Tim was a kind, compassionate person; it's why he took the job in the first place. But now she was beginning to think that he had taken Bailey for *her.* Because Bailey *was* the evidence – or part of it. Tim had been trying to please her until the end.

Self-reproach sent waves of nausea through her and all Jude could do was lean her head back until they passed. She made herself sick sometimes. So single-minded in her fight for animals, she left people by the side of the road like so much unwanted baggage. God, why hadn't she pulled him off right away, or at least when Gordon told her to?

Her phone rang. Probably Gordon again, or Lucas. *Where are you? Why aren't you returning my calls? Come back or you're out of a job.* She glanced at the caller's number. Didn't recognize it.

"Hello?"

"Um, is this Gillian?"

Sorry? Jude felt as though she were coming out of a fog. Oh, right. "Yeah, this is she. Who's this?"

"Pete from True Service Auto Body. You spoke to Charlie the other day? Said you were looking for a blue car we might have done some work on?"

"Yes, thanks." She was about to stop the guy from going any further since she'd already found out about the work on Bobby's car.

He was too quick for her. "Well, last week I did a job on a 2018 BMW ... an M4. The whole right side was banged up. Think I did a half decent job, if I do say so myself."

A zinging sound began to reverberate in the back of Jude's head.

"A BMW?"

"Yeah. I repainted the whole car. Couldn't match it exactly because the guy didn't want to wait for the manufacturer's paint. But it was close. A nice cobalt blue."

That's it, thought Jude. The name of the blue that had escaped her. *Cobalt* blue, a stunning, aggressive color – the BMW in Davidson's driveway.

"Did you get the name of the owner?"

Pete chuckled. "That's the thing. It was some kid, so at first, I thought he'd taken his daddy's car and didn't want him to find out about the accident. But he came back to pick it up a few days ago. Paid cash."

"Cash?"

"Yeah, doesn't happen a lot."

"Did he give you a name?"

"Hold on ... here it is. John Rivers. He gave me an address in Brattleboro, which I happen to know pretty well. I never heard of the street."

"He gave you a phony name and address?"

"Can't swear to it. With the cash and all, it smelled funny, but it's not my business to grill the kid, know what I'm sayin'?"

"Sure."

"Wish I could be more help."

"You've been a big help, thanks."

"Good, hope you nail the a-hole who hit you."

"I'm working on it."

Jude hung up, her weariness falling away as adrenaline began to pump through her system. Cobalt blue BMW. Fake name, fake address. Cash. Jesus, why didn't she get the license plate number when she went by Davidson's? It might belong to Ostrovsky, although even if he could afford it, he didn't strike her as a BMW enthusiast. That kind of car was more up his partner's alley. Dillon Byer and his $50,000 "enduring timepiece."

She got out of the car and marched up the driveway, praying that this was the one.

The vet's practice was set up in the old tack room of the barn, presumably so he could keep horses and other large animals overnight. After being assured that Jude was not selling anything, the vet's assistant told her that Dr. Packer was in back with a patient and that he'd be out shortly. It gave Jude time to look around the small but bright waiting room. One wall was covered in photos of pet owners with their dogs, cats, rabbits, and horses, most of them inscribed, *Thank you, Dr. Packer!* There was one picture of a young girl, her arm around a three-hundred-pound hog. *We love you, Dr. Dana*, it said, the word "love" drawn as a big, curlicued heart. Jude decided she liked him already.

And when he emerged, her feelings were confirmed. He was slight of build and had a kindly face with large ears. She had a soft spot for people with overly-big or oddly shaped ears. To her, they spoke of vulnerability. "What can I do for you? Miss ...?"

"Brannock," replied Jude, preparing once again to recite from the script. "I'm looking for a dog, a beagle actually, that a friend of mine might have brought here last week. The dog would have been quite ill."

The tips of his ears turned pink and he said, "I'm not sure. Let me think ... no, I don't recall that." He was a terrible liar.

"Dr. Packer," said Jude urgently. "This is very important. I really need your help."

His brow furrowed, he eyed Jude with some trepidation. "Why are you asking? Who are you?"

"I am not from the lab, if that's what's worrying you."

"Then you need to explain yourself."

She did, leaving out certain details. But she told him about The Kinship, about Tim working undercover at Amaethon, and of her belief that he had taken one of the dogs. "It's not legal, I know," she defended. "But Tim has disappeared and we're very worried about him. I had a hunch that he would have left Bailey with someone who could help. And that would be you, right?"

Packer took a deep breath and nodded. "Come with me."

He led her out of the barn and toward the back of his house. His wife, or so Jude assumed, was folding laundry on a back porch that overlooked the swing set. Nearby was a boy, about five or six, sitting on the grass playing with a beagle. The child wore glasses and, unlike his father, had short, round ears. A huge grin was plastered on his face and his tongue protruded slightly from his mouth; it appeared he had lost a couple of front teeth early. Packer stopped short of the lawn and watched the boy who seemed oblivious to anyone but the dog.

"That's my son Jackson."

It was clear, now that she had taken in the boy's appearance, that he was born with Down's Syndrome.

"And as you can see," said the vet, "he's fallen in love with Cooper."

"Cooper?"

"That's what we call him. Jack-o picked the name. I guess he's your Bailey."

"Well, a couple of the techs at the lab called him that, but it looks like Cooper fits just as well."

As they watched the two play happily together, Dr. Packer told the story. "I knew right away from the number tattooed in his ear that he was from a lab somewhere. And yes, he was very sick. He's doing better now, but I nearly lost him that first night."

"And Tim brought him in?"

"He didn't identify himself. He just pushed Cooper into my arms and said he'd be back in a couple of days to pay whatever fees. He said something about believing the dog wouldn't make it to Washington. It was late, around dinnertime. I heard him pounding on the front door of the house. I occasionally get emergencies at that hour, but they usually call first."

"And then Tim left?"

Packer turned to look at her. "Your friend was in a bad way. He was extremely agitated, and he didn't look well. I advised him to go to a hospital. I even offered to drive him, but he said he had to go back – he didn't say where to – and get his stuff. He promised to see a doctor the next day."

"Did he say anything else?"

"He insisted I treat Cooper right away and asked that if I did blood tests, to save the samples."

"Did he tell you anything about the dog's condition?"

"I could see that Cooper was lethargic, and your friend told me that he'd seen blood in his stool and in his mouth. He also told me what they were testing at the lab." Packer's eyes hardened and the muscles of his jaw rippled with tension.

"It's some kind of heart drug?" asked Jude.

"You could call it that. But it can't be a beta blocker or vasodilator. I can't say with a hundred percent certainty, but I'm pretty sure they're testing an anti-coagulant."

"Why would that be a heart drug?"

"It keeps blood clots from forming, usually to prevent pulmonary embolisms from causing a heart attack or stroke. When someone is put on drugs like warfarin or heperin, they're monitored carefully so there's only enough drug in the system to decrease the clotting tendency, not to stop it altogether."

"But I don't suppose the animal test subjects are monitored that way, other than to simply see what happens."

"That's right." He nodded to Cooper. "The poor thing was hemorrhaging internally. Any bump or cut that might bleed was going to keep bleeding. For God's sake, they make rat poison out of the stuff. It's a good thing that Tim gave me a heads up on the substance they're testing, because it allowed me to skip a few steps and get the bleeding under control."

Jude's mind spun crazily as she remembered what Bobby G told her about Tim's reaction to seeing Ostrovsky in the field ... the razed cornfield ... he who walks behind the rows. Recombinant proteins for large scale production. She finally asked, "Did Tim tell you *how* it was being tested at the lab?"

"They're feeding it to the dogs. Mixing it in with their other food."

"And what if ... what if a person ingested that food?"

"If he didn't need it? And wasn't being monitored?"

Jude nodded.

"He'd be in serious trouble."

"Like bad nosebleeds?" she breathed.

"Sure. There might be other symptoms too, like bleeding gums, an unusual rash, or bruising." When Jude didn't respond, he became alarmed. "Did Tim eat any of what they were testing?"

"I think he might have."

"He would eat dog food?"

"I ... I don't know."

"What makes you think he ingested the warfarin?"

"He was complaining about having nosebleeds that wouldn't stop." But Jude was not thinking only of Tim. She was thinking about the boy at the farmer's market and his nonstop bloody nose. She was thinking about Heather and the odd rash that covered her arm.

"Christ!" exclaimed Packer. "I hope he got to a hospital. Warfarin is nothing to fool around with. What are you going to do?"

"Go to the police."

Packer's son looked up finally and saw his dad. He wrapped his arms around Cooper and his smile grew even bigger. The vet waved, and Jackson waved joyfully back.

"You know, of course, that if you go to the police, they'll come and take Cooper back to the lab," said Packer. "He's stolen property. He belongs to Amaethon."

"Tim is gone," said Jude bitterly. "And I need help figuring out what the hell happened."

The doctor drew his hands roughly down his face. "They'll take him back to the lab and euthanize him."

"I can try to convince the cops not to do that," Jude said, her voice rising. "But I think there may be other victims besides Tim."

"Jude, I don't see how the drug could get out of the laboratory," cautioned Packer. "Maybe something happened in the lab with Tim. He ingested it by accident or inhaled it somehow."

All at once, she felt the sickening ache of guilt return. She hadn't listened to Tim. And if she was halfway right, this thing was too big to fight.

Packer was saying, "Look, if you feel you have to go to the police, then I suppose you have to. But can you wait a couple of days before telling them about Cooper? If something happened in the lab, they'll have the other animals there to examine. Please, just a day or two," he pleaded. "Give me a chance to find another suitable dog. I haven't seen Jackson this happy in a long time. He deserves some happiness."

Jackson's mother stepped down from the porch and walked over to her son. She crouched down and began to pet Cooper, who promptly rolled over, luxuriating in the grass. She and Jackson rubbed his soft, white belly as his tail whipped back and forth. It looked as though they were all laughing.

"You're right," said Jude. "Your boy deserves some happiness. So does Cooper. I won't say anything to the police. They think I'm out of my mind, anyway. If they do trace Tim's movements to you, just … tell them that Tim took the dog with him."

Dr. Packer gratefully took her hand in both of his before joining his family. The young beagle scrambled to his feet and licked the face of the man who saved his life. For a young dog, Cooper hadn't yet regained that frantic puppy energy, but as he got better, he would. And she felt sure he was with the right family, not only because Dr. Packer would take care of his physical health. Jackson's slow, deliberate moves and the simple joy that bubbled up from his core were just what this dog needed to heal.

Cooper was finally free of the confines of his breeding facility and the testing lab, free of the sterile cages and the latex-gloved hands – the only ones he had ever known until now. He was finally home.

Jude turned and walked back down the driveway, vowing never to tell a soul. At least she could do one good thing.

# CHAPTER 22

Katherine climbed the stairs with heavy feet and a heart even more burdened. She'd just gotten off the phone with the school which informed her that Heather had not come in and no one called to tell them she was sick. She'd have to bring in a note for tomorrow. "Of course, I'll make sure she does," Katherine reassured the administrator, her hands forming tight fists.

She expected to see her daughter listening to music with earphones clamped to her head and didn't bother to knock. But when she swung open the door, the room was empty.

"Heather?"

No answer. Tinny music was coming from the bathroom down the hall.

"Heather, I need to talk to you," called Katherine irritably through the closed door. A country-pop song continued to beat out an insistent rhythm from the iPhone, but there were no accompanying sounds from inside. "Heather?" Katherine tried to open the door and found something blocking it. "What's going on in there?"

But even as she asked, her chest constricted in alarm. She shoved harder on the door and felt it give a little. Through the crack, she saw her daughter's legs on the floor. Katherine began to scream.

The next fifteen minutes were a stampede of sounds and images. The pounding of Kurt's boots on the stairs, Heather curled up in a ball on the tile floor, the ambulance siren, her daughter lifted onto the stretcher, pale as death … and oh, God! The blood. So much blood on her flowered PJ bottoms and on the bathroom floor.

Then came the interminable, torturous wait in the hospital. Katherine took turns staring at the toes of her shoes and at the double swing doors where they had been stopped from following the gurney. Her husband hovered around the admitting desk, inquiring every few minutes if they had any information.

Finally, the ER physician came out to tell them that they had stabilized Heather as best they could. "She's lost a lot of blood," he cautioned.

"What happened to her?" Kurt implored the doctor.

"We don't know yet."

"Did she … try to kill herself?"

"We don't see any indication of that, but …."

Katherine offered up lamely, "She was having her period."

"Is Heather a hemophiliac?"

"No, no."

"On any type of blood-thinning medication?" he pressed, slight accusation in his tone.

Her parents looked dumfounded and shook their heads. The doctor frowned. "We're giving her an infusion now and running some tests. We'll know more in a little while."

"So, you don't know what's wrong with her?" asked Kurt.

"We'll know more when the tests come back."

Running a hand over his face, Kurt said, "I suppose we should tell you that about ten days ago she ... she shot up some heroin. Maybe it was a bad batch or something in the needle?"

"I doubt it."

Kurt felt it necessary to throw in, "It was just the one time. Crazy kid's mistake."

The doctor looked curiously from husband to wife before saying, "Mr. and Mrs. Buck, I don't think it has anything to do with this bleeding, but your daughter is a regular heroin user." He gauged their reaction. "I thought you knew. From the marks on her arms, she's used dozens of times. I'm sorry." Then he recognized the shock on their faces and added, "Don't be discouraged, we'll get her some help ... when she comes out of this. Hang in there."

He turned to go, leaving Kurt and Katherine dizzy with the realization that they didn't know their daughter at all. Worse, they might never get the chance to find out.

* * *

Now what? thought Jude, after she left Dr. Packer's practice. *Go to Haydon with her suspicions?* Speeding back toward Half Moon, she barked out a laugh imagining how that might go. *Well, you see, Sergeant, Amaethon's testing a freakin' blood thinner by feeding it to dogs. One of them nearly died of internal bleeding according to a source which I cannot reveal. And then Tim had all these nosebleeds that wouldn't stop. Probably from the same drug. And there was this kid at the farmer's market. And I have a theory about how they ingested it ....* She didn't even want to imagine his face when she told him what that theory was.

Maybe she could get Jim Davidson to talk. He knew what had gone wrong. And she guessed that the owner of one cobalt blue BMW knew as well.

The dried grasses and razed fields flew by. God, it was hot. Summer in Vermont was supposed to be over by now. Her car's air conditioning was malfunctioning again, and Jude rolled down all the windows to let the wind cool her. Feeble attempt. She was sweating bullets, her mind ricocheting from one idea to the next. She had to get something solid to bring to the cops. Something besides a license plate that *might* back out to Ostrovsky or Byer – if she could find the BMW. If she did, and the car belonged to someone at Amaethon, Haydon might speed up the paint chip analysis, and then—

Her phone sounded on the seat next to her. Jude glanced at the incoming caller and snatched up the phone quickly.

"What is it, Madelyn? " she asked anxiously. "Finn? Is he okay?"

"He's fine, Jude. He misses you, but he's fine."

"I miss him, too."

"Listen, I have to tell you something."

"Say again?" It was hard to hear over the noise of her wheels on the road.

Madelyn upped her volume. "It's about Rocky. I'm really sorry, but I had to let him go."

"I can't hear you."

"I had to let Rocky go," yelled Madelyn into the phone. "We tried. But he bit one of the volunteers, and he was wreaking havoc in the kennel."

A truck passed Jude, its rumble drowning out Madelyn's voice. "He bit somebody?" Jude bellowed back.

"Yes, we had to let him go."

"What do you mean 'let him go'?"

"We had to send him to County."

"You what? When? Is he still there?"

"I'm sorry. They ... they put him down this morning."

"No!" wailed Jude. "You promised."

Madelyn argued, "I know I did. But you haven't been here for over a week. I can't just hold on to everyone that you want to rescue. I have to look out for all the others, too."

"Shit!" Jude pounded the steering wheel. "Shit, shit, shit!"

She didn't hear what Madelyn said in response, if anything, because the sky had suddenly darkened, and she could barely make out the road. There was a stop sign ahead and she braked, but the road curved at the last second. Didn't it? Jude spun into the sign with a frightening crunch of metal on metal. She was aware only of her head snapping forward and hitting the steering wheel.

"You okay, ma'am?"

Jude came to and blearily looked into the craggy, pockmarked face of an older man peering through her window. "Can you move?" he asked.

She attempted to lift each of her legs and arms, one at a time. They seemed to function given her limited ability to maneuver behind the wheel. Her right knee was sore and her head pounded like a demon, but she felt generally whole.

"Let me help you out," said the man. "Easy now."

She took his sinewy hand and inched herself out of the car. The front headlight looked as though it was embedded in the pole of the stop sign. "What happened?" she asked, still foggy.

"You drove into the stop sign."

"Why?"

"Damned if I know. But to be honest, I've always felt it was a dumb place for it. It's not like there's an intersection here, just a tractor crossing, and any farmer with half a brain – and those are most of the farmers I know – would wait until there wasn't any traffic."

Jude remembered losing her vision just before the crash. But it seemed to be returning somehow and she zeroed in on the man in front of her. He wore baggy jeans and a green t-shirt that read "Don't Blame Me - I Voted for Bernie." The effort of standing upright, however, was making her dizzy and she put her head down and groaned.

"You got a nasty cut there, young lady. I think we should take you to the hospital."

She felt sweat drip down into her mouth. But when it touched her tongue, she tasted blood, not sweat. "Oh," she said, touching her forehead. "No, no, please. I'm fine."

"You don't look fine."

"I'm okay." Jude was beginning to get her bearings. "I couldn't have hit it all that hard because the air bags didn't inflate."

"They shoulda. Anyone I can call for you?"

"No, thanks."

"If you say so."

"Do you think the car will start?"

"I'll give it a try. Here," he said, handing her a bandana. "It's clean. You go sit over there while I give it a spin." He pointed to the flatbed of his truck a few yards away.

Jude complied, grateful for the old man's assistance. Holding the bandana to her head, she watched as he got the engine going and backed away from the stop sign. She winced more from the smashed headlight and dent in the grill than from the pain in her forehead. Her good Samaritan opened the hood and took a careful look inside, touching this and tweaking that as if he knew what he was doing. Then he closed it up and wiped his hands on the back of his pants.

"Think you'll be okay to get it to a garage. But I wouldn't do any long trips 'til you get it checked out."

She walked toward him. "Thank you so much." She pulled the bandana away from her face. "I got blood on this, I'm sorry."

"You keep it. What's your name, young lady?"

"Jude."

He smiled and his eyes creased into countless tiny folds. "Jude, eh? The patron saint of lost causes."

She looked balefully at the car. "You got that right."

His face turned serious. "The thing is, Jude, I can't let you just drive away until I'm sure you're okay.

"I'm not going to a hospital," she insisted.

"Very well. But I'm gonna insist that you see a doctor. I happen to know a good one about two miles up the road. He's a friend of mine. John Harbolt's his name. You follow me, and I'll take you there."

"I really can't ask you to do that."

"Don't matter what you can or can't ask," he replied. "It's what's gonna happen."

It wasn't until she found herself in Dr. Harbolt's waiting room that she remembered about Rocky. She doubled over and hung her head between her knees, letting the red-hot pounding in her head punish her for abandoning him. *Poor dog. Poor frightened, frustrated, angry dog. You get put in situations that you can't handle and when you react the only way you know how, by scaring people away, they call you aggressive and put you down.* She rocked for Tim. *Oh God, I didn't listen to you either. I'm sorry, I'm sorry, I'm sorry.*

"No, Miss Brannock, I'm the one who's sorry."

She lifted her head to the visage of a country doctor straight out of a Norman Rockwell painting, complete with starched white coat and stethoscope around his neck. Had her thoughts voiced themselves? She clamped her mouth shut in case more of them escaped into the outside world. They were bad thoughts.

"Sorry I've kept you waiting so long," said Dr. Harbolt. "Come on back."

She followed him into an examination room and he motioned to the paper-covered table. "Have a seat. Mack told me you had a little car accident," he said, dabbing at the cut with a moistened cotton ball. "Looks like you hit your head."

*Brilliant diagnosis*, Jude thought. But fighting the angry maelstrom in her head, she said, "It's not that bad."

"Not bad. But you will need a few stitches. Anything else hurt?"

"No."

"You got lucky then. Wait here while I get my sewing kit. It's about quittin' time, so I'm going to let my assistant go and put the 'do not disturb' sign on the front door. We'll have you out of here in two shakes."

She wanted to like him because he was a friend of Mack's and because he had big ears. But feeling perversely antagonistic, his folksy vernacular made her want to punch him in his face instead. He came back and had her lie down. Then he explained what he was going to do, numbing the area and putting in some sutures. "It's right at the hairline here, so it's not going to be noticeable."

"I don't care."

He looked surprised. "No? Lovely girl like you?"

"Are you hitting on me?" she asked testily.

"Would if I was unmarried and forty years younger." Unflappable, he went on chatting as he sewed up her wound.

Jude had little choice but to submit to the sting of the needle and his friendly patter. She closed her eyes and breathed in the cool, disinfectant smell of the room while his practiced hands did their work. And then it was over. The doctor covered the stitches with an adhesive bandage and told her to lie still for a few minutes.

Jude sat right up and asked, "Do you treat a lot of the people around Half Moon?"

"Guess I do."

"Have you recently run into some unusual cases of bleeding that won't stop?"

He froze for a fraction of a second, just long enough to set Jude's heartbeat going like a freight train. "You have, haven't you?"

"Why do you ask?"

"Because a friend of mine has been getting nosebleeds that are out of control."

"Mmn." Harbolt looked down, busying himself with his instruments and the bloodied gauze.

Jude stood firm. "Just tell me. Have you?"

He replied, "You're awfully pushy for someone who came for treatment after hours."

"You have, though, right? Treated people for unexplained bleeding." When he didn't answer, she blurted out, "What if I told you I know why it's happening?"

He looked sharply back at her.

She didn't know what in the world she was doing opening up to him. Harbolt was a complete stranger. Even as she spoke, she tried to tell her mouth to stop, but it wouldn't obey. "My friend Tim was working at Amaethon. They're testing a heart drug, and I have it on good authority that it's likely some type of warfarin, an anti-coagulant. I think it's escaped from the lab somehow and is affecting people in town."

"What are you talking about?"

"*Escaped* isn't quite the right word because it didn't come out of the lab so much as get *into* the lab."

He gazed at her sternly. "I think maybe you should lie down for a little while."

"Please, don't pretend I'm crazy because I hit my head. You know what I'm talking about."

"Can't say that I do, Miss Brannock." But he didn't try to stop her from continuing.

"Let me start over. Are you aware that certain foods have natural blood-thinning properties?"

"Yes," he replied. "There are a number of them ... uh, cranberries, ginger, pomegranate. Quite a few others."

"What if the genes that carry those blood-thinning properties could be inserted into another plant through genetic modification in such a way that the effect is magnified?"

He wagged his head yes and no. "I don't know much about genetically engineered plants, but I suppose it's possible. What are you getting at?"

*Shut up, Jude.* But she said, "Do you know the Amaethon Laboratory on Route 107?"

"Sure."

"Right now, they're testing what they claim is a new drug. It's an anti-coagulant, which I gather is a class of heart medications."

"Your point?"

"Amaethon is not a run-of-the-mill pharmaceutical company creating new chemical compounds. They're in the business of developing new *processes* for producing existing drugs – a process that involves plants. I think that they have genetically engineered corn plants to grow enough anti-coagulant that the consumption of a small amount of corn effectively works like a prescribed dose of medication. This is what they're testing on animals at the lab. And it's working. They're mixing in the corn with dog food, and the dogs – and I'm sure the other test animals as well – are showing signs of internal bleeding. With this drug in their systems, their blood can't clot."

"Hold on a minute," exclaimed Harbolt, putting up his hands to stop her. "Why in the world would Amaethon do this?"

"First of all, it's not just Amaethon. It's an entire industry: plant made pharmaceuticals – PMP's, they're called. Biotech companies are experimenting with growing antibodies, vaccines, and drugs in plants. Why? That's easy. They can be manufactured on a much larger scale and way cheaper than trying to create them in chemical factories or bioreactors. Think about it. Acres and acres of free-growing corn or tobacco – just let nature do its thing."

He shook his head vehemently. "No one would cultivate something that potentially dangerous here in Vermont."

"Don't count on it," Jude replied. "Not if there's a profit motive and an anti-regulatory environment. Go ahead and pay a local farmer to grow it. Maybe someone who's struggling financially and would welcome a company offering the right money."

Harbolt eyed her keenly. "What makes you think that your friend or folks around here have ingested any of this … this genetically engineered corn? If what you say is true, it would all go directly to the laboratory."

*He's listening, paying attention.* "I think they've eaten corn that's been *cross-pollinated* by the GE corn. An ear of corn has to be pollinated to grow kernels. The tassels at the top of the plant—"

"Release pollen, yes I know," interrupted Harbolt. "I grow a little corn myself."

"So, then you know that any individual ear of corn doesn't pollinate itself. It happens from other nearby corn plants, and it doesn't have to be from the same field of corn, pollen can drift in the wind from other fields. This wouldn't be the first time."

Jude shifted on the table to find a less uncomfortable position, then continued, "Several years ago, a company called Prolifitech genetically engineered a batch of corn to produce a pig vaccine. When the corn crop failed, they plowed it under and planted food grade soybeans. But some of the corn stalks got mixed up with the soybeans which made them, of course, unfit to eat. Now, who could have *possibly* foreseen something like that?"

"And what happened?"

"They caught the error and managed to intercept the soybeans before they got to market. Thousands of bushels. The company got lucky."

"And Amaethon didn't?"

"There's an organic farm near the one that was growing the GE corn, and he sells *his* corn at the local farmer's market."

"Are you talking about Kurt Buck?"

"His is the neighboring property to this particular local farmer."

"And you're saying that the pollen of the GE corn with the drug was blown onto Kurt's field and infected his crop."

"I think so, yes. Maybe other fields, too. All I know is that people have been eating bad corn. First, my friend Tim who told me that he was getting bloody noses all the time. Then there was a kid that I saw at the market whose nose wouldn't stop bleeding, and a girl with strange rashes all over her arms. Plus, the cases that you're obviously seeing. How else can you explain it?"

Harbolt's frown creased every line in his face. "If you're right, why isn't everyone in this community getting sick?" he asked. "Like lots of people, I've eaten Kurt's corn, and I haven't been affected."

"I wondered about that myself. But then I thought, most people cook their corn, and maybe if it's exposed to heat, the drug gets broken down and has no effect. But what if you ate the corn raw? Tim ate raw vegetables all the time. And he would have had the opportunity because he was shacking up with Kurt Buck's daughter. Probably not many people eat raw corn, but you might not have to eat much to have it take you down."

The doctor tried one more time. "There must be regulations to prevent something like this from happening."

But Jude was one step ahead of him. "Oh, there are. There's supposed to be a buffer zone between the drug plants and crops raised for human consumption. But who says the government is enforcing that? And besides, even if Amaethon thought they had secured a sufficient buffer zone … they were wrong, weren't they?"

Buying time, Harbolt took off his glasses to clean them on the hem of his lab coat. But Jude wouldn't give him the respite. "So, I'm asking you again," she pounced. "Do you have any patients who can't stop bleeding?" She registered his stricken face and concluded, "I guess you do."

She got down from the table. She'd lied – everything hurt, and she sagged against the table.

The doctor reached out to keep her from slipping to the floor. "Where do you think you're going?" he admonished.

"I have to find my friend." Even to herself the words sounded mythical. Tim was gone. She hoped that he had run and run far, but she didn't really believe it. Still, she had to know.

As if she had again spoken aloud her buried thoughts, the doctor cautioned, "You're not going anywhere right now. It's highly likely you have a concussion."

"But—"

"Slow down, m'dear. I want to help you."

"You do?"

"I do. What you've told me is very disturbing."

Harbolt's pager went off. He unclipped the relic from his belt and glanced at the incoming number. "I have to make a phone call," he said. "I'll be right back."

Jude waited on the examination table, the pounding in her head beating out the moments he was gone. She clung to the bright side. Harbolt believed her. There was someone who understood the craziness of what was happening and wanted to help.

The door opened and he came back in. "I have an emergency at the hospital," he announced. "But I'll be back shortly. This will be a good time for you to rest. Here's a couple of Tylenol," he said, handing her two white pills, "for the pain. You shouldn't be driving. When I come back, we can talk about what our next steps should be."

He handed her a plastic cup of water, and she swallowed the pills. All at once, Jude felt so tired that lying down was the *only* thing she could do. She nodded meekly. He led her to his office where a small sofa beckoned like a pool of water to someone dying of thirst. She succumbed to its plush fabric and curled up with her hands beneath her cheek.

"You rest now," said Harbolt.

She wasn't sure that she'd fallen asleep, only that she had gone somewhere else, a place of nothingness, and that it hadn't been long – an hour? Five minutes? The sound of a car door brought her back ... along with loud, hurried voices outside.

Pushing herself groggily off the sofa, Jude stepped over to the window and peered through the blinds. Harbolt was talking with another man by a car in the parking lot. The man's back was to her, but he seemed upset, clutching his fists against his abdomen. Something about the gesture made her think she'd seen him before. At that moment, the doctor glanced up in Jude's direction. She drew back, the metal blinds making their whispered tinkling as they settled. When she dared look again, Harbolt was striding towards his office and the other man turned to watch him. It was Stuart Ostrovsky.

It felt as though she'd been punched. Ostrovsky? Was Harbolt lying about a hospital emergency? After spilling everything she knew about Amaethon, had he rushed to call Ostrovsky? She looked around for a means of escape. There was no way out; she was trapped.

When Dr. Harbolt came into the office, Jude was feigning sleep in the same position. She tried to breathe slowly, while she mentally rehearsed how she might overpower him to give herself time to run. He went to his desk and unlocked a drawer. He took something out and re-locked it. Then there was silence, and she could feel him watching her. It was all she could do to keep her breathing even and sleep-like. A moment later, he left.

She waited until she heard the outer door close again before rushing to the window. Ostrovksy was still there. The doctor had a piece of paper in his hand. Holding it against the top of his car, he wrote something on it and handed it to the scientist. He looked at his watch and said one last thing before they both drove off in separate cars.

Jude was rocked completely off course. She flipped through what-if's in her head but couldn't come up with a credible scenario that would explain the country doctor's connection to Amaethon. Unless, because of his patients, he'd figured it out and Amaethon was paying him to keep quiet. Or maybe there was a more sinister explanation: he was being paid as a medical consultant and had been in on it from the very beginning.

That thought triggered a new blitz of panic. What were the pills he had given her? Tylenol – or something else? Her head still felt as though she had slammed it on a doorframe, but adrenaline was bringing her back to life. If he'd drugged her, it hadn't yet taken effect. She had to get out before Harbolt came back. Or sent someone.

Her car started and she coaxed it onto the road. There was an odd noise coming from the right front wheel, but for now, it was operable. Jude began to drive back to her hotel. But as she got closer, she questioned whether she'd be safe there. Stupidly, she'd noted the local address on the insurance form she'd completed at Harbolt's office. She drew in behind a Dunkin Donuts and called Lucas.

*Leave a message.*

"It's me. Uh … think I'm in trouble, Lucas. I … uh … I don't think Tim's alive." Her voice cracked, and she had to take a few swallows to get it under control again. "I think I know why, but not how. I have to know. If anything happens to me, it's about what they're testing at Amaethon. It's … fucking insane. They're growing an anticoagulant drug in corn, and it's gotten out, and now people are getting really sick. I don't know, maybe–"

A rude beep signaled she had come to the end of her allotted time. What was the point in leaving another message? Lucas was in Washington and she needed someone in Half Moon, now. It was time to call Haydon.

# CHAPTER 23

He was waiting for her when the Subaru limped into the motel parking lot. Jude couldn't figure out how he'd gotten there already, it had only been a few minutes. But she felt relieved. No one would come after her after seeing a state police car in the parking lot.

The sun was setting, leaving behind a golden-hued horizon, which would have been stunning had it not been for Haydon's silhouette against the farewell light. He appeared bigger and more rigid than she remembered.

"Thank God you're here," said Jude.

"Jesus, what the hell happened to you?"

"Nothing ... I just hit my head."

"You should see a doctor."

"I did."

He took a moment to take in the bandage on her head, the gray hollows in her cheeks, the grimy jeans, and the fever-like glaze in her eyes. "I've been looking for you," he said.

She huffed, "Really? You couldn't get rid of me fast enough at the diner."

"Why don't we sit down?" He walked over to one of the benches overlooking the valley and motioned for her to sit, which she did. He remained standing.

"You can cross Bobby Gravaux off your list," she said, brushing away the bench's flaking white paint. "That is, if you were ever interested in following up on that lead. I know what happened to Tim. Well, not what exactly ... but I'm pretty sure it was someone at Amaethon."

It was as if she hadn't spoken. Haydon said, "I need to ask you a few questions, Jude."

"Okay," she answered hesitantly.

"When did you last talk to Tim?"

*Good. Haydon was on it and finally putting his own timeline together.* Her jaw relaxed a bit. "I guess it would have been ... let's see, Sunday before last."

"And how did that conversation go?"

"He sounded drunk and messed up."

"The two of you fought?"

Jude was surprised by his question. "I wouldn't call it a fight. It was an argument."

"About what?"

"It was personal. But if you must know, I thought his involvement with Heather Buck, although I didn't know her name at the time, was getting in the way of his assignment."

"And the personal part? You were involved in a relationship with Tim, weren't you?"

"Yes, but it wasn't serious." Jude flushed, as much from Haydon's peering into her intimate relationships as from the knowledge that she had lied. If she were telling the truth, it had been serious. She just refused to acknowledge it at the time.

"And when did you arrive in Half Moon to look for him?"

"Thursday. That's the day I reported him missing, remember?"

"That would have been Friday, Jude. You didn't report him missing until Friday."

"Okay. Yes, Friday." Jude shook her head in confusion. *Why was his timeline focused on her? This was about Tim.*

"Where were you earlier in the week?" he pressed.

"What are you talking about? I was at work."

"That was on Wednesday and Thursday, yes?"

"Why are you asking me all this?"

But Haydon didn't answer. Instead, he said, "And you told Mr. Silverman that you were in New York visiting a friend the previous weekend. The weekend, plus the early part of the week, which is why you didn't get in to work until Wednesday." When Jude didn't respond, he continued, "In fact, you told your office that you were visiting a friend named Alice Cantrell."

She was beginning to catch on to his line of questioning. "What the hell is this? You think I had something to do with Tim's disappearance?"

"But I contacted Alice Cantrell who is, in fact, living in New York City. But she told me that she hasn't seen you since last May."

Jude glared at him, bristling with anger.

"Why did you lie to your colleagues about where you were?"

"I … was having some medical tests done, and I didn't want anybody to know."

"What kind of tests?"

"It's none of your goddamn business. And you have some nerve to question me this way. *I'm* the one who brought Tim to your attention."

"I just need to get some facts straight."

Jude had enough. She started to get up, but Haydon blocked her. "Where were you on Monday and Tuesday of last week?"

"I told you where I was," she fumed.

Haydon kept his calm. "Someone saw you and Tim together on Tuesday. In Half Moon."

"What? That's a lie! Who told you that?"

Pulling out a cellphone from his pocket, Haydon said, "This person also found Tim's phone and turned it over to us. You sent off some pretty angry texts to him."

"Give me that!" she cried.

But he held it out of her reach and said, "You didn't like that he wasn't calling you back like he was supposed to. And there was the issue with Heather."

"Okay. I was angry at him, but that wasn't … who found his phone? Where?"

"It was at the lab."

Jude scoffed, "That can't be true. He sent me some photos from his phone after he left the lab on Tuesday. I showed them to you, remember?"

"You don't know that he sent them from his phone. In fact, I have two witnesses who say that he clocked out of Amaethon on Tuesday evening and later returned because he'd left it there."

It stopped Jude short. "No, no," she stammered. "He went back to the lab to get Bailey. He only *told* Sylvia that he came back for the phone. It was a pretext, don't you understand? Whoever supposedly found his phone at the lab is lying to you. Maybe they got it out of Tim's car after driving him off the road. Was it Stuart Ostrovsky? Or the other one. Dillon Byer." There was a slight movement at the edge of Haydon's mouth that gave it away. "It was Byer. He drives a blue BMW, doesn't he?"

"Why do you ask?"

"The paint chips, Sergeant. Remember those? That sonofabitch ran Tim off the road and then got his car repainted. Call the autobody shop."

"Which autobody shop?"

Jude was so confounded by the accusations being thrown at her she couldn't think straight. "I don't recall right now. But I have it, I can get it for you." And then, she exploded. "This is bullshit. Byer's lying because he killed Tim. Their fucking experiment went off the rails and Tim threatened to expose them. Now Byer's trying to set me up. Screw this. I'm out of here."

She tried to brush past Haydon, but he caught her arm. "Afraid not," he said. "I need to take you in and get you on record."

Jude tried to wrest herself from his grasp, yelling, "You're crazy! You think I killed Tim? Fuck you!"

"I don't want to have to cuff you," said Haydon. "But I will."

And he did, forced to drag a screaming Jude to the back of his squad car. Haydon stayed mute while Jude kicked the back of his seat and cursed roundly. He had intended to take her to the barracks, but even after she stopped yelling, she started with the real crazy:

Genetically engineered corn;

Growing a blood thinner on a local farm;

Cross pollination, people getting *sick*;

People in town who *know* about it and are *keeping quiet*;

*Dr. Harbolt part of the conspiracy*;

*And he tried to DRUG her!*

Haydon changed his mind and drove directly to the hospital.

\* \* \*

Stuart Ostrovsky flipped on the overhead light when he entered the office. The long fluorescent bulbs began to hum softly overhead, sending an uncomfortable electric sensation through his veins. It intensified into a jolt when he saw Byer.

"Jesus, Dillon," he exclaimed. "What are you doing here in the dark?"

Byer swiveled in the desk chair to face him. "Thinking," he replied grimly.

"What's wrong?"

"The animal rights gal found the dog."

Ostrovsky could barely breathe. "Where?"

"Mains took it to a vet in Roxbury."

"*Mains?*"

"Jeffries. Tyler Jeffries."

"How do you know all this?"

Byer brushed some imagined lint from his chinos and said, "Jeffries must have told her. Either that, or someone from the lab is talking. But earlier today, she spent an awful lot of time with a vet in Roxbury."

After processing what Byer had said, the scientist reluctantly asked, "You've been *following* her?"

"She's asking way too many questions."

Ostrovsky began to look wildly around his office as if searching for a way out. He could feel the tremors getting worse. "We … we have to report it."

"Report it to who?" Byer demanded.

"The USDA, the police, I suppose. Tell them the truth. The cross pollination wouldn't have occurred unless some freak winds came up. It was completely unpredictable."

Byer jumped out of the chair. "No, no. My father invested eight million dollars into this project, and I sunk every penny I have, too."

"But people are still getting sick."

"No one has died."

"That we *know* of!"

"Chill, Stu. I've been following the local news. We would have heard. Listen, by the time the process is approved, this little incident will be history. All the animals will be gone. It'll just be your records. There will be nothing else to find."

"Nothing?" croaked Ostrovksy. "You don't get it. Kurt Buck is an organic farmer – he keeps his seeds. Even if he doesn't, there's pollen in his soil. The drug will be in his corn for years and could cross-pollinate someone *else's* field. No, Dillon, we have to come clean. It's the only way."

Stepping over to his partner, Byer grasped Ostrovsky's shoulders to look him square in the eye. "There's no need to panic, Stu. We're okay."

"Too many people know," groaned Ostrovksy. "Jim Davidson."

Byer leaned in closer, saying, "We give him another ten grand and Davidson will keep his mouth shut. He knows what's going on. He's in as deep as we are."

"What about Jeffries? He's out there somewhere."

"Don't worry about him," said Byer, waving him off.

The scientist backed away from Byer as he discerned his meaning. "Oh, my God," he whispered. "How did you know his real name? Oh, Dillon, Dillon, what did you do?" Feeling his hands go out of control, he fumbled in his jacket pocket for the new pills that were supposed to help. He shook out two and popped them in his mouth.

"Listen to me, Stu," said Byer, becoming frustrated with his partner's whining. "This is no time to fall apart. We can contain this, okay? The protocol is, for all intents and purposes, finished. The ninety days are over. We just have to wrap it up, and fast."

"How do we do that?"

"You do what you would have done anyway. Get rid of the animals and clean up the lab."

Ostrovksy nodded feebly. "I need a few days."

"No. Do it tonight."

"Tonight? That's impossible. I have twenty-three dogs down there, and more than a hundred rats. It takes time to euthanize them all."

"There's the incinerator."

Ostrovksy looked up at him, horrified.

"Whatever you have to do," pressed Byer. "Who's scheduled to work tomorrow?"

"Sylvia and Lester," he replied dully.

"Any chance they know what's going on?"

"No. They're aware of what we're testing, not where it came from."

"Fine. I'll call them and the others and tell them not to come in. I'll say there's a delay because of the USDA or something."

The pills hadn't kicked in yet. Ostrovksy shoved his shaking hands into his pockets so Byer wouldn't see. He was about to ask what his partner intended to do about the animal rights woman but decided he didn't want to know. The overhead lights thrummed on, the sound softly burrowing into his brain, like maggots on rotting food.

\* \* \*

"Why won't you listen to me?" cried Jude, as an orderly took over from Haydon. "Give me a chance! I can prove it to you."

The head nurse pointed to the last cubicle in the emergency room, and they brought her in there, sat her on the bed, and screeched the curtain closed. Haydon stood at the entrance with his arms crossed.

"Are you on Amaethon's payroll, too?" she accused him. "Call Gordon Silverman. Where's my phone? Get your fucking hands off me!"

The orderly stepped away and the nurse moved in, hands on hips, a few inches from Jude's face. "You're disturbing the other patients. If you don't knock it off, we're going to have to give you a sedative."

Her hands still cuffed at her waist, Jude straightened her shoulders in an attempt to salvage some dignity. "You probably shouldn't do that," she warned.

"And why not?"

"Because ... I took some pills before."

"How many?" the nurse wanted to know.

"Two."

"What were they?"

Jude calculated: maybe Harbolt had really given her Tylenol because her headache *was* better. On the other hand, she didn't know for certain. In any case, she sure as hell didn't want to be injected with anything that would knock her out. Let them worry they might be on the hook for a negative drug interaction. She finally said, "I don't know. I found them," adding, "I'll be quiet."

"I'm holding you to that," said the nurse, and then to Haydon, "Are you staying to watch her? Because I can't spare anybody."

"*I'm* not babysitting, but I'll send someone over. For now ...." He unlocked the handcuffs and rerouted one of them to the upper bar of the metal bed frame.

Jude shot him a hostile glare.

"It's just for a little while," he apologized, "until you get yourself under control."

As he was leaving, Jude said, "Haydon, I remember the name of the shop – True Service Auto Body. A few days ago, a guy there named Pete worked on a blue BMW with the right fender smashed. Some kid brought the car in, paid cash and gave him what he thought was a fake address. The kid was clueless. I'll bet that the owner of the car paid him to bring the car in – so no one could identify him. Would you check it out? Please? See, I'm being nice."

The sergeant stared at her for a moment before walking out. A minute later, she saw his feet below the curtain and then his hand deposit her backpack just inside. "Another thing?" called Jude. "My neurologist? He was doing the tests. His name is Michel Amin at Columbia-Presbyterian in New York. He'll vouch for me."

Jude heard him tell the nurse that he'd leave the handcuff keys at their station. And then Haydon was gone.

Left alone, Jude eyed her backpack intently. She had a metal nail file in one of the pockets that might do the trick. It had been a long time, but back in her protest days when she and other activists would handcuff themselves to the front doors of a university lab testing on baby monkeys, they practiced the art of cuff-picking. Under normal circumstances, she thought she could unlock them. If she could get to the nail file. The nurses' station just outside her cubicle was a problem, however. She'd have to drag the bed over, which would make a lot of noise.

She risked it. There was constant activity at the station which left it unmanned on occasion. And each time she saw more than two pairs of orthopedic shoes trot off to answer calls, with one wrist still attached to the upper bar, Jude pulled the bed an inch or two closer to the possibility of freedom. She'd managed a few feet when she heard a voice behind her, "Good Lord!"

She twisted around to face Dr. Harbolt.

They stood staring at one another in utter surprise until Jude said, "Don't come near me or I'll scream."

"Whatever are you talking about?" he asked.

Fearful that if she did scream, they'd label her as hysterical and permit Harbolt to drug her, she kept her voice low, answering, "Nothing. Nothing." *Don't let on that you saw him with Ostrovsky. Try to get rid of him.*

"Did something happen? Are you alright?"

"I'm fine," she said, stupidly.

"You're handcuffed to the bed," he observed.

"Ah … yes, so I am." She scrambled for something to say to get rid of him. "It's a misunderstanding, that's all. When I had the car accident."

"Are you under arrest?"

"No." *Shut up and go away.*

"Do you need me to talk with someone? I honestly don't think your injuries are serious enough to be hospitalized." But rather than seek out a nurse, he stepped into the cubicle and drew the curtain behind him.

She was about to call for help when Harbolt said in a hushed voice, "You're right, Jude. It's the corn. Kurt Buck's daughter is here and is in serious condition. She's been eating it raw for nearly two weeks. And I reached one of my other patients on the phone. He had eaten the corn without cooking it, too."

Jude was stunned. Was it possible there was some other explanation for his meeting with Ostrovsky in the parking lot? Warily, she asked, "Why are *you* here?"

"I told you, I had an emergency. Heather Buck was brought in hemorrhaging."

"Heather?"

"She's still critical. The on-call doctor wanted to know if I'd ever put her on blood thinners."

"What were you doing with Stuart Ostrovsky?"

"You saw him?"

"I saw both of you."

"And you thought ...."

"Damn right."

"He's a patient. I treat him for a problem with tremors. Stuart wanted to come in, but I was afraid he'd see you, so I wrote him a prescription outside and sent him away. I think we should call the police."

Jude searched his face for deception but could find none. His concern was either entirely genuine or he was a brilliant actor. She decided to jump off the cliff and replied, "Not unless you want to end up handcuffed in the next cubicle. I tried to tell them what Amaethon is doing, and it only landed me here. Probably would have been a psych ward if there was one closer. Ostrovsky and his partner Dillon Byer know that I'm on to their disaster. Byer went to the cops with a story to get me out of the way." She lifted her restrained hand as far as it would go. "And here I am."

"So, what can we do?"

"Get me out of here for starters."

Harbolt gave a shake of his head. "We should work with the police. They'll get to the bottom of this."

"Even if they believe you, it'll be too late," insisted Jude. "The protocol is over, the testing period done as of today. What do you think Amaethon's going to do? Sit around and wait for the cops to show up? No, they're probably back at the lab cleaning everything up and getting rid of the animals. By the time the cops get a search warrant – if they can get one without solid evidence, which we don't have – there will be no way to connect Amaethon to Heather Buck or anyone else who doesn't understand why they can't stop *bleeding to death*."

The head nurse poked her head in. "Is everything alright in here?" she asked.

"Of course, Sarah," said Dr. Harbolt. "Just checking on Miss Brannock's stitches, which I did at the office."

"She told me that she took some pills."

When Harbolt glanced back worriedly at Jude, she piped up, "Oh, right. The Tylenol."

"I thought you didn't know what they were," Sarah accused.

"But then I remembered."

The nurse grunted her displeasure with the difficult patient and shut the curtain.

Harbolt turned back to Jude. "I suppose you have a plan?"

"We have to talk with the people who will believe us," she replied, her eyes narrowed in thought. "And I'm going to need your help. But first, see if you can find the keys for this," she held up her shackled wrist, "at the desk out there."

# CHAPTER 24

Ostrovsky's shoe coverings made a stealthy, shushing sound as he wheeled his cart down the hall. As a matter of habit, he'd donned a plastic cap and latex gloves, but it didn't matter if he brought germs into the kennel now. He was both scared and feeling sorry for himself. The scientist in him had been looking forward to examining the tissue samples under a microscope and poring over the data that was sure to prove the PMP experiment an unequivocal success. The rodents he'd already necropsied attested to that. But he'd wanted the canines, too. Now he'd never get the chance.

He backed into the kennel and flipped on the light switch. The dogs erupted in the excited panting and strangled whines that met anyone who came through the door. To Ostrovsky, it wasn't nearly as annoying as the sound of two dozen beagles barking at the top of their lungs, which is why he'd had them all de-barked at the breeder before being sent to the lab. Some people thought it cruel, but he rationalized the procedure by believing that they'd lived with their vocal cords surgically removed for most of their lives — it was all they knew.

Still unable to deviate from pattern, he checked the thermostat. It read 68 degrees but felt much colder. He shivered and turned to the task at hand, arranging his instruments on the cart to prepare for the first canine. He knew that he should have an assistant to hold the dogs while he inserted the IV; if he didn't get the vein right away, the dog might struggle and make it that much more difficult. But he was on his own.

He laid a towel on the stainless-steel cart as he eyed which one he'd take first. Best to go for the sick ones, he thought. They were less likely to thrash, and it had been months since he'd done this procedure himself. By the time he got to the control group, he'd have it down. He eyed one in particular — a female who lay listless in her crate.

But as Ostrovsky prepared the pentobarbital injection, he found his hands were shaking and he had difficulty getting the needle through the rubber seal on the vial. He jabbed the syringe at it a few times, succeeding only in breaking off the needle tip. The tremors became more pronounced. What had Harbolt given him? He said this new prescription might act differently than the meds he'd been taking but assured him it would help.

He secured a new needle shaft and tried again. This time he got it through and drew up the pink liquid. Once injected, within a couple of minutes it would slow the brain, lungs, and heart until they stopped. But as he held up the syringe to clear any air bubbles, it shook back and forth in front of his face. This was hopeless. He wouldn't be able to get a clean shot at a vein, not like this.

The syringe went back on the cart, the dog in its crate. Ostrovsky hustled out of the room, thankful to be back in the silence, away from the dog noise once more. He stopped in the hall and took the new anti-seizure medication from his pocket. The doctor had told him to start with one tablet at breakfast and one with dinner, but he'd said that eventually the maintenance dose might be as high as 1000 milligrams or more. Ostrovksy had already taken two and it obviously wasn't doing anything. He popped two more. The shaking had to stop.

\* \* \*

There were about twenty people now, all crowded into the Buck's living room. Jude stood by the fireplace, sizing them up. Equal numbers men and women, many with a farmer's life etched onto their faces, the marrow in their bones made up of hard work and the inevitable failures brought on by pests, weather, and fluctuating markets. All these were tolerated as part of the world they had chosen. But tonight, what they were hearing was an abomination. Rumors had spread, and they were getting restless and anxious. Jude looked for Kurt Buck who had been next to her moments before. She couldn't proceed without him.

She ducked into the kitchen where he was on the phone, his wide back to her. He mumbled something into the receiver and then let it dangle by his side.

"Mr. Buck?" asked Jude quietly.

He turned, startled. He'd been crying.

"How is she?"

"Holding on," replied Buck.

"If you want to go back to the hospital—"

"No. My wife will call me if there's any change."

Voices of the neighbors from the next room filtered into the kitchen, but Jude saw that he wasn't ready. His face was a deathly shade of gray, fear and anger siphoning off his lifeblood. He set the phone down and turned away again, leaning on the kitchen counter, as if his legs couldn't quite support his body. "The worst of it is," he said in a voice choked with emotion, "it was my corn."

"We don't know that for sure," volunteered Jude.

"Unlikely that Davidson's crop could have cross pollinated anyone else." He stared out into the dark. "She could die because of *my* corn," he said. "My whole life I've tried to farm the right way. And not just because I wanted my family, my community, to eat healthy, but because it's the right thing to do. What happens to the soil, happens to us. If it dies, we die. I fought Monsanto when they pressured me to use their seeds. I fought the government when it labeled poisons like glyphosate safe just because the pesticide manufacturers told them it was safe. I've even fought my own neighbors who got sucked into the Monsanto quicksand. And I survived ... until this. My corn," he said, shaking his head. "My own damn corn."

Jude wasn't sure he was aware that she was still standing behind him. She cleared her throat and said, "It wasn't your fault."

"I should have seen it. The crows. I should have seen it was something in my fields." Slowly he turned back to her. "I owe you an apology. I was wrong about your friend Tim. My wife was able to talk to Heather a little while ago. Your friend didn't get my daughter hooked on heroin. She did that all by herself long before he showed up."

"There's help out there," offered Jude.

Buck dipped his head, not quite a nod. "Did you ever find him? Tim?"

"No. I think he found out what happened and confronted Amaethon. I'm not giving up hope yet, but …."

"Well, then, we should get started."

With leaden legs, Buck went over to the living room door and held it open for her.

It took a few moments to settle the crowd. When he had everyone's attention, Buck began to speak. "Thanks, everyone, for comin' over on such short notice. I wouldn't have called if it wasn't an emergency. As some of you may know by now, my Heather is in the hospital tonight. The doctors are saying she's bleeding inside and they're not sure if they can stop it. It wasn't a fall or accident or anything like that. She just started bleeding." He cleared his throat. "Maybe someone in your family is also suffering from the same thing. A wound that won't stop bleeding, unexplained bruises or rashes. Maybe somebody you know …."

A woman with gray hair tied back in a ponytail called out from the back, "I got two dead heifers this week, and the vet says 'internal bleeding.' Never saw that in my whole life."

Someone else spoke up, declaring, "My niece Tori has something like that, too. She had to leave school because of some crazy bruising on her feet, and they don't know what's wrong. What the hell is going on, Kurt?"

"This lady here," he answered, nodding to Jude, "is going to explain it to you." He stepped aside to let her take the lead.

All eyes bored into her as she began. "I ought to start by telling you that I'm an investigator for an animal protection organization." Responding to the collective exhale of bewilderment, she explained, "We try to document animal abuse that's occurring on a large scale and do what we can to correct it. We heard there was mistreatment and neglect of some of the animals being tested on at the laboratory on Route 107. You've probably all passed by it; it's run by a company called Amaethon. We sent an undercover investigator in there to try to video the problems, and he disappeared about ten days ago. When I last talked with him, he told me that he had damaging information on Amaethon. Unfortunately, he never got a chance to tell me what it was. But I did learn that he, too, was having recurrent nosebleeds that wouldn't stop, much like some of the incidents here in Half Moon."

No one saw the side door open and a man squeeze into the back of the group. He quickly scanned the people in the room until he landed upon Jude. Pulling his black cap even lower over his brow, he took cover in a dim corner, never taking his eyes off her.

"The more I looked into our undercover's disappearance," she was saying, "the more I learned what Amaethon is doing. We know that they were testing an anti-coagulant intended ultimately for people who have suffered heart problems or a stroke. Of course, such drugs already exist. But they're working on a new process for making it, and they're testing on dogs and rodents by putting it in their feed. I have good reason to believe that the technology is something called plant made pharmaceuticals – PMP's or cellular farming. Drugs derived from a biological source, in other words, grown in plants."

Most of the group stared at her with undisguised skepticism, and Kurt Buck interjected, "When Jude told me about this, I looked it up. I read that they can grow vaccines and contraceptives in tobacco plants."

Nodding, Jude added, "Many of the big pharma companies are doing similar tests on their own properties. But everyone wants to get into this new market and it's drawing smaller start-ups who are paying farmers across the country to grow their seeds – seeds that have been genetically modified to contain the drug. I read that they are not required to tell the farmers what's in these seeds, either. Their growers only have to take care of the plants, and when it's time to harvest, the pharma people come in and take it all. Amaethon is one of these start-ups and we believe they contracted a local farmer here to grow an anti-coagulant in corn."

A man a few feet away scoffed, "What evidence do you have?"

"We knew from our investigator Tim that Amaethon was putting the drug in the animals' feed. As expected, many of them began to show signs of internal bleeding. At the same time, multiple cases of unexplained bleeding started to appear in Half Moon. Then I learned that our investigator and another witness saw a man named Stuart Ostrovsky in a corn field here in Half Moon. Ostrovsky is the Chief Scientific Officer running the study for Amaethon. A few days ago, I walked that field myself. It's all been cleared now, but I'm sure it's where they had grown corn engineered to produce the anti-coagulant."

It was as if a fuse had been lit; in the ensuing silence the entire atmosphere became charged, waiting for the explosion. Finally, the gray-haired woman in the back said, "I know who it is." All heads turned in her direction. "Jim Davidson. I'd bet anything. He's been walking around town like suddenly he don't know anybody. And when I told him about my cows, he looked like he was going to puke. I thought it was all the talk about blood, but now I don't think so. I think he knows something." She stared at Jude and asked, "Am I right?"

Jude nodded. "I'm quite sure of it."

Someone else spoke up, challenging, "If Davidson did this, we'll settle with him. But I don't get what it has to do with us. You said that the seed companies come and harvest all the plants."

Kurt Buck answered, his arms tightly crossed over his chest as if to keep his emotions from detonating. "Davidson and I share a border," he said grimly. "Can't be but a half mile from his corn to mine. Now any of you that grow organic know that you have to keep a buffer zone a lot bigger'n that to keep the GMO crap from coming on your property."

No one had to explain further to the roomful of farmers. His statement landed with the dull thump of a distant bomb: cross-pollination. Yet, there were still a few quizzical looks.

"Half the town buys Kurt's produce at the farmers market. How come we're *all* not sick?" someone pushed back.

"I don't know. It's possible that once the corn is cooked, the heat exposure kills the active ingredient in the drug. But anyone who eats it raw, even a small amount, can be adversely affected. I talked with Dr. John Harbolt, and he has five bleeding cases that he believes are a result of this corn. I think we're going to find out that there are a lot more."

"Oh my God," cried the gray-haired woman. "I fed my heifers some of Kurt's corn, right off the cob." She clapped her hand over her mouth.

Above the rumblings, the man in front erupted, "That sonofabitch! Get Davidson over here."

"No. Not yet," said Buck.

The questions came fast and furious.

"Then what?"

"What are we going to do?"

"Maybe Davidson didn't know."

"How could he not?"

Buck scowled and said, "Maybe Amaethon didn't tell him what he was growing. But if he found out later and didn't say anything, I will personally beat the living crap out of him."

"Amaethon has to pay for this."

Someone else called out, "I agree. But apart from burning it down, what do you have in mind?"

"Call the cops."

"Put 'em in jail."

"Sue them."

Buck put up his hands. "Believe me, we will. But I don't have to tell any of you that companies like Amaethon have the USDA and the federal government on their side. You know what it's like to try and go after *them*. Unless we have proof, we're screwed."

"How do we get proof?"

"I'm going to get it for you," announced Jude, stepping forward. "Inside the lab, I'll get a sample of the feed. An analysis of that, the residue from Davidson's field, and Kurt's harvest will likely show the same drug proteins in all. And if I can also get one of the animals out, blood tests should pick up the same drug that has been consumed by the people who are sick in Half Moon. But I have to get in *now*. Amaethon has been trying to keep the cross-contamination a secret, and obviously, it isn't anymore. I wouldn't be surprised if at this very moment they're trying to clean up the mess. If we wait too long, there won't be any evidence at all."

A man's voice rang out from the back, "None of it will be admissible."

Jude recognized the voice and nearly smiled, despite the opposition. She peered over the turned heads to see fellow investigator Lucas Matz. He pulled off his black cap and eased his way through the group to the fireplace. Then he turned to face them. "Sorry to say, but you're on shaky ground, folks. My colleague here," he said, motioning to Jude, "ought to know better. No one is getting into that lab. They have an electrified fence that will fry anyone who tries to go over. And even if she could get in, the law doesn't look kindly on people who break and enter for the purposes of stealing evidence, especially if it's just a fishing expedition. Whatever she came out with would be illegally obtained and therefore worthless in a criminal prosecution."

But Jude had already thought it through. "There's a way around that," she replied. "If someone broke into the lab for another purpose – say, an animal rights activist who wants to free the animals – and she just happened to take some of the adulterated dog food with her – say, for the dog she's just liberated – it could be admissible evidence in an unrelated proceeding. From a legal standpoint, just because something is stolen doesn't make it inadmissible for all purposes."

"I think that's correct," said the gray-haired woman. "My husband's a lawyer."

"And besides," added Jude, feeling empowered by the support, "if you sue Amaethon for negligence, that's a civil matter and the exclusionary rule of evidence doesn't apply in civil suits."

"All well and good," noted Buck. "But how in hell are you going to get inside the lab?"

She spent the next ten minutes telling them.

* * *

The sound of tires on the Buck's gravel driveway was still in the air when Lucas steered Jude out through the kitchen to the back yard. He didn't speak until they had gotten to the old swing set, then burst out, "What the fuck are you doing?"

"Good to see you, too, Lucas."

"Look, I got your message that said you were in trouble, and I snagged the next plane. Then, the only thing from you is a text that you were at some farm in the middle of nowhere."

"How much did you hear?"

"Enough. Are you sure?"

"As sure as I can be without a sample of the feed."

He ran a hand through his shaggy hair. "If it's true, it's some crazy shit. Why would anyone take the risk of drugs getting into the food chain?"

"Because they can produce a lot of it for far less cost – the story of American capitalism."

"Any news on Tim?"

"No. But I think he was able to piece it together: the dogs' bleeding, his own symptoms. Something else, too. I spoke with Katherine Buck earlier and she told me that one day she was grinding cornmeal, and apparently, Tim showed an unusual interest in it, asking a lot of questions. Maybe what they feed the dogs looks like cornmeal. He grew up on a farm and after seeing Ostrovsky in Davidson's corn field, I think he started making connections. The photos that he sent me were just a heads up."

"Why didn't he call you and tell you everything then?"

"He was trying to put a ribbon around it, for me," she sighed. "Right after he sent me the photos, he went back to the lab after most of the staff had left. He knew it was his best chance of taking one of the dogs and wanted to get one of them out for blood tests, believing that the results would match his own. But something happened. I talked with the tech who was still there when Tim came back. She said that he told her to go home and he'd finish up for her. Dillon Byer was in the lab waiting to lock up. He must have seen Tim with the dog."

"And Tim confronted him about what was going down."

"Maybe, yeah."

"And you think Byer got rid of Tim?"

"Not then. Tim was able to get out of there with the dog. I think he intended to bring the dog to DC. But he saw that the dog was too sick, so he took him to a vet right away. He went back to the motel to pack up ...."

"And Byer was waiting for him."

"He would've known where Tim was staying. I'm sure, though, that Byer drove him off the road and ... I don't know what happened after that."

Lucas began to pace in a tight circle. "Jesus, Jude," he exclaimed, "we're in way over our heads."

"Not if I can get inside that lab."

"You can't be serious," Lucas barked angrily. "You want to get yourself killed, too? And even if you get in and out successfully, talk about American capitalism ... this is big pharma and the agriculture industry wrapped into one package. Amaethon will have the entire U.S. government on its side. Don't think for a minute that federal agencies won't do everything in their power to make sure no one even finds out about this."

Jude retorted, "Kurt Buck's daughter is in critical condition. He won't let it go, and neither will the others."

"You're fooling yourself. A couple mil in settlement fees and people will let a lot of things go. Amaethon throws enough money at this and everyone in Half Moon is walking around saying, 'what drug?' while you're serving eight-to-ten in federal prison. That is, of course, if Byer doesn't get to you first."

"Since when did you get so cynical?"

"I'm not even going to respond to that."

Turning away from him, Jude reached out to one of the swings. Clouds had blotted out the stars, and the light from the farmhouse windows couldn't reach them. She thrust her hand forward in the dark, searching for one of the swing seats until her fingers closed around it. She sat in the rubber tire and rocked back and forth as Lucas pressed on. "You know, I found street level photos of the lab. You can *see* the high voltage fence around the whole property. You'll never get past that – not alive, anyway. And even if you could, breaking into a lab is exactly what they want, to brand animal activists as criminals."

"Dillon Byer went to the cop who's looking into Tim's disappearance – a state trooper named Haydon – and told him that he had seen me with Tim here in Half Moon the day he went missing."

"That's ridiculous. You were in New York, right?"

Jude coughed. "Yes, but not for the reason I told you."

"What do you mean?"

"It's not important now. But I was nowhere near Half Moon. I tried to tell Haydon, and if he checks it out, he's going to find out that Byer was lying, and Byer must know that. He was trying to deflect suspicion onto me so he can buy some time.

"Time enough to clean out the lab, alter the records, and get rid of the animals. They're probably doing that right now."

She dug her heels into the grass to stop rocking. "There are two dozen beagles in there, Lucas. And I don't know how many rats and mice. Some are sick and suffering. And think about the control group that's not getting any of the drug. They're all still healthy. And Byer and Ostrovsky are going to kill them all."

Lucas clapped his hand to his head and groaned. Finally, he said, "I hate it, Jude. I hate it. But there are tens of thousands of animals in labs all over the country—"

"Well, I'm here, right now. And I'm going to get as many as I can out."

She could hear Lucas taking deep breaths through his nose. Finally, he said, "I admire your passion and your courage, my friend. You know I do. But what you're proposing is a suicide mission. Nothing less. Let's go to the cops."

"Can't do that."

"Why not?"

When Jude didn't respond, Lucas muttered, "Ah, shit. What did you do?"

"A few hours ago, I was in custody … technically speaking. And I escaped."

"You what?"

"I tried to tell Haydon," argued Jude. "And I suppose I did get a little heated, but he thought I was so delusional that he brought me to the hospital and handcuffed me to a bed. I got Dr. Harbolt to uncuff me and we left. Haydon's probably got a warrant out for me right now. He's going to sort it out, but by the time he does, it'll be too late. I'm going in as soon as the light comes up."

"The light won't matter," said Lucas gruffly, stepping in front of her. He held up two fingers. "What do you see?"

"What are you talking about?"

"How many fingers am I holding up?"

"Cut it out."

Holding his ground, Lucas asked again, "How many fingers?"

Jude jumped up, leaving the swing's chains clattering. "How would I know? It's pitch black out here. Why do you always do this to me? I thought you were my friend."

"I *am* your friend. Which is why I'm trying to stop you from sabotaging your whole freaking life."

"I don't need saving, okay?"

He grasped her by the shoulders. "You need something, Jude. Because what you're doing is not working."

"You have no faith in me," she exclaimed, wrenching herself from his grasp. "This will work."

"I'm not talking about getting into the lab. I'm talking about your life. It's not working."

Jude swiped back, blurting, "You don't know the first thing about me."

"Really? You really believe that?" He took a step away and put up his hands as if to ward her off. "Never mind. Maybe you're right, because I can't tell anymore who you are. You lie to me and everyone about being in New York, about you and Tim. Who knows what else you're lying about? The truth is you don't *want* anyone to know the first thing about you. You're so trapped in your one-woman show trying to fight animal abuse, you can't see anyone or anything around you. And sometimes I think you're so busy trying to out-run yourself that you don't even really see the animals."

She wheeled around and stormed back to the farmhouse, throwing over her shoulder, "I don't have time for your dime-store BS psychology."

Her stiff back and determined stride gave Lucas little hope that going after her would do anything but make her more obstinate. Nevertheless, he called out, "How many fingers, Jude?"

# CHAPTER 25

The laboratory halls were tomb-like. *I'm being buried alive*, thought Byer as he continued searching for his partner. Breathing the stale air was claustrophobic and the silence back-breakingly oppressive. *Get me out of here* was a chant that had been going through his mind like an unwanted pop song for the past few hours. As he packed files into cardboard boxes and downloaded electronic files onto a thumb drive, the song kept repeating and repeating. *Out of here, get me ...* When he was done, he wiped the hard drive and went to look for his Chief Scientific Officer.

The door to the room where the rats and mice were housed was ajar, but it was dark inside. He'd directed Stu to keep the lights off as much as possible. The last thing they needed was a cop to swing by to ask if everything was all right. Byer opened the door a little wider and heard the scrabbling of their feet. It was a bad sound, and not just because Stu was supposed to have taken care of the lot. He hoped at least the dogs were done with.

Gripping the door knob tighter, Byer called out. The rustling of sawdust was his answer.

*Where is he?* Byer continued down the hall and checked two other rooms. His frustration level was rising. They were running out of time. He came to the end of the hall by the reception area where glass windows looked out on the parking lot. At first, he saw only his reflection in the night-backed glass, but a second look told him that the horizon was getting lighter. Byer checked his watch and was surprised to see that it was 5:30 a.m. He'd been cleaning up for hours and hadn't noticed the time. *Jesus Christ, get me out ...*

Then he smelled burnt coffee and hurried toward the break room.

As he flicked on the overhead lights, Byer saw the coffeemaker was on and that the smell was coming from the blackened bottom of its glass pot. Ostrovsky was splayed on the cheap vinyl sofa next to a vending machine. His mouth was open, and one arm dangled over the side. Byer walked slowly over to him. "Stuart?" he asked tersely. "Stu?" A little more tentatively. He reached out to see if he could detect a pulse, and as his fingers made contact, Ostrovsky made a phlegmy noise in his throat. Byer stepped back in alarm.

The gurgling became louder and Ostrovsky began to cough. It woke him and he struggled to sit up.

"What the fuck, Stu?" cried Byer. "What's the matter with you?"

Ostrovsky managed to push himself up and he blinked at the harsh fluorescent lighting. Rubbing his face, he mumbled, "What time is it?"

Byer didn't bother to answer. "What have you been doing?" he demanded. "You're supposed to be taking care of the animals."

"I … uh … I started to."

"You *started?* Where?"

"The kennel. Everything was ready. I tried to do the injections, but I had a little problem," he said, licking his dry lips. "I took some new medication for the … you know. It made me dizzy and I had to lie down."

"Son of a bitch. Come on, already. We have to get out of here."

"Yeah, okay." He rose a bit unsteadily to his feet, and once he got his balance, he held his hands out to check them. No tremor. "I'm good to go," he confirmed.

"Then go."

They walked out into the hall and Byer began his angry trek back to the office. Ostrovksy stopped him, saying "Wait a minute."

"What now?"

"You hear that?" asked the scientist, his head snapping towards reception.

Byer listened for a second, waiting to hear footsteps or a car driving into the parking lot. But he heard neither of those things and shook his head.

"You don't hear that?"

"What?" asked Byer, exasperated.

"Out there. On the road," explained his partner.

Byer finally heard something, but it didn't make any sense. It sounded like a group of people yelling in the distance. And they were getting closer.

\* \* \*

Some held signs they'd made with magic marker and poster board. Others brandished long corn stalks that waved like strange and unruly banners. A few had brought cow bells and weren't afraid to bang on them. Several cars and flatbeds crawled behind them, purposefully honking their horns. About a dozen farmers, their neighbors, and some of the townspeople marched down Route 107, materializing out of the early morning mist like apparitions. Noisy ghosts, they chanted, "No drugs in our food," and "Our kids are eating your drugs!"

The gray morning carried an early September chill that would wear off by midday. But at this hour, most of the marchers wore boots, flannel shirts, and fleece, which made them look like countrified zombies as they neared Amaethon's perimeter fence. Kurt Buck and Lucas were in the lead, Jude buried somewhere in the middle of the crowd.

It had taken a sustained effort throughout the night. Those gathered in Buck's living room reached out to their neighbors who called their friends who texted others. No one got much sleep. But no one cared. A monster had snuck into the wrong community, something Buck had underscored when he addressed the assemblage at their appointed meeting place. Theirs was a community where farm-to-table meant more than a restaurant slogan – it meant pride, livelihood, and sustenance. The corporate lobbyists in Washington had all but shut down Vermont's attempt to have genetically engineered food labeled so you could know what you were feeding your kids. And now, the federal government was supporting this insane experiment that had gone horribly wrong in their town. Children were bleeding, animals dying, and the landscape being poisoned.

Time had limited their ability to reach more people in the community, but latecomers kept adding to the back of the line. Cars going by on Route 107 slowed to see what the fuss was about. Some of the high school kids, friends of Heather, took up stations on the road's solid yellow line and told them. A few of the drivers pulled over to the side and joined up.

Amaethon's front gate was locked and the building dark. When the group reached a critical mass, Kurt Buck and Lucas went into action, organizing the citizens to stretch out along the fence's perimeter. *Keep making noise, keep moving, create chaos.* Jude weaved in and out of them, looking for her entry point. Tori Ann Lacey's aunt ran Melissa's Cleaning Service which cleaned the lab twice a week. Except for the rooms where the animals were kept and only the techs were allowed, Melissa knew every inch of the place. She'd come over to the farmhouse to share what she knew and draw out a rough map. There was one possible entrance into the building.

Jude made her way to the westernmost edge of the hi-voltage electrified fence. She plucked a blade of grass and tossed it onto one of the lower wires where it snapped and leapt into the air. The line was live, but she hadn't expected anything else.

She turned to see Kurt Buck at her shoulder. A few hours earlier, his wife had called to tell him that Heather was going to pull through. Buck's fear turned to fury, mobilizing him to help Jude plan her entry. They made eye contact. "This is it?" he asked. And when Jude nodded, he produced a five-foot metal stake onto which he'd welded a thick copper wire near one end. Using a mallet, he drove the stake into the ground, and from his back pocket he pulled out a bottle of water and poured it on the ground around the stake. Then he fit a large crocodile clip taken from an old battery onto the end of the copper wire.

Just then, Lucas found them. He tried one more time, imploring, "Please don't do this. You'll be subject to prosecution along with her, Kurt. Aiding and abetting."

But the farmer nodded and said, "Fine. Let 'em come after me."

Jude turned to Lucas and said, "We need your help."

For a moment, Lucas hung his head in defeat. She was going to do this no matter what. "Okay," he replied reluctantly.

"Then let's go."

Kurt warned them both to stand back and shoo away the nearest protesters. He donned rubber gloves and with his arm extended, connected the crocodile clip to the fence. He ducked. A brain-rattling buzz reverberated around them, sparks flew up into the air, and the acrid smell of short-circuited wires filled their nostrils.

A few seconds later, Buck repeated the test, throwing blades of grass at the wires, and this time they fell lazily to the ground. He nodded to Jude and pointed to his watch. She had 15 minutes – the minimum time they'd calculated it would take for the security company to respond to the silent alarm. Then he cupped his hands to give her a leg up and over.

From the fence to the southwest corner of the building was a forty-yard sprint. Jude made it and flattened herself against the building. Behind her, at Lucas's signal, the chanting from the protesters intensified. Crouching low, she moved quickly along the rear of the building, searching for the window described to her. This part of the lab was built partially underground, and the high windows cut into the concrete blocks indoors were at knee level where she ran. The one she was looking for was supposed to be the third from the corner. One, two, her breath coming fast. This had to be it.

She lowered herself to her knees and pushed on the lower edge of the casement. It didn't budge. The coffee she'd consumed all night came up in her throat. Could Melissa's count be off? Was there a room or window she hadn't accounted for? Jude pushed harder this time, and with a rasp, the window moved. Another few shoves and inch by inch, it opened inward.

When she thought it was wide enough, she slid on her belly and backed herself into the opening, her feet feeling cautiously for the shelf unit Melissa had described. Jude could only hope that she wouldn't knock any of the cleaning supplies over and make a racket. As she eased farther in, she began to lose her grip. She clung to fistfuls of dirt which crumbled in her fingers and she felt herself falling backwards. Just then, her right foot hit the metal shelf. She made a final, futile grab at the casement rim before dropping to the floor.

A sharp pain shot through her ankle. She shook it out and waited for the burn to subside, listening for footsteps. She also pretended that a few moments would allow her eyes to adjust to the dark. But in fact, her eyes weren't working all that well. They hadn't been since her fight with Lucas at the swings. Translucent gray clouds seemed to sail across her visual horizon like smoke. No, she didn't see how many fingers Lucas put up. And no, she hadn't told anyone. This was the only chance they had.

Finally, she made out a sliver of light underneath the door and mentally reviewed where she was – in the storage room where cleaning materials and empty crates and cages were kept. Melissa had sketched the corridors and stairway she'd need to navigate to get to the kennel. There she would find a metal cabinet that held the dogs' feed and vet supplies. Jude put some weight on her injured foot and found it would support her; it was sore but serviceable. She took a deep breath and ventured into the hall.

\* \* \*

Dillon Byer grabbed Ostrovsky's wrist. "What are you doing?" he demanded.

"Calling the police."

"No, not yet."

"Listen to them," cried Ostrovsky. "They're going to break in."

"No one's getting across the fence, Stu. Calm down."

Ostrovsky put his hands over his face and moaned, "Oh my God, they know. How did they find out?"

His partner knew exactly how they'd found out – Jude Brannock. But he didn't say. He took the phone out of Ostrovsky's hand, cautioning, "They don't *know*. They're speculating. Listen to me, if the cops show up, they can't search anything without a warrant. Just in case, I want to get rid of the corn feed. It's kept in the kennel, right?"

"What about Jim Davidson?"

"Davidson is on board."

"What about the animals?"

"Nobody takes them without a court order. And by that time, we're all cleaned up. Now, where's the feed?"

Ostrovsky nodded. "The big red container. In a cabinet."

"Locked?"

Looking around wildly, the scientist tried to remember. "No," he said. "I opened it last night. I … don't think I locked it again."

"And what about the rodent stuff?"

"Same thing, a red container in their housing area."

Byer didn't particularly want to go in there, but right now, his partner on the loose was a liability. "You sit tight. If the cops show up, they'll call you to open the gate. Don't let them in the front door. Ask to see a warrant. I need a little time."

"What are you going to do with the feed?"

"Put it in the freezer."

"What?"

"The big freezer in the basement – that's where you put the carcasses, right? In plastic bags. I throw the corn in the same bags and stuff them in the freezer underneath. No one is going through a pile of dead animals, and the disposal company is coming soon for pick up. By the time they think to look there, it will all be gone."

"We'll never get away with it."

Byer rushed at his partner and threw him against the wall. With his forearm at Ostrovsky's throat, he said roughly, "Yes, we will, Stuart. We will get away with it – unless you fuck up. Do you understand?" He pushed harder against Ostrovsky's neck until his face turned bright red. The scientist gave a strangled assent and Byer let go. He left him slumped against the wall, heaving for breath, before he made his way toward the animal housing. But first, he had another stop – something he should have done days earlier.

He had never killed anyone before. But afterwards when he thought about it, he decided that he hadn't killed Jeffries … not really. The guy was already one head bump away from an intracerebral brain hemorrhage. Just walking into a door frame might have done it. And even if he *had* killed him, it was partially Jeffries' fault.

Jeffries shouldn't have come back to the lab to get one of the dogs. A whining dog was hard to conceal. And for damn sure, he shouldn't have mouthed off about going to the cops and telling them everything he knew – about the corn and Amaethon's gross negligence. That Jeffries had himself eaten some of the cross-pollinated corn was just plain bad luck and evidently made it acutely personal for him. His nose began to bleed as he threw off Byer's restraining hand.

But he'd made even more mistakes. Assuming he wouldn't be followed, for one thing. And then, when he finally did spot the tail, trying to make a run for it on back roads.

Byer had thought the crash would kill him outright. But when he got down to the car, Jeffries still had a pulse, though his pupils were fixed and dilated which meant that blood vessels in his brain were probably leaking. There was a good chance he would die if left there. Byer couldn't take the chance that he would wake up and try to get help. He had to finish the job. He thought of strangling him in the car or hitting him on the head with a rock but knew that when the cops found him, they'd see marks inconsistent with the crash.

It took nearly ten minutes to drag Jeffries far enough away that he wouldn't be found easily. If anyone discovered the car, they'd have to assume the driver had climbed the embankment for help. By the time Byer thought he'd gone far enough, Jeffries was already dead.

He cleaned out the car and removed the license plates, shoving the contents into plastic garbage bags. He took them to one of the abandoned quarries nearby and threw them over a cliff where they joined the broken TV sets and other rusted junk that the local dump refused to take. All but Jeffries' phone, which had turned out to be a good move. It revealed him to be the animal rights bastard Byer suspected he was, and the litany of angry texts from Brannock could deflect suspicion onto her.

Then just before dawn, he returned to bury Jeffries in the woods.

All in all, Byer figured that Jeffries had basically dug his own grave with his missteps. Byer, on the other hand, knew he'd made only one, and he was going to fix that now. He'd torn off Jeffries' t-shirt to wrap his sore hands while he shoveled and forgot to throw it in with the body. He couldn't leave it at the scene; it would have his DNA all over it. And he didn't want to keep it in his own car while it went to the body shop. So, he tied it up in a plastic bag and shoved it in the back of a file drawer at the lab. He'd been meaning to dispose of it long before now – now that there was an angry mob outside the lab, soon to bring the police into the picture.

# CHAPTER 26

The cool lab air felt rough against her skin and her sneakers sounded too loud in her ears. Jude moved quickly down the hall toward the red exit sign above the door to the stairwell. The animals were kept on the floor above. The plan was to get into the kennel, fill the ziplock baggie in her pocket with feed, and take one of the dogs – more if she could. Then she was to make her way back to the storage room, where Kurt would meet her at the window.

Jude focused on the exit light like a beacon.

She had no sooner opened the fire door of the stairway when she heard the clatter of footsteps coming down. Hastily, she reversed course. No way to get back into the storage room in time. She had no choice but to duck into the first door she came to. It was marked "Mechanical."

Emergency floor lighting revealed that she was in an area that housed the lab's cooling and air purification systems. The drone of machinery and its thrumming vibration penetrated her body until it felt like it was rattling her bones. Ahead of her was a large box-like appliance with the "Turbo Air Cooled 2000" plaque identifying it as the system's air compressor. Against the wall to her left were two seven-foot stainless steel freezers. But what stood out were the frantic blinking lights of an electric grid mounted on the opposite wall. She cursed her bad luck in seeking refuge here. Whoever was coming down was sure to come in here to check on the short-circuit.

Jude dove behind the air compressor just as the door opened. She crouched low and peered around the compressor, able to make out a man's legs from the knees down. He went over to the freezers and set a heavy bucket on the floor. She recognized the figure of Dillon Byer. He reached up and punched in a code on the panel of one of the freezers. Then he wrenched open its door. A blast of frigid air came whooshing out. Only then did she remember what the freezers were there for: the storage of dead animals waiting for pick up. At the very thought, bile rose up in her throat. But she barely breathed as she watched what he did next.

Byer pulled out a heavy black garbage bag from the freezer and placed it next to the bucket. He put on rubber gloves and cut the fastening on the bag. When it was open, he withdrew from it a smaller plastic bag. This one was clear and marked with numbers drawn with a thick black Sharpie. It was filled with dissected rodent bodies, flesh and fur frozen into a distorted, sickening clump. He laid it on the floor. Then withdrew another. *What was he doing?*

When he had taken out about a third of the bag's contents, he looked around as if he thought someone might be watching. He dug into the bucket he had brought and pulled out a big rag. Except that it wasn't a rag. Bursting through her cloudy vision, Jude saw that it had sleeves and a neckline, and it was printed with the swirling tail of an "M" and the iconic tips of the Manhattan skyline. The New York Mets logo. Yet the familiar, faded orange and blue colors were distorted, clotted with dark red blood. Jude clapped a hand over her mouth to keep from screaming aloud. Tim's favorite t-shirt – the one she had so often rested her cheek against. And now, Byer was stuffing it into the bag and hurriedly covering it with the bloodied rat bodies.

Jude let out an involuntary moan. Byer heard it and whipped around. Taking advantage of his moment of surprise, she leapt out from behind the compressor. His eyes filled with fury and he grabbed at her. But she dodged his reach, threw open the door, and began running down the hall.

As she raced up the stairs, Jude fought her emotions. *He killed him, he killed him!* Until this moment, she'd clung to the barest of hope that Tim might still be alive, perhaps in a hospital somewhere trying to process what he knew, maybe scared of what he might believe was his failure and what she would say. In the far reaches of her fantasy, he'd struck his head in the car accident and had amnesia. More than once, she'd imagined telling him it was okay, she didn't blame him, she understood what he was trying to do. But now, the truth tore through her like a searing hot poker. He was gone, and the possibility of reconciliation had been trashed along with the frozen animal bodies. Reason roared at her to get out – get out and tell someone what she'd seen. But rage overtook self-preservation. Not until she got her hands on the feed.

Jude threw open the door to the ground floor hallway and thundered toward the canine housing. What had Melissa told her? Second on the left? A few more steps and she spotted the steel door with a ventilation louver. Throwing her shoulder against the door, she burst in.

The first thing that hit her was how un-noisy it was, certainly compared with the cacophony of a normal kennel. Yet it was far from silent. There were the sounds of tails whapping against the sides of metal crates and the strained yelping of de-barked dogs. Jude had seen many horrific things done to animals. She'd worked undercover in factory farms and once at a slaughterhouse. She'd seen videos, hundreds of them – dog fighting, elephant poaching, dolphin killing. And even though she knew that it was a standard practice to remove the vocal cords of laboratory dogs, she had never heard what they sounded like. Never been surrounded by the smothered, garroted cries of animals that had been bred to be man's best friend. *Sweet Jesus! They were trying to greet her.*

The clouds in front of her eyes grew thicker, darker. She squinted at the crates, stacked two-high on both sides of the room, and could identify the moving shapes of the dogs pacing inside. At that moment, the door behind her flew open. Byer had found her.

Jude backed away, trailing her fingertips along the metal bars to guide herself. She needed time. Just a few seconds until her vision returned. It always did.

"You didn't have to kill him," she breathed, feeling him close in on her.

"I don't know what you're talking about," replied Byer.

"I saw his shirt. Tim found out about the corn, didn't he?" she challenged, even as she inched her way back. "And he was going to expose you. But you drove him off the road. What did you do to him, you sonofabitch?"

"Didn't have to do anything. He was already bleeding internally."

Jude screamed at him, "Because he'd eaten the fucking corn! What did you do with him?"

"It was his own fault," replied Byer. "He made a big mistake – one that all you animal activists make. He came back to rescue a dog."

Jude's hip connected with something hard. Instinctively, she reached out and felt some kind of metal shelf that began to roll away. As it did, her fingers brushed against a row of slim cylinders and their needles. She knew what they were: euthanasia injections lined up, any one of which would provide a lethal dose of pentobarbital to a dog.

He didn't speak right away, but when he did, his voice came from a place off to her right. "Hellooo?" he sing-songed.

She whipped around to face him.

"I'm over here," he taunted, this time from her left.

Straining to hear his steps or the rustling of his clothes, Jude struggled to come up with something to say to keep him from hurting her.

But he quickly filled the gap. "This should make it a little easier, I suppose. The bleeding-heart animal activist devastated at witnessing the death of all the doggies. It's too much to bear. She'll never save all the animals. Better to end it all now."

With that, he picked up one of the syringes and came at her, grabbing her arm and twisting it to give him a chance at a vein. Jude lashed out with a punch in the direction of his face. It barely connected, but in the instant that he dodged, she wrenched from his grasp. When she turned to run, she knocked into the cart. Spinning it around, she rammed it into Byer's knees. The impact sent him flying backwards amidst the jangle of glass vials and metal instruments falling to the floor. It gave her enough time to get through the door and into the hall.

Her panic escalated as she realized that she didn't know which way to turn. She could hardly see anything, just the barest of light from the ceiling and a long tunnel of black ahead. How could she possibly get away? Clinging to the walls, she stumbled down the hall, shouting for help. Her cries died into the baffling overhead.

Another doorknob in her hand. Turning it hard, she shoved her way inside. By now, she could see nothing. The blackness and panic became one and threatened to swallow her whole. Frantically feeling along the walls, she sought to take cover. She'd gone a few steps when she collided with something hard and cold. The sound of tiny, scurrying feet reacted to the contact. She ran her fingers along an eight-inch length of smooth plastic, then a break, and then another. Moving her hand upward, she reached more boxes. She could feel movement inside them and realized she was touching the stacked bins of rodent housing. This was where the rats and mice were kept. She tried to remember some of the photos that Tim had sent her. There would probably be six to ten of these racks in the room, each holding storage bins. Inside each bin, little bigger than a shoe box, would be two or three rats, maybe more. Jude felt her way past the first rack, her hands desperately exploring the air in search of the next one. When she found it, she crouched behind and held her breath.

The door opened with a crash, and Byer was in. She could sense him surveying the room and could hear the moment when he spotted her. It was just a small grunt, but it resonated with victorious fury. His footsteps grew closer, and she threw up her hands to protect herself. Useless attempt.

He pulled her up roughly and pushed her back, pinning her against the wall. She fought, kicking at his legs, but he held her hands in a vice-like grip and pressed them over her head against the cold plaster. His smell was strong and sour. It flashed through her mind that it wasn't coming from him. It was the smell of her own death. She felt the sting of the needle in the soft crook of her elbow. *No!* She screamed and aimed a vicious kick at his groin. This time she connected, and he fell back, doubled over.

Jude lurched around him, but he grabbed her leg. She fell onto the floor. Scrabbling on her hands and knees, she tried to crawl away. She clutched at the linoleum tiles, clawing for anything to hold onto. As Byer dragged her back, she writhed and kicked. In the struggle, one of the racks toppled and fell with a crash, storage bins scattering on the floor, lids flying off.

Byer threw himself on top of her and pinned her with his entire body. "You bitch!" he rasped in her ear. There was a moment when Jude felt the tingling of small claws cross her hands and the brush of fur against her face. He wrenched her arm behind her back and twisted it. She felt the needle once again, piercing her skin. "You fucking b—"

Right then, Byer let out a yelp and rolled off her. Jude heard the rodents' feet, now scratching on the floor. It sounded like hundreds of them. And Byer screamed. He screamed like a terrified child and began slapping at his clothes. The sounds of rats screeching and hissing were all around them.

Jude didn't wait. She squirmed away from him again, got to her feet, and ran toward the door. Or where she thought the door was. She banged hard into the wall. Ignoring the blow, she frantically felt for her escape until she found it. Behind her, Byer was making strange noises.

Jude stumbled down the hall and ran directly into a pair of strong arms. In her terror, she swung her fists, trying to break away. But the arms held her fast, and she heard his voice. "It's me, Jude. You're okay. It's okay."

"Lucas?" she whimpered.

"Are you okay?" he asked.

"He's trying to kill me," she cried, looking futilely over her shoulder.

"Who?"

"Byer. He killed Tim." It was only then that she took in the other footsteps running down the hall. At first, she thought Byer was coming after them. "We have to get out of here," she cried.

And then she heard heavier boots coming from somewhere else. And shouts. She didn't understand.

"It's alright," said Lucas. "Come with me." He guided her away from the chaos down the long hall. Without being able to see where she was, each step was excruciating. And he sensed her pain because he finally stopped and took her by the shoulders, repeating, "Jude, are you hurt?"

She felt his face close to hers, his eyes looking for injuries. He smelled of wood smoke and damp leaves. Of some sort of safety. "Lucas," she said, her voice cracking, "I can't see."

He pulled her in against his chest, saying, "I know. I know."

* * *

Outside, the sun glinted off the early frost as protestors, turned curious onlookers, gathered in groups outside the fence.

They talked among themselves and speculated about the police activity going on. The gate was thrown open, but a somewhat confused security guard was there to prevent all but official vehicles from coming through. A knot of state cruisers with active rotating bubble lights was clustered at the building's entrance.

Looking grim, Haydon hovered near his vehicle. He glanced over his shoulder at Dillon Byer who was hunched in the back seat, arms handcuffed behind his back. Stuart Ostrovsky was similarly positioned in a nearby car.

Trooper Willison came out of the lab, lugging a heavy plastic garbage bag. He brought it over to Haydon and when he opened it, both men recoiled. Then Haydon donned latex gloves and searched the contents. After a moment, he removed Tim's t-shirt, put it into an evidence bag, and labeled it.

Other officers were busy controlling the throng of Half Moon residents. One was taking down the ladders that they had used to breach the fence. Another was directing the odd assortment of animal ambulances and pet transports that were showing up. A few of them had come all the way from Burlington. Still other police officers helped Kurt Buck's crew carry the animals out. A young woman emerged from the shadows of the building, cradling a beagle in her arms. She marched up to one of the animal emergency trucks and gently handed him over to a vet tech. She was followed by Buck himself who carried a dog under each arm. One by one, the beagles came out – each one quickly checked, then placed in a crate where they would be taken to a veterinary hospital for evaluation and treatment.

Lucas was inside supervising the removal of the rodents. When he felt the officers were organized enough to do the job right, he left the building and headed over to an EMS van parked behind a string of other emergency vehicles. He passed a paramedic coming the other way. "Is she showing any signs?" Lucas asked her.

"A little groggy," answered the paramedic, "but he couldn't have gotten a vein or she wouldn't be conscious."

Lucas thanked her and walked to the back of the van where Jude sat, her shoulders draped with a blanket. They'd cleared her of any life-threatening conditions and had asked a lot of questions about her blindness. But she'd waved them off with a vague reply, letting them think it was a lifetime disability. Inside, however, Jude was doing everything she could to keep the frightening sightlessness at bay, hoping that it would clear up at any moment.

Lucas announced himself as he came near and sat next to her. "We've only got a few more to go," he said.

"What's going to happen to them?" she wanted to know.

"We'll get it sorted out," he said. "I got in touch with the beagle rescue people in Massachusetts and they're on their way. If anyone can get the dogs healed and adopted out, it's them. I don't know about the rats and mice, but I'm going to do everything I can to keep them from going back into a lab."

"They saved my life, Lucas. I felt the rats all around me, but they went right for Byer, I don't why."

"Don't know either. But they're a lot smarter than we think."

"Who went in after I did?" asked Jude.

There hadn't been time to tell her what had gone down from his end. "Me and Buck," he replied. "He saw Byer's BMW parked in the back and we were afraid he'd find you. But there were a half dozen people right behind us. They heard you talking last night – about the animals being euthanized – and decided on their own to get them out. We couldn't stop them from going in. It really was an amazing thing to see all those people helping each other get over the fence."

"Putting themselves at risk."

"That's right. By the time the cops got here, I can't tell you how many people had stormed the building. Somebody found the office and stood guard to make sure nothing left the building until the police got there. Others helped get the dogs out."

"And the police? They're letting you go in and get them out?"

"No, they're helping, too," said Lucas.

Jude made a small sound of surprise as her mouth curled into the glint of a smile.

"There's a black trooper in charge."

"Haydon," said Jude.

"You know him?"

"Yeah. He's the one I told you about."

"Well, he's got Byer and Ostrovsky in custody. I heard one of the cops saying that Ostrovsky was falling all over himself trying to admit to everything, including what he suspects about Byer. I'm so sorry about Tim. I really am."

Jude nodded.

"And," said Lucas, looking over his shoulder. "Here's the trooper now."

Into the aura of Jude's blackness stepped Haydon. "Mind if I have a word?" he asked.

Lucas nodded curtly and went back to help the cops in the lab.

When he'd left, Haydon asked quietly, "How're you doing, Jude?"

She let out a weak laugh.

"We found Tim's t-shirt where you said. And we recovered a syringe on the floor in a room full of rats."

"What about Byer?"

"He isn't talking. But his partner gave us a damaging statement, and I'm going to guess that Byer has left trace evidence all over the t-shirt and the syringe. We're working on getting a paint match on the BMW. So, Byer can lawyer up all he wants, but it's not looking too good for him about now."

"Will he tell you what he did with Tim's body?"

"Guessing he will."

They stayed silent for a moment. Finally, Haydon said, "I owe you an apology. After I left you in the hospital, I tracked down your doctor and the mechanic at the auto body shop. They backed up your story, but by the time I got back to the hospital, you'd ... *fled*, as we say in police lingo. You should have stayed put and let us handle it."

"There wasn't time. I didn't trust that you'd follow up that ... *expeditiously*, as we say in activist lingo."

"Why did you lie to your boss about where you were in New York?"

Jude let out a weary sigh. "I didn't want them to know that I was undergoing an MRI and all the neurological tests. I just ... didn't want anyone to know about my vision."

She couldn't see Haydon nod in understanding. "Let me ask you something," she said. "Why are you letting us take the animals out? Technically, it's theft of property."

"They can't stay in the lab, can they?" Haydon reasoned. "Besides, as far as I'm aware, you and Matz are the only *professional* animal activists who got in. The rest are just regular folks from Half Moon. No one's pressing charges against them – not even against you – not with Byer and Ostrovsky under arrest for murder. And no court around here is going to return the animals to Amaethon."

"Thank you."

He stood to go. "Well, I better get back. I hope …" She could feel the heat of his sympathy. "I hope you recover, and all goes well for you, Jude. I mean that. I'll be in touch. We're going to need formal statements, of course. And normally, I'd ask you to stick around until we get them. But you need to look after yourself. I know where to find you. And to be honest, even though you got it right, you've been a pain in the ass. I'd just as soon you finally get the heck out of Half Moon."

Jude heard the smile in Haydon's voice, and then the creak of his gun belt as he walked away. She stared after him into a darkness that was already becoming familiar.

# CHAPTER 27

"Jude? Come on in." Over the gentle humming of the noise machine, Ruth Harris's voice brushed against Jude's cheeks like a warm breeze.

Many sounds now had a similar effect. She felt them more than heard them. The ticking of Finn's nails on her apartment floor like someone tapping the back of her hand. An airplane overhead as if something was pushing down on her head. Every day she was assaulted with a multitude of new sensations, not all unpleasant, but overwhelming. Blindness was not for the faint of heart. Every step, even if she had a steady arm to hang onto, took courage.

She pushed herself up from the chair in the reception room and waited for the psychologist to guide her. Jude knew better than to try and make it into the office alone. She hadn't gotten the hang of a cane yet and Finn, although in training to be a guide dog for her, was still an unreliable narrator in this new story. She slipped her arm through Harris's.

"Do you want to sit in the armchair again or on the couch?" asked Dr. Harris.

"Chair, please." It had more definition to the arms and seat. When she lowered herself, the door clicked closed and the psychologist's shoes whooshed softly on the carpet, heading to her seat a few yards away.

"How's it going?" asked Harris. Her voice was empathetic without being pitying. Of course, Jude had never seen what she looked like. But she sounded as if she were in her early fifties, long hair pulled up in a twist or a braid. She would have some lines around her eyes and would dress in muted colors, like soft gray and mauve. Jude imagined that she had a husband at home who read voraciously with glasses perched atop his head. And from the comfortable way she'd greeted Finn, there was probably a dog in the mix. She'd be meaning to ask but hadn't gotten around to it.

"How are you managing, Jude?" asked Harris again.

"I can make it from my bed to the kitchen sink without crashing into anything, so ... I don't know, is that a milestone?"

"Given what you're going through, I'd say it is."

"Pretty low bar."

"Sounds as if you expect an awful lot of yourself at this point."

"I'm not used to being incapacitated."

"You have some help? Lucas seems like a good guy."

Jude rubbed her palms against the nubby fabric of the chair's arms. "Yeah, he is a good guy. Too good for me, anyway."

"Why do you say that?" asked Harris.

"Lucas is one hundred percent there for me, all the time. And I haven't been a very good friend. I lied to him about Tim." Her hands picked up speed against the chair's arms. "Did I tell you that they found him? Tim. Dillon Byer buried him not too far from the crash site."

A sharp intake of breath from Harris before she said, "I'm so, so sorry, Jude."

"The medical examiner said that the cause of death was internal bleeding. Haydon told me that Tim probably was unconscious from the time of the accident and … uh, wouldn't have suffered. But I don't know if he said that to try and make me feel better."

"From what you've told me, Sergeant Haydon seems like a pretty straight shooter. Did you go back to Vermont when they found Tim?"

"No. I thought I wanted to be there, but in the end, I didn't see what good it would do."

"It might help you deal with your grief."

"We did go to the funeral in Maryland, and then afterwards to his sister's house." Jude turned her face to the cool breeze from the air conditioner. It was such a contrast to the murkiness she felt inside. "I … I have a lot of time to think these days," she continued. "And I've been going over and over what happened the last week Tim and I were in contact. I didn't handle it well, but I don't think he did, either. If he had given the slightest hint that he was in danger, I would have done anything to help him."

"Of course, you would."

Jude's train of thought was jumping all over the place. She said, "When Haydon called about recovering Tim's body, I suddenly couldn't stand the thought of going back to Half Moon. Especially with Lucas having to drag me all over the place."

"Does that make you feel like a burden to him?"

"I *am* a burden to him."

"A good friend is usually okay with being burdened sometimes."

"But it's always been that way with Lucas."

"How so?"

"Because he's in love with me."

"And you don't feel the same way?"

"I don't know. I'm just more comfortable in a situation that is …"

After a long enough pause that the psychologist figured Jude was not going to finish her thought, Harris prompted, "… that is what?"

"Oh my God, you really get personal, don't you?" accused Jude.

Harris chuckled softly and answered, "That's the whole point."

By this time, Jude's palms had begun to sting. She stopped rubbing and clasped them together tightly. "Do I have to answer?"

"No, but I would really like to hear what you think."

"Well, then. I think I'm just happier in a relationship that can't go anywhere."

"And why is that?"

"Because, like I used to tell Tim, the animals will always come first, and I don't believe that you can build a love relationship when one person feels like that. Hell, I ought to know. I was head over heels with a man who did two years in federal prison for releasing mink from a fur farm. Even after he got out of prison, he was busting up the government traps they use to kill wolves and coyotes. I don't know what he's doing now, but he can't stay in one place for more than a few weeks because the FBI has a warrant out for him." Jude snorted derisively at herself. "Now, that's the kind of guy I can really commit to."

"And you believe that you can't have both? Have a loving relationship *and* work to help animals?"

Jude shook her head but couldn't articulate why she knew this.

"Well, I know many people who have both," continued Harris. "Strong relationships and fulfilling work lives. I think it's very possible."

Jude had to find a new place for her hands and folded them into fists as she crossed her arms. "Could we get down to the reason I'm here?" she asked. "My alleged psychosomatic blindness?"

"Sure. The last time you were here, we had begun to talk about your history. Do you remember ever having trouble with your vision when you were a child or an adolescent?"

Jude thought she heard the street door open and wondered if it was the next patient arriving early. Or maybe Lucas willing to wait until her session was over. The psychologist read the anticipatory tilt of her head and said, "We have plenty of time."

*Oh.*

"What were you asking?"

"If you had problems with your eyes before."

"Once," said Jude.

"When was that?"

"I was ten or eleven."

"And what happened?"

"I'm not sure if it did really happen or I've manufactured the memory, but it was in my second foster home. The dad was like Jekyll and Hyde. He could be very nice, but when he drank, he turned into a monster. One night, he went on a tear and started beating on my foster mom." Jude's voice, even to herself, came from a place she could barely discern as she became lost in the memory. "They were screaming and throwing stuff at each other. I ran into my bedroom and hid in the closet. It was dark inside, but there was a space at the bottom of the door and you could see light through it. And I was watching the light to see if his feet came close and he'd find me. I knew that as long as I could see the light, I was safe. But it started to get dark, just the way it happened in the lab, the blackness closing in like a collapsing tunnel. And I got scared because I thought it was him. But then I heard him in the kitchen, so I knew he couldn't be outside the closet. And it got darker and darker until I couldn't see any light at all."

"When did your vision return?"

"I don't remember exactly. But I think I went to school the next day, so I must have been fine."

"That must have been very frightening."

"Do you think what is happening to my eyes now is related to that?"

"It could be."

"How?"

"You were confronted with violence that no child should have to witness. That must have been overwhelming. Sometimes the body has a way of compensating. You couldn't bear to see your foster mom being hurt and were scared that you might be hurt, too. So, your body made sure that at least you couldn't see it."

"Okay. But I'm not a child anymore. I can fend for myself. Why is this happening now?"

"We'll need to explore that, but I can throw out some ideas. You told me that your sight went completely when you saw the dogs in the lab, and you heard the sounds they made having had their vocal cords cut. You told me how deeply sad it made you because humans have domesticated dogs to trust us. Perhaps that kind of betrayal and suffering was something that you couldn't bear to look at."

"But I've witnessed far worse animal abuse. And besides, it had started before that. Here in D.C. and when I first got to Vermont."

"Maybe *seeing* is more than just what our eyes do. Maybe you were recognizing some things about yourself. Like recognizing that it hurt you to keep secrets from Lucas and from your colleagues at The Kinship. And perhaps recognizing that sometimes your passion for animals eclipses your own needs. A need for friendship and love."

"In other words, I should strive to be a normal person?"

"Nothing wrong with being human. Besides, is *normal* something you would associate with your line of work?" Jude could hear the smile in her voice.

"I need to keep fighting for animals. To do that I really need to see again."

"I would like you to see again, too."

"It is possible?"

"No guarantees, but I think we have a good chance."

"How? How do we do that?"

"By doing the work."

"What work?"

"The work that therapy entails. Committing to the process, getting personal, trusting each other, and being willing to accept help."

Jude took a deep, courage-seeking breath, and when she let it out, she could feel the sting of tears. It startled her. From the moment her sight had completely left her, her eyes had felt nothing. No pain, nothing, as if they had been deadened to all sensation. Until now.

Maybe it was a sign of healing. Maybe it was an awakening of something else. Whatever it was, she had a choice to make. And she made it, letting herself fall, just hoping there were arms to catch her. "Okay, I'm ready," she said. "When do we start?"

And Harris replied, "We already have, Jude."

Made in United States
North Haven, CT
02 December 2021

11874511R00174